Nikki's eyes widened, the blood draining from her face. In another life, he would have told her, "Honey, when a guy points a gun in your direction, duck, dive, run, anything, just move and keep moving." But it was all over before he could have even gotten the word "honey" out of his mouth. The other killer cleared the hall; Kid covered him and squeezed the trigger twice, rapid-fire, on his Heckler and Koch .45—body shots. The guy dropped like a stone behind her.

Perfect. Now everybody in a five-block radius knew somebody was shooting something. More likely, if Juan Conseco had sent more than two guys to murder him in his sleep, and they were paying attention, they knew *el asesino fantasma* was shooting something, probably their guys. The man he'd strangled had been carrying a silenced semiautomatic pistol. The guy he'd shot had been carrying the same, and he'd just squeezed off two full, hot loads with plenty of bang.

Aiming at the dead guy's head, he rose to his feet and, standing between the man and Nikki, fired off another hollow-point bullet. He wasn't taking any chances. He never took any chances.

He was across the living room and had Nikki by the arm and out of the chair before she could even get her mouth closed, let alone wipe the stunned expression off her face. Holding her close, he shielded her off to his right side as he put another bullet in the other killer, head shot. Neither of the bastards was ever getting up again. When Kid cleared a room, it stayed clear.

Turning her around, he hustled her back out the door to the patio. The house had been made. He'd been made, and that left only one thing to do: run like hell.

CRAZY
KISSES

Tara
Janzen

A DELL BOOK

CRAZY KISSES
A Dell Book / March 2006

Published by
Bantam Dell
A Division of Random House, Inc.
New York, New York

ISBN-10: 0-440-24261-4
ISBN-13: 978-0-440-24261-1

Printed in the United States of America
Published simultaneously in Canada

www.bantamdell.com

OPM 10 9 8 7 6 5 4 3 2 1

AUTHOR'S NOTE

Anyone familiar with the beautiful city of Denver, Colorado, will notice that I changed a few parts of downtown to suit the story. Most notably, I took Steele Street and turned it into an alley in lower downtown, a restored historic neighborhood in the heart of Denver known as LoDo.

CRAZY
KISSES

$\mathcal{P}$ROLOGUE

ONE HUNDRED AND FIFTY-FOUR *fucking inches of rain a year*—and this little corner of the Colombian jungle was getting all of it tonight.

Geezus. Kid Chaos Chronopolous shifted his gaze from the deluge outside the cantina's door to the other patrons in the smoke-filled bar: one old man he could take on his worst day—and today was definitely headed in that direction; two young whores he wouldn't take on a bet; and half a dozen rats who looked like they could take him without breaking a sweat.

Tightening his arm around his waist, he checked the door again. The river was rising like a sonuva-bitch, but according to the bartender, the *Garza* was still out there, chugging her way downstream, which meant there was still a chance to catch a ride out of this hellhole tonight.

Thank you, God and C. Smith Rydell. Even if he had to swim for it, he wasn't missing that damn boat. No way in hell. Screw the piranhas. If they wanted a piece of him, they were going to have to get in line.

He glanced toward the bar. C. Smith had gone up to talk about hot food and cold beer. It was a long shot this time of night, but Kid's money was on Smith. The guy didn't look a day over nineteen with his blond ponytail, scruffy beard, and shit-eating grin, but if there were two plates of rice and a cold beer left in this rat-infested backwater on the banks of the Rio Putumayo, the hippie gringo with the Sig Sauer .45 strapped to his hip and the U.S. Drug Enforcement Agency ID buried in his pack could be counted on to get them.

Something cold would be great. Anything cold. Sweat was running down his face, down his body, and it was all he could do to keep from fainting dead out on the table.

Shit.

Taking a steadying breath, he looked down and slowly tilted his hand away from his side.

Okay. He was a little chewed up, but it wasn't so bad—except for the blood running through his fingers. The bullet was still in there, just under his skin, and might have skittered off one of his ribs, which would explain why he hurt so goddamned bad. That wasn't so good, but the blood . . . yeah, the blood was a problem. He'd lost too much. Smith had done a quick patch on him when he'd gotten hit, but he'd lost that an hour back, and they hadn't dared stop long enough to really bind him up, not with eight armed men on their asses. Getting shot was one thing, but actually dying on the job went against every order they'd been given. A baby-faced DEA agent and a black-ops soldier from the Department of Defense showing up dead in the South American jungle was the sort of thing the U.S. government did *not* want to have to explain to anybody.

On the plus side, he and Smith had successfully located the airfield where Juan Conseco was transporting semirefined coca from the south to be processed in his big labs in northern Colombia. They'd also found opium latex, but the real prize had been a SAT-COM phone number tacked to the wall with a flight schedule and a ship's lading document. Smith had recognized the number, which was bad news for the U.S. government and good news for every junkie in the Western Hemisphere. Fresh off the DEA's "Operation Containment" force in Kabul, Afghanistan, Smith had been transferred to their Heroin Task Force in Bogotá, Colombia, to follow a lead on Middle Eastern narco-terrorists looking to broaden their market base. Finding an Afghan opium warlord's phone number tacked to the wall in an illicit airfield shack just north of the Putumayo was about as broadly based as drug trafficking could get. Smith had grinned from ear to ear. The last thing the U.S. needed was for somebody to start running Asian heroin through the Colombian cartel's cocaine pipeline—but it had felt damn fine to follow a gut instinct halfway around the world and hit pay dirt.

Drugs and thugs, from one side of the globe to the other, with every terrorist group in the world getting a piece of the black-money action. Snort heroin or cocaine in Los Angeles, feed a terrorist in Kabul, Tehran, or Medellín, Colombia—the connection was pretty damn straightforward.

"Chico." A cold beer came down on the table, the bottle dripping with icy condensation. A plate of food followed as Smith settled into the chair next to his.

Kid reached for the beer. "How long have we got?"

"Five minutes max," Smith said. "Then the generator goes out like last year's lightbulb, the rest of the beer gets warm, and this whole town disappears back into the jungle until dawn. Eat."

Kid took a bite, then shoveled in another.

"Town" was an undeserved compliment for Banco Nuevo. He was sticking with "hellhole" to describe the mud street and two dozen ramshackle buildings doing their damnedest not to slide into the river.

"What about the boat? The *Garza*?" The food tasted like sawdust, and his gut was churning, but he'd be damned if he threw up. Food, water, beer— the three essentials. If he couldn't get it down and keep it down, he wasn't going to have the strength to do what had to be done. They weren't home free. Far from it.

Hell, the only reason Smith had dragged him in here was to get him out of the rain long enough to slap another battle dressing on him, and if possible, shove a little hot food in him. They were sitting ducks in the cantina.

"If there's still a dock in half an hour, the boat will be at the dock." Smith was pulling first-aid stuff out of his pack with one hand and spooning food into his mouth with the other. It wasn't a pretty sight, but neither were they after ten days of jungle recon and three hours flat-out on the run. "Can you hold on that long?"

"Absofuckinglutely."

The *Garza* was the only thing that could get them as far as Santa María by morning, and Santa María was the last place left on the river where they could call in a plane to pick them up. They could be heading back to Bogotá tomorrow.

But first they had to get through the night, and considering the number of people they'd pissed off today, that wasn't going to be easy. The pack of rabid *pistoleros* they'd been outrunning had no sooner stopped for the rain than they had.

No, they wanted their shit back, all the papers and documents he and Smith had stuffed into their packs at the airfield, all the data Uncle Sam and the Colombian government needed to shut them down or blow them off the map. The only question was who was going to get to Banco Nuevo first, the *Garza* or the narco-guerillas?

Kid was praying for the *Garza*. He knew guys like Conseco, and he knew for a fact that torture would figure pretty heavily in any death they dished out, especially for agents of the U.S. government.

Smith knew it, too.

"Lift your arm," Smith ordered. "And I can guarantee you this is going to hurt."

That was Smith. Right to the point. No candy coating.

Then Kid saw the bottle of *aguardiente* rotgut Smith had brought from the bar along with the food and beer.

Oh, fuck.

He put his fork back on the plate and swallowed the rest of the food in his mouth. "I don't think—"

"Good idea," Smith said, interrupting him and lifting the bottle. "Don't think." Without another word, he poured the alcohol on Kid's wound.

Fiery, blazing pain flashed across his left side, burning like a friggin' hot poker from one edge of the bloody torn wound to the other—and it didn't stop. The pain just sat there on him and burned.

Oh, fuck. Oh, fuck. Oh, fuck. His eyes crossed, and he almost went down. The only thing stopping him was Smith grabbing the front of his shirt and forcibly holding him in his chair.

"Come on, Chico," Smith said, his voice low and hard. "You're tougher than this."

No. No, he didn't think so. Not right now.

Right now, it would be easier to just pass out. To just let his eyes roll up inside his head and let go.

Smith splashed him again—the sonuvabitch—and

set the rotgut back on the table. He started pulling Kid's shirt away from his skin.

Oh, shit, it hurt.

"If I have to carry you out of here, it's going to get ugly."

Yeah. Real ugly. He had twenty pounds on C. Smith, and they were each humping fifty-pound packs and thirty pounds of guns and ammo—all of which they needed, every single ounce of it.

"You couldn't carry me out of here on your best day," he said, his voice barely a whisper, which did damn little to increase his confidence. *Please, oh, fuck, don't let me pass out.*

"Lucky for you, Chico, this isn't my best day." Smith gave him one of those shit-eating grins, and Kid almost grinned back—almost, but not quite, because Smith was opening a Sani-Pak bandage, and the only reason Smith would be opening a Sani-Pak bandage would be to press it onto his wound to help seal out infection.

Great fucking idea, but he didn't want anybody *pressing* anything on him.

"Uh, Smith—"

Too late. The Sani-Pak went on, and Smith sealed the edges, and Kid felt his own edges get a little blurry and start to turn black. He tried to remember to keep breathing . . . and forgot.

Beer brought him back around in a snap—cold beer being poured on his face.

"D-dammit, Smith," he spluttered. "You're wasting the beer."

"I'll buy you another one in Santa María." Smith ripped open a roll of gauze and started winding it around Kid's waist—real tight.

Kee-rist. That hurt, too, but the last thing he wanted was to bleed out in Banco Nuevo—or be captured alive by Juan Conseco. The cocaine baron would have a bounty on them by dawn.

Not that anyone needed the added incentive to take him out. The glory alone was worth the risk.

El asesino fantasma. He knew what they called him—the ghost killer. He didn't have a problem with the name. He'd earned it. He'd earned it the hard way, one death at a time, until all the Colombian narco-guerrillas who had butchered his brother had been put in their graves. But the name had started following him like a hungry dog, with every half-cocked gunfighter from Cusco to Cartagena snapping at his heels. If he didn't cut himself loose and get the hell out of South America, he was going to die here. It was time to leave.

Past time.

"Are you okay?" Smith asked, tying off the gauze. "Steady?"

"Like a rock." Yeah. Right. That was him, rock steady. He was going to leave finger dents in the tabletop, he was holding on so freakin' tight. The sweat was pouring off him now, and if he didn't keep himself real still, he was going to lose his rice and whatever monkey meat had been in it.

Over behind the bar, the bartender set a lantern next to the glassware and fired up the wick. Time was running out.

"Then keep eating," Smith said, letting go of him and pulling a battle pack of ammo out of his rucksack.

No way. Not yet. Kid needed to get ahold of himself first.

Smith was moving fast, pulling empty magazines off Kid's web gear and replacing them with full ones off his own tactical vest. Kid had already eased his M4 off his back and onto his shoulder.

"You're not planning on us going out of here like Butch and Sundance are you?" A sniper by trade and training, compliments of his hitch with the United States Marine Corps, stealth was always Kid's preferred modus operandi.

"Nope," Smith said, reloading Kid's magazines out of the battle pack, sliding one 5.56mm cartridge in on top of another with quick, efficient precision. "Butch and Sundance were packing six-shot, single-action Colts. You're going to cover me with half a dozen spare magazines and your M4 on semiauto."

Kid didn't like the sound of that. *Cover him while he did what?*

"Where are you going?" Kid's orders were clear: Get the DEA guy into southern Colombia, help him find the frickin' airfield, and get him back to the Bogotá office in one piece.

"Out in the dark with a knife."

And that would be Kid's absolute last choice in the plan department, for Smith to go out alone to take on Conseco's guys. He'd never actually come out and asked, but more than once, as tough as the guy was, he'd wondered if maybe C. Smith really was only nineteen or twenty, wondered if somehow he'd slipped under the DEA's age requirement. He looked damn young, and nineteen-to-twenty-year-olds, even tough ones, didn't have the kind of experience necessary to go out in the dark with a knife—not when there were more than half a dozen badass banditos out there waiting for him.

On the other hand, he sure as hell was in no condition to go hunting himself. It was going to take everything he had to get to the dock—and maybe even everything he had wasn't going to be enough. He was trying so damn hard not to hyperventilate. Really weird, bad shit happened to you when you'd lost a lot of blood and started hyperventilating.

"Maybe we could set up a diversion, draw them out." It was a better plan, a safer plan.

Smith just grinned and kept shoving cartridges into the M4's magazine.

"Don't worry, Kid. The only person in this town I can't take with a knife tonight is you." He pushed the last cartridge in and switched the full magazine with the half-empty one in Kid's carbine. "Come on. Let's get you set up."

Smith bent down enough to get his shoulder under Kid's good arm and helped him get to his feet. Then he grabbed both packs one at a time and slung them over his other shoulder.

Tougher than freakin' titanium.

"You can see the river from the back door. There's sort of a porch," Smith said, heading them both across the cantina, toward the back. "Not much cover, but once the generator goes off, it's gonna get real dark out there. I'm going to put a light on the dock, try to keep the *Garza* from missing us. If she pulls up, get your ass down there pronto. Give me two minutes. If I don't make it back, tell the captain to push off. Nobody else gets on the boat from Banco Nuevo. Nobody."

Okay. Now Kid really hated the plan. Leaving Smith behind was not an option.

The generator went off just as they made it to the porch, and the whole world went dark. Smith was right. In this kind of rain, and without the generator lighting the place up, the *Garza* would float on by and never know she'd missed Banco Nuevo.

Smith propped him up on the porch and checked the magazine in Kid's pistol.

"In case somebody gets too close," he said, slapping the magazine home, before shoving it back in Kid's holster. "No matter what happens, you get on that boat. I'm counting on you, Chronopolous. Don't let me down."

And then he was gone, melting into the dark.

Shit.

Kid leaned up against the wall and settled into his carbine.

Damn, it was dark, and the rain was pouring out of the sky like one big upended bucketful. The racket alone was enough to shake a guy's brain.

This wasn't the way he'd planned his big exit, bleeding to death in the middle of nowhere on the back porch of a flea-bitten dive on the Putumayo.

Hell.

Seven months in South America, half in the Colombian jungle, half spent going in and out of the Peruvian highlands, bushwhacking his way across the Cordillera range, and all he had to show for it was another friggin' bullet wound, a reputation he'd never live down, and a kill list as long as his arm.

And two gold wedding rings he kept on a silver chain around his neck.

Yeah. He still had those.

It was the only illegal thing he'd ever done in his life, taking the rings off the finger bones of the skeletons he'd found in an ancient Incan ruin above Cusco, Peru. Two sets of bones, one male, one female, buried under five feet of earthquake rubble. He'd taken both rings. He'd taken them for Nikki. If anybody owned them, she did.

But that was a place he definitely wasn't going

tonight—the Nikki McKinney files. No, thinking about the girl he'd fallen in love with last summer wasn't going to help him get out of Banco Nuevo alive. She belonged to somebody else now, some "fiber artist" she'd met, and that hurt worse than the slug buried next to his ribs.

He should have called her, or written after he'd left Denver. Or at least gone back to Colorado for Christmas. Would that have been so freaking hard?

Apparently, because he hadn't done it, and she'd gone and gotten herself engaged to some other guy. Fucking *engaged*.

There was no way in hell for him to even think about it, let alone figure it out. So he'd been ignoring the fact for four long weeks, ever since he'd heard. Just plain ignoring it.

But he'd found the rings, and no freaking fiber artist from Boulder, Colorado, could have done that. And what the hell was a "fiber artist" anyway?

A basket weaver, that's what it was. "Fiber artist" his ass. He took a breath and refocused his attention on the edges of the street.

And the rain stopped. Just like that. The jungle was dripping, but the deluge was over.

One by one, a lantern came on here and there in a few of the shacks. They didn't cast much light, just enough to get everybody in trouble—which worked out fine for Kid. Suddenly, the night was his.

He chambered a round into the M4 and did what he did best: waited in the dark to take his shot.

It was less than a minute before a steady stream of light cut through the dark down by the river. Smith had gotten his flashlight lashed to the dock. Somebody immediately fired off a short burst and tore up one of the dock's planks. And that somebody's muzzle flash was like one big spotlight for Kid. He saw movement, held his breath, and squeezed.

Two and a half pounds of pressure and a heartbeat later, the guy went down.

The narco-guerrillas with the automatic weapons hadn't been nearly as far behind them as he and Smith had thought. Kid wasn't really surprised. Fucking demoralized, but not surprised. It was going to be hell getting out of Banco Nuevo.

He reached down to his .45 and flipped the safety off. It wouldn't take long for Conseco's guys to lock in on his position, and then the whole porch thing would turn into "Kid's Last Stand."

Shit.

At least Butch and Sundance had gone out on their feet.

Something, a movement in the dark, an instinct, drew his attention to the third shack up from the river on the far side. Light from an adjacent doorway cast a thin sliver of illumination down the shack's thatched wall. There wasn't a sound, no crying out, no shot, but between one breath and the next a body fell out of the shadows and landed facedown in the mud.

It wasn't Smith.

The appearance of the dead man brought another

guy running up the street in a low crouch, rifle at the ready.

Ready for what, Kid wanted to ask him, but he already knew the answer—ready for the last mistake the bastard would ever make.

Kid raised the M4, sighted, squeezed—and he and Smith were up by three.

Two shots from the same hide were enough to set his warning bells ringing. He had to move, no matter what it cost him.

Using his pack for support, he pushed himself to his knees—and then he heard it. The soft sucking sound of a footstep in the mud. A quick glance back into the bar proved the old man, the bartender, and the two girls were still inside, huddled together on the floor, too smart to get into the middle of what he and Smith were bringing down on top of them.

The rats were on their own.

He pulled his .45, and when a rifle muzzle edged out around the corner of the cantina, he took up the slack in the trigger and waited. The instant the man showed himself, Kid fired—twice in rapid succession, blowing the guy to hell and back.

And now he was really screwed. Everybody in town had to know where he was, and God, the pain in his side was like a knife—a knife with a serrated blade. *Geezus*. He couldn't catch his breath.

A fresh burst of shots, coming from a couple of directions, slammed into the cantina's walls, showering him with splinters and bits of wood. He'd definitely been found. A piece of a board buried itself in his upper arm like a stiletto. Something sharp and hotter than hell caught him across the face. He felt the skin tear and burn. He smelled it. Swearing under his breath, he grabbed one of the straps on his pack and half stumbled, half dragged himself and the pack down the porch steps. He made it as far as the nearest tree before a slug caught him in the leg and he collapsed into a heap. His heart was pounding like a jackhammer.

Fuck! He wasn't going to die here. No way.

Then the shooting stopped, and there was nothing but the sound of water dripping off the trees.

Bracing himself, he reached up and pulled the splinter of wood out of his arm. He tossed it aside without looking at it. He didn't want to know how big it was. He just wanted the fuck out of there.

Easing the weight off his side, he checked the street. There were still two bodies in the mud and no sign of Smith or the other shooters.

An engine coughing and chugging its way down the river brought his head around. The *Garza* was pulling up to the dock, her cylinders misfiring, the paint-peeled letters on the bow sliding through the beam of Smith's flashlight.

A wave of dizziness washed across the back of his skull—not the first of the night, and sure as hell not the last. He carefully lowered his head, fighting it, focusing on his breathing, making it deep, making it count, and he held on. He wouldn't last thirty seconds if he passed out.

A whippoorwill sounded behind him.

A freakin' whippoorwill in the Colombian rain forest. Oh, God, if he hadn't hurt so badly he would have laughed. Smith needed his head examined.

He dared to glance up. Out on the dock, somebody stepped off the boat with a bow line and tied her off—and there she sat.

Gringo bait.

He took another breath and tried to keep himself as motionless and quiet as possible. Conseco's guys were still out there, waiting for him and the whippoorwill to make a try for the *Garza.*

He didn't hear Smith come up behind him, but neither was he surprised when Smith slid into view. Smith looked a little worse for wear himself. He had blood on his face and a gash on his arm.

Nothing was ever easy.

Smith held up three fingers and pointed at three different places along the street.

Kid gave a short nod and pointed to his six o'clock position. There had been shots coming from behind him.

Smith drew his hand sideways across his throat.

Okay, Kid thought, impressed as hell. That was two for the boy wonder and his knife. Unless Conseco's guys had called in reinforcements, they were down to just the three guys on the other side of the street.

And the *Garza* was still out there, looking about a million miles away.

"They're going to cut us down, if we try the dock," he said quietly. The damage report would have to come later.

Smith nodded. He was breathing heavily, the blood running down his arm. "We're going to have to swim for it. Come up on the starboard side."

Yeah. Swim.

Swim a flooded river, upstream, with him carrying two slugs, bleeding like a stuck pig, and praying to God the piranhas weren't looking for a midnight snack.

Nothing was ever easy.

Smith shouldered Kid's pack along with his own, stopped for just a second to catch his breath, then signaled him to move out.

Yeah, he was right, and if C. Smith could carry the gear, the least Kid could do was get himself down to the river. It was crazy to worry about the piranhas. *Shit.* He'd probably sink like a stone and drown long before the piranhas got hold of him.

Right.

He got his one good leg under him, and the effort instantly cost him his dinner. He lost it all on the jungle floor.

Oh, geezus, that hurt. He grabbed for his side, and that hurt, too. Every single part of him hurt like a sonuvabitch. He wiped the back of his other hand across his mouth and tried not to feel so friggin' awful—and suddenly, he knew he was in real trouble. He didn't have to look down at his wound. He knew what he felt. He'd bled through the Sani-Pak. Already.

When he didn't move, Smith looked back.

It took Kid a moment to find his breath, another couple of moments to work through the pain and find his voice, but when he did, he outlined the facts for Smith as neatly and succinctly as possible.

"We . . . we need . . . I . . . fuck, Smith. It would take Superman to get me out of here tonight."

C. Smith knew who Superman was, everybody did: a guy named Christian Hawkins who worked with Kid at SDF, Special Defense Force, a clandestine unit of special-forces operators nobody at the Pentagon or the Department of Defense would ever admit existed. He was a legend with a well-deserved reputation for getting himself out of the kind of situations that killed mere mortals—himself and whoever was with him.

He was also over three thousand miles away from the Rio Putumayo.

Smith understood, though.

"Well, tonight's your lucky night then, Chico," he said, dropping the packs back into the mud. "Because tonight I *am* fucking Superman."

In one tortuously painful move, he had Kid on his shoulders and was headed for the river.

CHAPTER

1

Panama City, Panama. Four days later.

THERE WAS A BIKINI BOTTOM in his bathroom.

Curious as hell, Kid picked the tiny scrap of green-and-purple cotton up off the towel bar and turned it over in his hand.

It wasn't unusual for him to come home and find somebody crashing at his place. He'd known the instant he walked in that someone was there. The house in Panama City had belonged to his brother, and J.T. had always had an open-door policy.

But the bikini bottom was unusual.

Combat boots, surfboards, cases of beer—that's what he usually found. Not outrageously green bikini bottoms with purple palm fronds printed on them.

It was enough to make a guy think.

About sex.

And about death.

He swore softly and put the swimsuit back on the towel bar. J.T. had been the kind of guy who took care of people, a lot of people. Some of them had been women—mostly friends, but a couple of ex-lovers had shown up over the last few months. Kid didn't think he could face one of them tonight, and have to be the one to tell them J.T. was dead. He still felt about half dead himself.

Easing himself around, he limped back out to the living room. The house was pure tropical bungalow, with two bedrooms, two baths, a kitchen and dining area together, and a living room that opened onto a palm-shaded courtyard. It had lizards darting around outside, a housekeeper named Rosa who held the place together no matter how many unexpected visitors showed up, and neighbors who liked to party— tonight being a case in point. A salsa beat was coming from both sides of the house.

After his and C. Smith's adventure on the Putumayo, two days in a Bogotá hospital, and two days of debriefing with the DEA and the Defense Department guys, he wasn't in the mood to party. All he wanted to do was sleep in a bed he called his own. He hoped the bikini girl had picked the spare bedroom and not the one he usually took.

The thought made him pause.

Geez. No wonder he never got laid anymore.

He shook his head and continued on across to the breezeway and the south bedroom, the one he preferred, and sure enough, it was definitely *ocupado*.

There were clothes everywhere, and stuff, girl stuff, piled up on his dresser and draped over the chair, filmy stuff, bright colorful bits and pieces. The girl's suitcases were on the floor in a corner, and besides being the most amazing shade of crocodile-patterned hot pink leather he'd ever seen, they were overflowing with electrical cords, makeup bags, and shoes, like a "girl grenade" had exploded and sent her clothes flying in every direction and left the heavy stuff to settle.

That thought gave him pause, too, sort of reminded him of something else, but he wasn't going to spend the effort to figure out what. He was too damn tired to sort through anything tonight. All he wanted to do was sleep, and one bed or another didn't really make much difference.

He turned to leave, when a small torn white T-shirt hanging off the doorknob caught his eye, a plain white T-shirt with a paint smear on it—electric blue paint.

Everything inside him froze, except his heart, which plummeted into the pit of his stomach.

Impossible. It was absolutely impossible—but he knew that T-shirt, knew that paint smear.

His gaze slid to the clothes draped over the chair, and he saw something else he knew: a purple silk robe with a letter "N" painted in pink on the pocket. *Geezus.* He looked around the room, at all the stuff. But it wasn't just stuff, and it wasn't just any girl grenade that had gone off in here. It was a Nikki McKinney grenade.

He picked up the robe, brought the silky material to his face—and her scent flooded his senses. Hot sex, warm love, all the memories were there, so close to the surface.

Too close.

Nikki was here, and suddenly, he was in over his head. Way over.

Why in the world would Nikki be in Panama City?

And had she brought the freakin' fiber artist with her?

Geezus. He couldn't take that. No way in hell.

He looked up from the robe and checked the room. No, this was a one-person disaster, from the Panama hat and pink-and-green-striped sunglasses on his dresser to the pile of underwear on the bed. This was all Nikki, every square inch of it.

Underwear. Bed. Nikki.

And suddenly, he was wide awake, every cell in his body.

He dropped the robe back on the chair and headed out the door. In the courtyard, he turned toward the loudest music. Nikki would be at ground zero, which meant the Sandovals' walled garden next door.

Rico and Luis Sandoval were a couple of trust-fund twins whose daddy ran the biggest chain of car dealerships in Panama. They were great guys for a good time, a cold beer, and a Friday night poker game, strip poker if they could talk a girl into playing.

Kid always opted out of any Sandoval brothers scheme that included drunk naked women, but Rico and Luis wouldn't have had to use liquor or talk very fast to get Nikki in the game. There wasn't anything she liked better than naked men. Twins would be an irresistible bonus in her book.

Cripes. Nikki and a couple of Panamanian beach-boy hustlers with a marked deck. The thought had Kid limping at double time. It would serve Rico and Luis right if he just let her have them. They'd never get the drop on her, no matter how much they cheated, and once she pulled her "Gee, can I paint you naked" line on them, they wouldn't have a chance. She'd have them stripped out of their *machismo* faster than they could drop their skivvies. The trust-fund boys would still be looking for their balls come Christmas.

But he didn't want any other guys dropping their shorts for Nikki tonight, or any other night—Panamanian beach boys or fiber artist fiancés.

A fiancé—how in the hell had he let things get so out of hand? How had he gone seven months without calling her? Without writing her?

He stopped by the gate in the wall—stopped and made himself take a reality check. The truth was, he knew why he hadn't contacted her. He knew exactly why he hadn't gone home at Christmas. And nothing had changed.

He wasn't the man she'd fallen in love with, not anymore, not even close, and there was no coming back from the places he'd been.

But she was here, and he had to see her. He wasn't

going to fool himself into thinking she'd come to see him. He was the last person she would have expected to show up in Panama City, despite his owning the house. If she'd wanted to come to Panama, for whatever reason, Skeeter would have loaned her the key and given her the official situation report: He was in Colombia, working out of Bogotá.

And if he hadn't reached the end of his rope, that's where he'd still be.

No, she couldn't have come here looking for him. For the last seven months, no one except the men he was with had known where he was or what he was doing. In the beginning, that had been Hawkins, and later another SDF operator, Creed Rivera. After Creed had finished his mission, he'd gone home, but Kid had stayed.

He'd stayed too long.

Colombia wasn't safe for him anymore. People were looking for him. They just didn't know his real name or what he looked like, not yet, but that wasn't going to hold them off forever, not these guys, not if he kept doing what he'd been doing. The airfield on the Putumayo wasn't the first time *el asesino fantasma* had hit Juan Conseco's operation, and the drug lord knew it. News of the "Putumayo bounty" Conseco had put out on the ghost killer had hit Bogotá while he'd still been in the hospital. The cocaine baron wanted him dead or alive, and for half a million dollars, Kid figured Conseco had a pretty good shot at getting him.

It was a helluva lot of money, but Kid had done a helluva lot of damage, including a pair of sniper hits contracted by the Colombian government via the U.S. Department of Defense on two of Conseco's top lieutenants, a mission so black it had been black-on-black. Which all made Nikki's presence even more unnerving, if that was possible—which, honest to God, it wasn't. He was already unnerved all the way down to his gut and his toes by her being here. The situation with Conseco only made it worse.

And wasn't that just perfect? He hadn't been home five minutes, and the first thing he had to do was literally kick Nikki McKinney out of his bed.

Well, hell. At least now he had something to say that didn't begin and end with "I'm sorry." He'd said that to her so many times, especially when she was crying, and when they'd been together, she'd cried a lot. He had to admit that "Get your butt home" didn't sound much better, though.

He reached for the gate, then had to stand back when a couple stumbled through, their arms wrapped around each other, holding each other up on their way to the Ramones' place on the other side of Kid's yard.

From the looks of the two of them, a little drunk, a little disheveled, and both in drag with half their clothes falling off, the Sandoval party was in full swing—a fact proven when he stepped through the gate.

Every year, four days before Ash Wednesday,

Panama City hosted Carnaval, a sexually charged, anything-goes party leading up to Lent. Every Friday night, no matter what was happening on the next Wednesday, the Sandoval brothers did the same.

There were colored lights hanging in the trees, two transvestites crooning on a makeshift stage, well over a hundred other people crammed into the garden, some in costume, plenty of beer, and a bar serving *baja panties*—literally "panty lowerers," which in Panama translated to any drink made with hard liquor.

And there was Nicole Alana McKinney. He spotted her instantly. She was half in costume, with a pink feathered tiara in her black-and-purple spiked hair, and a blue sequined miniskirt with a matching stole to go with the top half of her green-and-purple palm frond bikini. She had a *baja panties* in one hand and five cards in the other. Her back was to him, and she was sitting at a table with four guys, two of them Rico and Luis, one of whom was already down to a pair of tighty-whities and an orange feather boa.

It was like the living incarnation of his worst nightmare—or at least his nightmare before she'd gotten engaged.

But this scene. Oh, yeah, he'd imagined it plenty of times: Nikki and a bunch of half-dressed guys well on their way to being undressed guys.

It was her work, taking naked guys and putting them through the wringer of her cameras and her paint brushes until she got what she wanted, which was always more than the guys ever thought they'd have to give.

She was practically famous now, her paintings showing on both coasts and selling in five figures. Three months ago, she'd done an *Esquire* magazine cover of Brad Pitt as one of her fallen angels. Kid had seen it in Bogotá, and it had been incredible.

Fucking Brad Pitt. Who would have believed? Nikki's mentor, Katya Hawkins, was taking her straight to the top of the art world, exactly where she deserved to be. He'd watched Nikki work once— work a guy over—and it had made him sweat and all but turned him inside out. He hadn't known a girl could be so freakin' fierce.

Yeah. He'd kept up with her career, with her life. He'd been discreet, but he'd kept up, asked a few questions. Her sister was married to another of the Steele Street operators, Quinn Younger, although Quinn hadn't gone out on many missions since he and Regan had hooked up.

It was a helluva price to pay for a woman, but under any other circumstances than the ones he'd found himself in last summer, he might have done it for Nikki.

She hadn't come straight out and asked him to take fewer chances, or even quit his job, but he'd seen it in her eyes every time she'd looked at him. He'd known it every time she'd cried because he was going away. So freakin' fierce, and yet so fragile.

Hell, she'd probably made the right choice with

the basket weaver guy, but yeah, sure, he could have done it, backed off on the job and turned himself into her boy toy, gone back to school, and become... something.

Something other than what he was: a highly skilled weapon of the United States government. The months he'd spent with Hawkins and Creed, tracking down and taking out his brother's killers, had changed him. Superman and the jungle boy had changed him. They'd taken everything the Marine Corps had taught him and honed it all to a razor sharpness.

He wasn't a bona fide superhero, not like Hawkins, and he wasn't three-quarters wild like Creed, but he didn't have to do much more than stand there and look at her to know he was still in love with Nikki McKinney.

God, what lousy news. And it didn't change a damn thing. It only made things harder.

He was going to have to keep his distance. Be professional. Stay cool. Play it smart. Get her back on a plane ASAP—and for God's sake not do anything stupid and spontaneous.

Like kiss her.

Or run his tongue up the side of her neck.

Or put his hand on her ass.

He took a breath, ran through the "don't" list one more time, and was good to go—up until she suddenly turned in her chair, startled like a bird taking flight, feathers flying, sequins shimmering, and looked straight at him. He saw the shock on her face, saw her mouth form his name, and his quickly laid plan started sliding out from under him like beach sand in a riptide.

In combat, "tunneling," focusing on one thing and losing track of everything else that was going on around you, was a good way to get killed.

Apparently, the same rule applied in love, because he was slain. The transvestites went into a butchered rendition of "La Vida Loca," and he could barely hear it. The other hundred people were laughing, talking, singing along, their glasses clinking, their sequins shaking, and all they were was a blur. Loose feathers floated in the air, beer spilled, women squealed—and all he could see was Nikki. All he could hear was his heart beating, slow and steady and strong. He knew what he felt, and there were no words for it. Not this.

Her tiara caught the lights and glittered in her wild, dark hair. Pure bed head, pink feathers, and a couple of purple streaks, strands going every which way. It wasn't an accident. She fixed it like that, moussed it and blow-dried it all into an artful mess. He'd watched her do it, teased her about it, kissed her between the moussing and the blow-drying—and loved every second of it.

She had five earrings in one ear and three in the other, always, and none of them ever matched. She sang in the mornings, and he'd been her first man.

All of that made her his.

He started forward, and she rose from her chair, her cards falling to the table, her hand coming up to her chest—a delicate hand with paint under the nails. There was no Nikki without paint. She painted men. She painted on her photographs. She painted angels and demons. She painted her clothes, and once, for him, she'd painted herself—in chocolate and caramel.

Oh, yeah. He was in way over his head.

Seven months without her, without her kiss, without her wrapped around him—by all rights, he should be dead.

He passed the last barrier of drunken dancers and found himself suddenly standing in front of her— with absolutely nothing to say. *Geezus*. All he could do was look at her. She was so beautiful. She'd knocked him senseless the first time he'd seen her, and he'd never really recovered—the wild color of her hair, the dark wings of her eyebrows, the shape of her face, the clear, sun-shot gray of her eyes. Her mouth. God, what she'd done to him with her mouth.

"I . . . I didn't expect . . ." she started, her voice trailing off breathlessly. Her cheeks were flushed. "Not tonight."

"Neither did I." It was the God's truth. She was the last thing he'd expected in this place.

"Kid!" Rico shouted a greeting above the party noise, above the singing and the music and all the chatter.

"*¡Chico!*" Luis put a beer in his hand.

"*¡Chuleta!*" someone else said, and tossed down their cards, laughing. "*La hermosa paloma tiene una* *flor y una escalerilla."* The beautiful bird has a straight flush.

"Nueve alto," Rico called out. Nine high. "Roberto! Take something off."

The conversation flowed around them in Spanish and English, the latter, he knew, in deference to Nikki. The Sandoval brothers were very inclusive, especially of beautiful women. They wanted to keep her in the game.

But she'd already left with him. They just didn't know it yet.

He took a short swallow of the beer, set the bottle aside, and reached for her hand.

There was absolutely nothing to say—not after she put her hand in his.

He needed to kiss her. He was going to kiss her, but not here at the party. He was taking her home.

Keeping her close to his side, he threaded a way through the wildly dancing crowd, heading back toward the gate in the wall. Catcalls sounded behind them, with Rico and Luis accusing him of all sorts of felonious kidnapping of beautiful *gringas*. He wasn't offended. They were laughing and cheering him on, and none of it made a damn bit of difference. There was nothing but Nikki, her hand in his, so small and strong, her skin not so soft, not on her hands. Too much paint, too much paint cleaning, too many hours in the darkroom, processing film to her exacting standards. Her hands were always rough, always nicked up.

But the rest of her was soft, ungodly soft.

He opened the gate and, once on the other side, shoved the bolt home, locking out the rest of the world. He wasn't worried about the Ramones. The traffic was usually one-way from the Sandovals'. By the time people ended up at the Ramones', they were done for the night.

No, all his attention was focused right here, right now, right where he stood.

His heart was pounding.

It was dark on his side of the wall, dark and sweet with the smell of flowers, with just the light from the party filtering in through the trees and across the tops of the climbing vines.

"Kid," she said, her voice still so softly breathless. "You're here. I hoped, but . . . my God, it's like I dreamed you."

Her face was turned up toward his, her hand touching his arm.

"Nikki . . . I—" he started, then gave up and simply lowered his mouth to hers. There was nothing to say, not right now, not when all he wanted, all he needed was to touch her, to slide his tongue in her mouth and taste her, to fill himself up with her.

Their lips met, hers parted, and a hundred emotions flooded through him. He'd expected the pleasure, electrifying pleasure—but he also got relief, bone deep. This was home, being with Nikki, their bodies touching. She came up on tiptoe, her mouth on his, her arms going around his neck, and he slid his hand down her back.

Then farther.

Two rules down in under thirty seconds. He was kissing her and had his hand on her ass—and it was incredible.

This was going to get crazy, fast. Real fast. He could tell. The kiss had gone from "home sweet home" to hot and deep instantly. He tried not to stick his tongue halfway down her throat, tried not to devour her, but she was already there, and he was drowning in the love he felt—in the edge of desperation pulling him under, the heat of her skin, in the all-consuming soft wetness of her mouth.

This was going to be more than crazy. It was going to be crazy hot sex, sweet and dirty up against the garden wall in less than five minutes. *Geezus*. He'd been so in love with her, *was* so in love with her. How had he ever thought he could live without this?

NIKKI opened her mouth wider, took him deeper, and it still wasn't enough—not even close.

She was doomed. Nothing should be this hot, this fast, and nothing ever had been, not in her whole life, except Kid Chaos. She'd come to Panama needing to see him. Her friend Skeeter had said he'd finished up a mission and would be returning to his house in Panama City, and Nikki had known she had to come.

She needed to tie up loose ends, close the books, get him out of her system so she could move on.

She had not come to kiss him.

She had not come for this. She swore it, but between one placed bet and the next, she'd known he was here, and her heart still hadn't stopped racing. It was crazy. She knew it—but, God, it was Kid, and everything she'd ever felt about him, everything he'd ever made her feel had washed through her and nearly dropped her to her knees.

She'd thought she'd gotten past him, but she'd gotten past nothing, not from his first kiss to his last, to this one. The way he felt, the way he smelled, the angle of his jaw, the nape of his neck, the way he held her in his arms, his strength—with his mouth on hers and his arms around her, she never wanted to let him go.

And *damn*, it wasn't supposed to be this way.

He'd left her, twice, the last time without a word for seven long months. No letter. No phone call. No e-mail. She'd missed him until she thought she'd die, been angry with him, longed for him. God, how she'd longed for him, all six feet of warm, smooth skin and ironbound muscle. He was so beautiful, a warrior with dark brown hair and hazel eyes, and a face stripped of all artifice. He was what he was, and he was the first man she'd ever given herself to—and God help her, she was about to do it again. The need was building in her, totally irresistible, damnably inevitable.

Doomed.

She held his face in her hands, covering him with kisses, and he slid his hand under her skirt—and all she could think was *Yes . . . yes. Please, Kid.* It had been so long since she'd had him, since he'd been hers, and it was so easy to fall for him again, to get just a little more naked with every passing minute. He pushed off her panties. She unzipped his pants. Her top came untied. She opened his shirt.

"You've been hurt," she whispered against his lips, her fingers gently touching an edge of gauze.

"No," he assured her, then backtracked a bit. "Well, just a little . . . maybe."

Probably more than a little, considering the size of the bandage, but his heart was beating strongly beneath her hand, his skin was warm, and his mouth was all over her, telling her how much he wanted her.

It was all she needed to know. For this moment, for now, it was everything.

IN the back of his mind, Kid knew the bedroom was only fifty feet away from the garden gate. He also knew they weren't going to make it that far, not the first time, not when she was soft and wet and his pants were half off, not when her hand was between his legs and he could hardly breathe for what she was doing to him.

"*Geezus*, Nikki." He rocked against her, then lifted

her in his arms and pressed her back against the wall. "Wrap your legs around me."

She did, helping him out, helping herself, and then he was pushing up inside her—and everything slowed down, way down.

It was so incredible, the sensations so intensely sweet, the rush of emotion overwhelming.

He swore softly. She felt so amazingly good. He nuzzled her neck, thrusting into her, and felt himself die a little from the pleasure—and the pain. His leg was killing him, and his side hurt like hell from lifting her, but God, there was no way on earth for him to stop.

With his arms under hers, he had one hand wrapped around a fistful of vines, holding them against the wall, and the other threaded through her hair, flowers crushed in his fingers. The whole thing was amazing, the heat, the smell, the softness—Nikki, taking him again and again. It had been so long. It had been forever since he'd been inside a woman, and this was her. All she had to do was breathe to make him hot.

But she did more, sealing her mouth over his and sucking on his tongue and just flat-out filling his whole body with the sensation of sex, from the top of his head on down. Everything. Consuming him. It was all sex and love and heat and Nikki.

He moved one arm down around under her bottom, holding her tighter, lifting her, pushing deeper—and then he came. He felt the warning signals, felt that first sweet edge of release and was helpless to stop it. He didn't have the strength. He didn't have the will. Not this time.

Oh, God. It was soul-wrenching, a melting orgasm that started at the back of his skull and the base of his groin and just flowed out of him, taking him deep inside himself, deep inside her. It was timeless sensation, and it lasted forever, and all the while she kissed him, holding him, her mouth on his so hot and sweet.

"Nikki..." he groaned, pushing himself deeper, his body shuddering. He'd needed her for so long—only her.

THE Learjet glided to a stop on the private airstrip south of the city. Inside, two well-dressed men commandeered the forward cabin, one thin and ascetic, his clothes austerely black, the other younger, more solidly built, with broad shoulders and an elegant, aristocratic face. The white shirt beneath his expensive gray suit jacket was open to reveal a diamond-encrusted gold cross. Both men wore large gold rings engraved with the letter C in the shape of a fer-de-lance, the deadliest snake in tropical America. Its mouth was open, ready to strike, its fangs showing. The C stood for Conseco, and the snake epitomized Juan Conseco's rise to the top of the drug cartel's ladder, a rise punctuated by a series of sudden, lethal strikes against his competitors, until he'd had none left.

Now he only had enemies, and they treated him with all the care and consideration they would have given any poisonous serpent in their midst.

"This is not wise, Juan," the older man said. "I cannot protect you in Panama the way I can at home."

"The way you protected Ruperto and Diego, Uncle Drago?" It was a cruel question, but Juan Conseco was a cruel man, and vengeful. Ruperto had been his cousin, blood of his blood, Drago's oldest son, and he'd been murdered a month ago at his breakfast table by an assassin's bullet—by *el asesino fantasma*. Diego had died the same day, outside Juan's own home, with twenty armed men guarding the walls. None of them had seen anything except Diego falling to the ground with a bullet between his eyes.

It was a signature shot, *el asesino fantasma* laughing in Juan's face, baiting the snake. Losing two of his lieutenants, two cousins, in one day had been a terrible blow to his family's heart, and a blow to his family's pride. The theft at the airstrip on the Putumayo four days ago had been one more blow, the worst in a series of recent hits on the Consecos, all of them making him look weak to his enemies—until, by the grace of God and a night nurse at the Bogotá hospital, Juan's prayers had been answered. The gringo who had been shot in Banco Nuevo, who had flown out of Santa María, had a name: Peter Alexander Chronopolous. It was a name Juan knew only too well, and it had lifted the mystery of *el asesino fantasma*. Finally, Juan understood the fierce ruthlessness that had driven the ghost killer the length of Colombia and into Peru, and brought him back again: revenge, hot with the same blood lust that drove Juan.

For what had been done to his brother, *el asesino* must desire to kill every guerrilla and *pistolero* in all of Colombia. Juan would, if J.T. Chronopolous had been his *hermano*.

He admired ruthless men, but the ghost killer, the gringo devil who dared to interfere with Juan Conseco's affairs, needed to die, an eye for an eye. When Peter Chronopolous had gotten on a plane to Panama earlier this afternoon, Juan and Drago had not been far behind.

Juan looked down the length of the cabin, at the other men he'd brought with him, two assassins of his own, men skilled in all manner of death, and four soldiers from his private guard. They would hunt this Chronopolous down and kill him like a dog.

CHAPTER 2

NIKKI WASN'T DRUNK.

Not even she could get drunk on half a rum-and-Coke. So that was no excuse.

Craziness might work, the old "sex by reason of insanity" defense. Loneliness was a definite contender. She'd never really known what loneliness was until Kid Chaos had loved her and left her.

"Damn," she swore quietly, watching the ceiling fan go around and around above the bed. She wasn't going to think about loneliness. She'd given it up months ago, given it up for good. She wasn't going to miss him ever again, especially when he was lying right next to her, sound asleep, not going anywhere for at least a few more hours. She wouldn't count on more than that. She knew the kind of life he led, and it did not include room for a woman.

At least it hadn't included room for her, but she wasn't going to think about that, either.

So what did that leave her to think about?

Her fiancé.

Which made her wince.

Actually, "almost fiancé" was a more honest way to put it, she decided. Maybe even ex-fiancé—she didn't know what label to put on Rocky anymore, not since the word "friend" had no longer been enough for him, which was one reason she'd come to Panama City.

The other reason was Paris, and what going there meant—but that was too hard to think about when she was lying next to Kid.

So sure. She could think about Rocky Solano. That ought to be enough to clear her head. Yeah, that should cut through the thick sexual haze she'd fallen into the instant she'd seen Peter "Kid Chaos" Chronopolous.

Stifling a groan, she rolled onto her side—and immediately changed her mind. She wasn't going to think about Rocky, dear sweet Rocky, no way in hell, not when Kid was stretched out naked next to her, looking like a god—and that led straight back to the insanity plea, because she hadn't just made love to him once. Oh, no, after the garden incident, they'd headed for the bedroom and started all over again—hot, sweet, and slow, until she'd nearly lost her mind.

She *was* crazy, which wasn't exactly the news flash of the century.

"Damn," she swore again. Wildly abandoned sex

hadn't been part of her plan. So what was she doing in bed with Kid Chaos?

Exactly what she wanted, she admitted, and that was the truth, and when he woke up, she'd probably do it again, her plans be damned. She wasn't to be trusted, not around him—and that was a helluva cold, hard fact to be faced with in the middle of the night.

"Nikki?" he murmured, his voice sleepy, not quite awake. He reached for her hand and brought it to his chest, their fingers entwined. "I love you, Nik."

She let out a heavy sigh, then took a deep breath, maintaining control. She wasn't going to lose it, not here, not now, not with him, but his declaration wasn't exactly a news flash either. He'd told her how much he loved her at least a dozen times since they'd made it to the bedroom, maybe two dozen. Love hadn't been their problem. Their problem had been death, the death of his brother. There'd been no way to get around how J.T. had died, or what Kid had been compelled to do because of it. He couldn't have left the job of tracking down his brother's killers to someone else, not when he was the best the United States government had to offer. It had been a sacred duty, and Nikki understood sacred duties. She'd known he had to go, but she hadn't known he wouldn't need to come back for her—ever.

Seven months without a word.

Not. One. Word.

She went back to watching the ceiling fan slowly slap the hot, humid air.

She wasn't going to fool herself. Despite what had happened, she still had a plane to catch in the morning. Four days ago, Skeeter had told her he'd be here, in Panama City, at his brother's house, but Skeeter had been wrong, and now she'd run out of time. She had to be back in Denver by tomorrow night, and as of yet, absolutely nothing had changed between her and Kid. If anything, they had more loose ends than ever. They hadn't talked. They'd had incredible, mind-blowing sex—again. This whole thing tonight had been an accident, like a train wreck, unplanned, unexpected, highly combustible, dangerously out of control—and completely predictable. They always had train wrecks. Their whole relationship had been a train wreck, the same train wreck over and over: Lay eyes on each other, make love all night long, Kid Chaos disappears. Either he was with her, or he was off the planet.

"Nikki," he murmured again, rolling onto his side, his breath leaving him on a sleep-filled sigh and warming her shoulder.

She turned toward him. God, he was so beautiful— and he'd been hurt, worse and more recently than she'd allowed herself to realize. Her gaze narrowed.

She untwined her hand from his and reached up to touch his chest. She'd noticed his bandages. It would have been impossible not to notice them, the white gauze so stark against his sun-warmed skin, but the gauze had come unwound in places and there was fresh blood on the lower layers, small smudges of it on his arm wrap and the bandage around his leg, a darker smear on the bandage around his torso. Plus he had two stitches on his face, right along the curve of his jaw.

She knew what it all meant. He'd been in a fight, and the only kind of fight Kid Chaos Chronopolous was ever in was a firefight—bullets flying, life or death, no quarter asked, none given, everybody out for blood. She'd once heard Skeeter refer to him as SDF's gunslinger. According to the kick-ass Goth princess, Kid was the best they had, and within that highly skilled group, that was saying a lot.

Skilled at what, other than "gunslinging," Nikki didn't exactly know. Everything about SDF was hush-hush. Kid had once told her he was a bodyguard, but she knew his job went beyond that. She just didn't know how far beyond, or in what direction. Nobody told her anything—especially Kid. So she'd stopped asking, and he'd left, and there it all had been, until tonight.

Crazy, crazy, crazy. She'd probably set herself back four months by sleeping with him, which would really suck big-time. The "three months without a word" mark last Christmas had been the absolute lowest point of her life. She'd barely survived.

No, she wasn't going there again, not even for Kid Chaos. She'd closed those doors for good.

A soft snore escaped him and brought a smile to her lips. As gently as possible, she tucked the end of his arm bandage back under itself, and then slipped her fingers underneath a pair of gold rings he was wearing on a chain around his neck. She'd seen the rings earlier and had been curious as hell about what he was doing with two gold wedding bands, but at the time she'd been too busy to ask—too busy trying to get enough of him.

Letting out a sigh, she turned the rings over in her hand, then let them slide back to their resting place against his chest. They were terribly scratched up, and engraved inside and out, but with just the moonlight to read by, she couldn't see what was written on them.

Damn, what a mess. She was wearing a ring, too, white gold and multijeweled, and he hadn't asked her about it either, thank God. She wasn't sure she had an answer.

Her ring didn't look like a traditional engagement ring, and given the state of her engagement, that was probably for the best. So there they were, lying naked in each other's arms, two people, three rings, no confessions.

Reaching up, she gently ran her fingers back through his hair, sliding a few loose strands off a face of high cheekbones and lean angles, and an incongruously cute nose. It was what made him look so young. Carefully, softly, she touched her mouth to his, then pushed herself away.

She didn't get far.

In an instant, he was awake, his hand coming up and holding her in the bed, his eyes wide open—every muscle and tendon in his body tight and radiating one single message: *Ready.*

Ready for what? she wondered, startled by his sudden transition into utter and complete wakefulness. Good lord, he'd been sound asleep, snoring.

"Don't go," he said, holding her gaze, his voice soft, a sleepy contrast to the alertness pulsing through him like a heartbeat.

"I . . . I wasn't going." At least not very far. She'd thought she'd get some space between them, get some air, give herself at least half a chance to think straight, something it was impossible to do when she was close enough to breathe him in—and they were close. One of his legs was half over one of hers, his right arm beneath her left shoulder. Every breath he took, she felt his stomach rise against her.

"Good." His gaze slid past her to the door leading to the patio and then to the door leading to the hall. His face was stark, his expression deadly serious as he quickly and methodically checked the room.

It gave her pause. It unnerved her. She knew what he was doing—searching for a threat. She'd seen him lay a pistol on the bedside table when he'd taken his clothes off. *Didn't he feel safe in his own house?* she'd wondered at the time.

Obviously not, was the answer, and the realization sent a small shiver through her.

"Are you cold?" he asked, his attention immediately coming back to her.

"No." She shook her head.

He looked at her for a second, an unreadable expression on his face, before his gaze slid away again.

"Nikki, I . . ." he started to say something but then didn't, and suddenly, she felt a little tongue-tied herself.

Oh, yeah, she thought, they were getting off to a great start. The silence drew out between them, then it drew out a little more, until she couldn't quite bear it.

"Your hair is longer," she said, reaching up and smoothing the dark strands lying across the back of his neck.

Longer than it had been seven months ago, before he'd disappeared out of her life.

Without saying anything, he closed his eyes and lifted her hand to his mouth, kissing the backs of her fingers—but he'd heard her. She could tell by the tension furrowing his brow.

"I think you're bleeding," she added, wondering how in the world sex could be so easy between them and everything else, like simple conversation, could be so damn hard. "Do you want me to check your bandages?"

He shook his head. "No." Then he kissed her fingers again and relaxed back on the bed. After a long moment, he opened his eyes and met her gaze. "What are you doing here, Nikki? Here in Panama?"

There it was, the perfect opening, the right question, but somehow, the answer was lodged in her throat. Somehow, it was too patently absurd, after what they'd been doing, to tell him she'd come to find out how she felt about him, or even stupider, to tell him she'd come to close the books on their relationship so she could move halfway around the world with a clear conscience.

Close the books. *Right*, when she smelled like him everywhere, when she still had the taste of him in her mouth and could still feel where he'd been inside her.

"I won a contest," she said, because honestly, what other reason in the world could she possibly have had for hauling her butt over two thousand miles south to the land of palm trees and *baja panties* than to see him?

"A contest?" he repeated, not sounding at all convinced, of course, because he wasn't a complete idiot—except when it came to her. He should never, ever have left her alone for so long, not when he still loved her.

"Yeah. The Skeeter Bang Bake-Off. First prize was a round-trip ticket to Panama City and the key to your house."

He grinned at that, a fleeting half-smile that didn't quite reach his eyes. "You and Skeeter couldn't bake your way out of a paper bag."

True. She was bona fide Take-Out Queen, a fact she'd proven to him numerous times during their brief but intense time together last fall.

"When she gave me the key, she said you'd be here."

"When was this?"

"Four days ago."

He seemed to think that over for a moment or two, before he spoke. "I was still in Colombia four days ago."

"You were in Colombia a long time," she said, then paused. To her surprise, the words had come out with just the barest bit of an edge on them, which was the last thing she'd expected. Honestly, she had not come all the way to Panama to lay blame on anyone. She was willing to listen to any explanation he wanted to offer—*any* explanation. He loved her. He'd said it over and over. He'd missed her like crazy, dreamed about her, dreamed about being with her the way they'd just been. So why hadn't he come home? Christian Hawkins had come home. Creed Rivera had come home.

But not Kid.

"Yeah, a long time," he said, not seeming to notice her bare little bit of edge—except he picked up her left hand. "Too long, I guess."

O-kay. Suddenly there were two small, bare little bits of edge lying between them, and she was beginning to see why maybe they'd instinctively made love first, because even the simplest conversation was going to hell in a handbasket at light speed.

He turned her hand over, and the faint light of the tropical night slid over white gold and diamonds, over an original Rocky Solano design of emeralds, sapphires, and rubies. The ring wasn't garish. It was stunning, art of the highest order, like everything Rocky did, its nature suffused with his genius. He'd had it made for her as a testament of his love and admiration—and up until tonight, she hadn't worn it since she'd gotten on the plane in Denver.

Bling. That's what she'd thought earlier this evening. She would put on a little bling to go with her sequins and tiara. She'd been in Panama for three nights, and for three nights running, she'd been hanging out with the Sandoval twins, waiting for Kid. It had been one party after another to keep from going crazy worrying about him, about why he wasn't home like Skeeter had expected, and about how she was going to feel if he didn't make it back before she had to leave—because she wasn't looking back. She had a life to lead, and she couldn't move forward if she was always looking back.

"What *are* you doing here, Nikki?" he asked again, lifting her hand between them, his meaning disturbingly clear.

"So Skeeter told you?" *Dammit*. She'd wanted to do it herself, in her own time, to explain her engagement in her own way, whatever in the hell that might have turned out to be.

"Yes." The word came out flat.

Hell. If she'd come and there'd been no connection left between them, if there'd been no chemistry, no heat, no love, she would have already told him everything, cleared the air, closed those damn books that were giving her fits, and be ready to catch her flight and move on in the morning.

But they'd gone nuclear.

And she'd just gotten busted for bling. She should never have put the ring back on, not after she'd taken it off. Given where she'd ended up tonight, she never should have put the ring on in the first place. That hadn't been a news flash four weeks ago when she'd done it, and it sure as hell wasn't a news flash when she was lying naked in bed with Kid Chaos.

"I needed to see you," she said. "When you said you'd be back, I thought you meant before I hit menopause."

Another grin touched the corners of his mouth, but just barely.

"You *did* say you'd be back, Kid."

YEAH, he had, Kid thought, and he'd meant every word when he'd said them, but things had gotten complicated.

"The mission took longer than we'd planned," he said. "Adjustments had to be made." And that was about all he could say about what he had done. Everything else was either classified or nothing he wanted her to know. She hated what he did, and she didn't know the half of it. Hell, she didn't know a tenth of it, a hundredth, and if it was up to him, that's exactly the way he was going to keep it.

"Even Creed made it home for Christmas."

"Yeah." It was true. By Christmas, Pablo Castano and Manuel Garcia had been dead; his and Creed's job had been finished. But Creed wasn't a black-ops sniper. "I was . . . uh, tasked with another mission." The assassinations of Juan Conseco's lieutenants had taken weeks of planning, recon, and rehearsal, but the results had been exactly what they were supposed to be: two shots, two kills, the perfect ratio. From there, he'd been tagged for the Putumayo mission, and almost before he'd realized it, he'd been gone for seven months—six of them spent thinking she was still there, somehow part of his life.

He'd been wrong. The proof was staring him in the face, the damn thing he'd been trying so hard not to think about for the last four weeks. The thing he'd completely forgotten the instant he'd seen her, and remembered the instant he'd seen her ring.

"So you're engaged," he said as casually as possible.

Fuck. It sounded so much worse out loud than it did knocking around inside his brain, painfully worse.

"No," she said. "Not really."

Oh, sure. Right.

He could see how she could have a few doubts at this point, but the ring looked damned real to him, and it made him feel goddamned awful, actually sick, and really fucking angry. A ring on her left hand said only one thing: She'd been sleeping with another man.

Sex. Like they'd just had. With another man.

Another man inside her.

Fuck. He rolled onto his back and stared at the goddamned ceiling fan.

He couldn't do this, this whole hash-it-out scene,

not without saying things he knew he would regret, probably not without breaking something—and that was the wrong goddamn impulse to give in to right now. He was way too primed for violence, and no matter what she'd done, she didn't deserve that from him.

With one move, he pushed himself out of the bed, and grimacing, headed for the bathroom. He didn't look back. Sure she had doubts, or she wouldn't have come to Panama, but before she'd had doubts, she'd fucked another guy—and he was in no shape to deal with it.

In the bathroom, he splashed cold water on his face, and then stood in front of the sink, forcing himself to keep his hands relaxed. He couldn't get back in the bed with her. He knew that much.

After another minute of just standing there, watching the water drip off his face, he realized that was the only goddamn plan he was going to come up with— not sleeping with her the rest of the night.

Fine. Great. He'd go with it.

But when he got back to the bedroom, it was a done deal. She and her little purple robe were gone.

He heard her banging around in the kitchen, and figured it was good enough. She could bang around all night long, what was left of it. He was going back to bed—alone.

CHAPTER

3

T HE MISSION TOOK LONGER.

We had to make adjustments.

Nikki banged a pot on the stove. *Damn him.*

He was angry. Well, there was plenty of anger to go around. Seven months and all he could say was "the mission took longer than we'd planned"?

She banged another pot on the stove just for the hell of it.

I was tasked with another mission.

She'd show him "tasked."

Another pot came down, and then she had to stop. He only had three pans. She started water for tea in one and slammed the others around a bit getting them back in the cupboard.

This had been their whole problem the whole time they'd been together: Peter "Kid Chaos"

Chronopolous was the most buttoned-up man she'd ever met.

Men gave it up for her—always, every time. She took off their clothes, put them under her lights, and deconstructed them, and up to a certain point, every man she'd ever painted or photographed had been glad to do it. After that "certain point" they all balked, except for Travis James. Her angel model simply didn't have anything to hide. But balk or not, she had never let a guy get away from her without giving up at least some of his secrets. More often than not, she got more than they ever meant to reveal.

Except for Kid Chaos.

He was incredibly self-contained. So self-contained, there wasn't room for her, except in his bed.

Damn him.

Two people could not make a life out of just sex, not even the kind of sex they had. In all the nights they'd spent together, there had been only one where he'd opened up, the night he'd gotten back from Colombia with his brother's remains. The experience had been shattering. He'd hurt so badly that night, and she'd hurt for him. But for all they'd shared, by morning, he'd had himself back under control.

He was the Ice Man, glacially cool Kid Chaos. In his line of work, that was probably considered an asset, but in a relationship, it was a definite obstacle.

Adjustments had to be made.

She'd show him adjustments. She was going to "adjust" herself back to Denver in the morning, and if *anything* he'd said to her tonight had been true, he wouldn't be too far behind.

And if he was too far behind, that would be the end of it, because she'd be gone.

KID knew three things the moment he woke up: Nikki wasn't by his side; he was crazy in love with her, which under the circumstances was a goddamn awful thing to have to admit; and something was wrong—more wrong than just Nikki not being next to him.

Sure, when he'd gone to bed, he'd wanted to be alone, but he didn't now, especially when something didn't feel right.

He pushed himself out of the bed, soundlessly, and slipped on his pants. Reaching for his pistol was automatic. Racking the slide and chambering a round was deliberate, something he usually did before he fell asleep. But last night he'd fallen asleep with Nikki in his arms, and he'd forgotten, which he hoped to hell wasn't indicative of the way things were going to be, that he'd be so sex-addled around her, he wouldn't be able to think straight. Guys like him did not fall asleep without their guns cocked, locked, loaded, and less than an arm's length away.

Yeah, he was hoping there was some way for them to work through this mess, despite that goddamn ring on her finger. A future together, that's what he'd been thinking, and he kept right on thinking it up until he got outside and had to face the fact that she was thinking something else.

There was light coming from the kitchen, illuminating the front half of the courtyard, and her hot pink mock-croc leather suitcases were stacked next to each other on the patio, both of them packed, zipped, and ready to go.

It didn't even take a second for what it all meant to register, and he couldn't believe it. She was walking out on him. In the middle of the night. What the hell part of "I love you, Kid. Oh, God, please, I love you," had he misunderstood? Or had all that just been the heat of the fricking moment?

Because there had been heat, searing, consuming heat when they'd made love. He'd been reborn in it, felt hope in it, up until he'd seen her ring—and now the suitcases.

Goddamn. This couldn't be right. It couldn't end like this. Something huge had happened to him when he'd seen her at the Sandovals'. Suddenly he'd seen a life for himself again, something beyond the day-to-day battle of staying alive, and for him, for the last seven months, it had been a battle every single fricking day. Somebody was *always* out to grease his ass.

He started toward the door into the living room, determined to do something, say something, anything, to make her understand, to apologize, whatever it took—and then he saw the body, a crumpled form in sequins and feathers lying next to the garden wall, drenched in blood.

Half a gallon of adrenaline instantly drop-loaded into his veins, switching on every survival instinct he had. He tightened his hold on the .45, wrapping his right hand around his left on the gun's grip, his gaze raking the yard. The dead person wasn't Nikki. He'd known that immediately. The body was too big, all long legs, muscular arms, and broad shoulders—the exact opposite of everything that was Nicole Alana McKinney.

The rest of the yard was clear. He ran his gaze over the body again, saw the mutilation that told him just exactly how much fucking trouble he was in, and all the while, he listened.

Listened for a breath, for a step, for any little snick of sound that would tell him where the killer was, where Nikki was, tell him she was still alive, still *here*.

Please, God. If she'd been taken from the house, the odds against them got so much worse. He wasn't even going to consider the possibility of death—not hers, not tonight.

Then he heard it, the scrape of a chair and the clink of a cup being set on the kitchen table.

The assassin heard it, too.

Kid saw a shadow slide across the window in the other bedroom, and he moved to intercept, silently, quickly, from the patio into the main bathroom. He was waiting for the bastard, his knife in his hand, when the killer came down the hall.

Shooting him at close range with the .45 would have been effective, easy—and loud. The five-inch, razor-sharp Spyderco blade was just as effective and far quieter, but it came at a cost when the man instantly countered Kid's attack and fought back, blocking Kid's first strike.

Kid would have fought, too, if someone had been trying to slip a knife up under his skull to sever his brain stem, or stab him in the neck to slit his throat. He would have fought like a sonuvabitch, and the guy was—fighting for his life. The assassin got in a good hit with his elbow, catching Kid right on the mother-fricking bullet wound in his side. Pain, white hot, flashed over him like a strobe light on speed. Stars flashed in front of his eyes, but he didn't make a sound, didn't let go, and didn't let up. The guy kicked and squirmed, until Kid body-slammed him hard into the doorjamb and stunned him enough to wrestle him to the floor. He got in one deep cut to the guy's gut and jerked the blade upward—hard.

As added insurance, Kid took the assassin's head in his hands and twisted, hard and fast, breaking the guy's neck. The sound was unmistakable. He heard the snap loud and clear.

So did Nikki.

Her gasp brought his head around.

She was sitting at the table in the kitchen, on the other side of the living room, staring right at him, frozen in shock. The look of horror on her face did absolutely nothing to ease the rush of adrenaline coursing through him, jacking him up. He knew how he looked: frighteningly fierce, kneeling on a guy he'd just killed with a knife—killed, he might add, with a fair amount of skill. The guy had gone *down*, and except for whatever screwup had alerted the guy, and the resulting grappling around, Kid had taken him down almost without a sound. If there were other gunmen in the house, they didn't know he was on the hunt.

But they knew someone was in the kitchen, someone who gasped out loud, and clinked her cup, and didn't have a clue what kind of danger she was in.

Kid knew. He heard the soft crunch of a footstep on the grass runner in the hall behind the kitchen, and drew his pistol, his knee still firmly in the dead assassin's back.

Nikki's eyes widened, the blood draining from her face. In another life, he would have told her, "Honey, when a guy points a gun in your direction, duck, dive, run, anything, just move and keep moving." But it was all over before he could have even gotten the word "honey" out of his mouth. The other killer cleared the hall; Kid covered him and squeezed the trigger twice, rapid-fire, on his Heckler & Koch .45—body shots. The guy dropped like a stone behind her.

Perfect. Now everybody in a five-block radius knew somebody was shooting something. More likely, if Juan Conseco had sent more than two guys to murder him in his sleep, and they were paying attention, they knew *el asesino fantasma* was shooting something, probably their guys. The man he'd strangled had been carrying a silenced semiautomatic pistol.

The guy he'd shot had been carrying the same, and he'd just squeezed off two full, hot loads with plenty of bang.

Aiming at the dead guy's head, he rose to his feet and, standing between the man and Nikki, fired off another hollow-point bullet. He wasn't taking any chances. He never took any chances.

He was across the living room and had Nikki by the arm and out of the chair before she could even get her mouth closed, let alone wipe the stunned expression off her face. Holding her close, he shielded her off to his right side as he put another bullet in the other killer, head shot. Neither of the bastards was ever getting up again. When Kid cleared a room, it stayed clear.

Turning her around, he hustled her back out the door to the patio. The house had been made. He'd been made, and that left only one thing to do: run like hell.

CHAPTER 4

Denver, Colorado

LIFT YOUR SIDE about two inches," Travis James said, leaning back a bit from his ladder to see if the painting was lining up on the wall.

"Cripes, Travis, two minutes ago, you told me to lower it two inches, and it's the middle of the freaking night," his friend, Skeeter Bang, bitched.

"Hey, babe, you knew the deal," he said, adjusting his side of the seven-by-five-foot painting after she moved her side. Then he tied it off.

The "deal," when they'd negotiated it, hadn't specifically included hard labor all night long, but Skeeter knew things didn't always go as planned when a person was hanging a show for Nikki McKinney. This wasn't pottery they were arranging. Nikki's paintings—most of them of him, naked and in angel wings—ranged from large to extra-large.

It was tough work, yeah, but no tougher than Skeeter. She wasn't going to walk. She needed him. For every hour she slaved for him, helping him put up Nikki and Rocky Solano's show in the Toussi Gallery, he was going to slave for her—bare-chested and shrink-wrapped in blue Lycra tights, a mighty sword in his hands, Japanese *kangi* tattoos running down his arms. Tattoos that were damn hard to get off, and that she got to choose. And she chose the good stuff, just what he wanted on his body—Blood Warrior, and Scream Reaper, whatever the hell that was, and Dagger Death, real weird shit. She'd let him choose the first time she'd drawn him, but then complained that Peace, Love, Compassion, and Joy had thrown her off her vibe.

He thought her vibe was off all by itself, without any help from him. The character she had him playing, Kenshi the Avenger from her *Star Drifter* series, was *not* him. She was thinking of somebody else. He didn't know who, but it was somebody who'd been places he couldn't get to even in his imagination, which was strange. Nikki took him straight to hell most of the time, and he didn't have any trouble getting there.

"How many more paintings are there?" she asked.

"Eight, and don't get your panties all in a wad. Just be glad Rocky's stuff is up." Rocky Solano's fabric art pieces were triple-extra-large, damned heavy, and unwieldy until they were in place. No place mats for that boy. No way.

"I . . . I feel faint," she groaned, stopping halfway down the ladder and resting her head against a step.

"Oh, right. Faint." He let out a short laugh. "You could kick my butt from here to Boulder all night long, which is why I called you. And you need me, which is why you're here. You can't afford to feel faint, Skeeter, and neither can I, not tonight."

SKEETER made a face behind his back, the slave driver. But he had a point. She did need him, if she was ever going to get her *Star Drifter* series finished, and he definitely needed her, if he was going to get this show hung before Nikki got home.

His other helper, a small piece of crumb cake curled up in a corner of the gallery, sound asleep, wasn't proving to be much help at all.

"What's her name again?" she asked, gesturing at the girl.

"Jane Linden," he said.

"And how much does Nikki pay her to sleep on the job?" The girl had been asleep since Skeeter had gotten to Toussi's.

"She doesn't work for Nikki. Hawkins hired her to help Katya around the gallery. She's staying in the apartment upstairs." The gallery was in LoDo, a restored historical neighborhood in Denver's lower downtown, the place where Katya Hawkins had launched Nikki McKinney's career last summer, super-launched it. Nikki was going places, and

Skeeter was keeping tabs—not for herself, but for Kid Chronopolous, the poor sap. She loved him, but he was being a total idiot when it came to Nikki McKinney, who'd turned around and thrown a real wrench in the works by getting herself engaged to Rocky Solano. Skeeter's own love life was far from perfect—well, actually, it was far from even existing—but even she knew you couldn't hold on to a lover by completely ignoring them, and Kid had completely ignored Nikki McKinney since he'd left for South America last September. It was now March. Seven whole months.

"Street kid?" she asked, tilting her head toward the sleeping Jane.

"If Hawkins hired her, you know she's got to be a certified juvenile delinquent with a rap sheet a mile long."

Yeah, Skeeter knew. That's what she'd been when Christian Hawkins, a.k.a. Superman, had pulled her in off the streets and given her a chance at a new life. Now she was a certified computer geek with a deadly roundhouse kick and a Heckler & Koch 9mm who did race-quality tune-ups on sixties-era muscle cars on the side.

She'd come a helluva long way in the last few years—and Travis was right, at five feet eight inches tall, and benching one seventy-five, she probably could kick his butt all the way to Boulder and back. It wasn't that he wasn't in shape. The guy was ripped— and plenty hot, with his golden, wheat-colored hair pulled back in a low ponytail, and ocean-blue eyes girls and gays seemed to just drown in—but he was also really, really nice, gave great neck massages, did yoga, for crying out loud, was a good listener, and believed with all his heart in conflict resolution, not confrontation.

In other words, he wouldn't have lasted five minutes in the places she'd been.

"Should we wake Jane up and put her to bed?" she asked. The girl looked a little crumpled and darned uncomfortable where she'd fallen asleep across a couple of upholstered chairs.

"I don't, well, uh, let's just get finished here first."

It was a subtle thing, just the barest hint of hesitation in his voice, but it was more than enough to fire up Skeeter's imagination. Fighting a grin, she slanted her gaze back to Travis. He was sweet on the crumb cake.

Fascinating.

Women mobbed Travis James. A couple of women had actually followed him home from Nikki's last show, presented themselves *en déshabillé* on his doorstep, and basically freaked him out. The risk was inherent. Over half of Nikki's work featured him, in angel wings, in agony or ecstasy, either descending or ascending, and always completely in the nude. When Nikki painted him in Hell, he was post-Apocalyptic, shattered from the inside out, his wings in shreds, his body bleeding. On his way to Heaven, he was a rising god, pure as the driven snow, nearly transparent with bliss and light—and looked good enough to eat, which she was sure was exactly what those two women had had in mind.

Nikki McKinney was a genius, and Travis was the muse.

Skeeter knew that in comparison she was just a graffiti artist who'd taken her stuff off the city's walls and thrown it on paper. But, hell, Travis inspired her, too, along with everyone else she knew. Unlike Nikki, she had a whole bunch of people she drew all the time, though a couple of them didn't know it.

"Eight more paintings, huh." She shifted her attention back to the stack against the wall. It was fine with her if he wanted to let the crumb cake sleep. Skeeter couldn't see her face, but from the size of her, she didn't think Jane could haul eight more paintings up on the walls.

"Three of them are a triptych," he said, as if that helped. "We'll hang them last."

Triptych, diptych, there were still eight paintings left to be hung.

"I'm going to need food." Carbs, herbs, protein bar, a triple-whipped-cream mocha latte with chocolate sprinkles and an extra shot—anything.

"There's a few things over on the table, next to . . . uh, Jane."

Sheesh. She didn't even bother to hide her grin this time. The guy was smitten.

Stepping down off the ladder, she went over to see what Mr. Twigs and Leaves might have brought for snacks. Skeeter liked an organic smoothie as well as the next person, and had more than one herbal concoction she swore by, but Travis was from Boulder, home of free-range supplemental fungi and antioxidant algae, and sometimes his idea of food looked more like compost to her.

And sometimes it looked darned good. On the table, she found a bag of tortillas, a container of organic herbal cheese spread, and a bunch of grapes—which solved her hunger problem beautifully.

Curious, she checked out the girl while she fixed herself some food. Jane had silky dark hair that fell halfway down her back. It was very shiny, and straight as a stick. Her shoulders were narrow, her butt definitely curvy under her designer jeans, and she had on a blue silk sweater to match her blue high heels—very uptown. She definitely looked expensive, at least from the rear. Travis seemed to have excellent taste in reformed delinquents.

Skeeter was halfway through her first tortilla and reaching for the grapes, when Jane stirred in her sleep. Taking another bite, she glanced over at the girl again—and came to a full-out stop in mid-chew.

Jane had rolled over onto her other side, revealing her face—and *oh, cripes.*

Oh, brother. Oh, cripes.

Jane. He'd said Jane Linden, as in plain Jane, and Jane's Addiction, but Skeeter and every gangbangin' wallbanger from the west side to the 'burbs knew her by her street name as Robin Rulz, as in Robin Hood and robbing fools, robbing them of their purses and their wallets, and for all the times she never got caught, that ruled. She was a grade-A pocket-picking genius whose mad skills included lifting people's car keys with no jingle jangle. She and her gang had staked out some turf in LoDo a few years back, becoming known as the Castle Rats, with a C-RAT tag marking their territory and enough light-fingered members to give the Denver cops a run for their money. For a couple of years, lower downtown had been notorious for the scrawny band of street kids who came out after dark and stole people blind, with their victims absolutely clueless until they got home and realized their cash and credit cards had gone missing—except, of course, for the really unlucky ones who couldn't get home because the Castle Rats had stolen their cars.

Then Robin Rulz had disappeared—poof—right off the streets. Not even her gang knew where she'd gone. Rumors said the legend had finally been busted, bottomed out in juvie, and been sent down to the penitentiary in Canon City for some hard time. Others had said no way. Robin hadn't been caught, not ever, but she'd been known to take a break now and then when the heat was on. That's all it was, they said, just Robin taking a break. Some folks had said she'd gone to Phoenix to wait out the cops, give them a chance to forget her, and then she'd be back and the fun would start all over again.

And here the hell she was, the leader of the pack,

with the run of a gallery full of thousands of dollars worth of art, hundreds of thousands with Rocky's work installed. It was enough to give Skeeter heart palpitations. Had Superman gone completely mad? Robin Rulz living in Toussi's?

And Travis thought he liked this girl?

Skeeter glanced over her shoulder at him, took a breath, and told herself to remain calm. Christian Hawkins was no fool. It was while he'd been doing his own time in Canon City that he'd acquired the name of Superman. He knew the score, and he knew people. Not even a legendary hustler like Robin Rulz could have pulled the wool over Superman's eyes, but Travis—*geez*—he was a babe in the woods when it came to this kind of action.

Somebody really needed to tell him who she was, or at least who she'd been.

Somebody, right. Dammit. Skeeter didn't need to look around to know she was the only one available for the job.

Well, hell. Maybe Travis was right. Maybe they should get the darn show hung first and worry about other things later, like leaving the gallery in the hands of a thief.

Jane, she thought, shifting her attention back to the girl. The name Jane Linden sounded almost wholesome, and no one who had ever seen them in action would have ever used the word wholesome to describe a Castle Rat.

Panama City, Panama

KID TOOK NIKKI through the Ramones' yard, avoiding the Sandovals' and the dead drag queen with the "Colombian necktie" lying next to the garden gate. There was a reason the guy had been drenched in blood. Having your throat cut and your tongue pulled out through the opening was a damned bloody business. It was also one of Conseco's signature pieces, his and every drug lord's from Tijuana to Medellín. But Conseco was the one after him, the one after the ghost killer.

He'd known his cover would be blown someday. He just hadn't expected someday to be today. His money said someone in the Bogotá hospital was a few thousand pesos richer tonight. There couldn't have been too many gringos with bullets in them this week, and he'd left enough blood in the Banco Nuevo cantina and on the *Garza* for Conseco's guys to know he'd been hit. Getting flight information on the plane he and C. Smith had taken out of Santa María wouldn't have been too damn difficult, not with money changing hands, and there was a lot of money waiting to change hands.

Fuck. Half a million dollars. What was he, the poster boy for the antidrug coalition? Conseco was out to make a statement, that was for damn sure. And if the cocaine baron got his way, the statement was going to be written in *el asesino fantasma*'s blood.

A man's shirt was hanging off a chair on the Ramones' patio. He grabbed it and jammed his feet into a pair of shoes lying next to the table. Besides the knife and the HK .45, he had a thousand dollars and his wallet in one of his cargo pockets. His passport and three extra ten-shot magazines were in another—standard urban battle pack.

Heading toward the Ramones' back gate, the one leading into the alley, he gave Nikki a quick glance. She was in shock, her face white, her expression dazed, and unbelievably, she had her purse clutched in her hand. He remembered seeing it now, on the table next to her teacup.

He was moving her too fast for there to be much conversation, which was just as well. The last few minutes had been pretty intense. Business as fucking usual for him, but completely outside her realm of experience, until she'd met up with him again—damn it. He could see his whole white-picket-fence fantasy going up in flames.

At the gate, he pulled her behind him and waited, listening, and trying damned hard to hear anything beyond her breathing. Nikki was hyperventilating. That sucked, but there wasn't much he could do about it right now. Conseco's guys usually ran in packs, but there was a slim chance those two guys had been on their own, a couple of freelancers out for the half a million. Everybody and their mother had to be after him for that kind of money.

His kitchen door slammed, and he swore under his breath. Hell, no, they weren't out of this, not yet. Voices were coming from his backyard, one yelling orders, another demanding answers, and in the middle of all the shouting, somebody made a threat and backed it up with Juan Conseco's name, the last thing he'd wanted to hear.

Shit. It was definitely time to get out of Dodge.

He eased the gate open, checked both ways, and pulled her out of the Ramones' yard and into the alley, into the jungle. There was a reason J.T. had bought a house in this particular neighborhood: escape routes and cover. The streets and alleys were a maze, and unlike other places in the city, the forest had been invited back here and nurtured with a vengeance. People in this insular section of the capital valued their privacy, thus the walled gardens and the profusion of vegetation, towering trees and thick shrubbery. Four blocks away, it all emptied into an urban landscape as much of a jungle as any on the planet. That's where he was taking her.

Keeping close to the sides of the overgrown alley, and a firm grip on her hand, he ran past the next two houses. As soon as they rounded the corner, he ducked across the alley, opened the first gate he came to, and slipped inside one of his neighbors' yards. There was nothing random about his movements. The route was planned. He'd run it a dozen times in the dark.

He didn't stop inside the gate to listen. He didn't need to listen. There was no mistaking the sound of men piling into the alley, or of the trash and refuse piles being torn through. Gates were being breached, dogs barking, lights coming on all over the neighborhood, and it was all happening with lightning speed, like an avalanche sweeping toward them.

So he ran, and he kept running, dragging Nikki with him through one yard after the next, lifting her off her feet when she stumbled, practically carrying her the rest of the time. At the end of the block, they crossed another street. A hedge on the other side provided cover until they came to a set of stone steps leading to a small, tree-enclosed plaza. He plunged the two of them down into the darkness, not daring to slow their pace until they'd reached the far end of the park.

As they came out from under the trees, he slipped his gun into the waistband of his pants. There were other people on this end of the park, some older kids messing around, groups of party-goers, couples sitting here and there on the benches, and the last thing he wanted was to draw anybody's attention.

Blending in—that's what they were doing now, not running their guts out.

Releasing the death grip he had on her arm, he slid his hand down to hers and gave her a quick glance. He'd been holding onto her pretty damn tightly—and sure enough, he'd marked her. Every one of his fingerprints stood out on her pale skin like a brand.

Damn, he hated that, really hated it.

Moving her along at a fast walk, he headed toward the street, toward the crowds of people making the scene in the Calle Uruguay, Panama City's club district. On Friday and Saturday nights it was the biggest party in the country, the safest place for them.

"We're almost there," he said, glancing over his shoulder. "You're doing great." That was a lie. She didn't look like she was doing great. She looked shell-shocked. He could imagine what was running through her mind, and none of it was good.

Letting go of her for a second, he did up a couple of buttons on the shirt. He had a round in the chamber of his .45, five left in the magazine, and thirty cartridges in his cargo pocket. Under the best of circumstances that was a damn short firefight. Under the worst of circumstances it was a goatfuck waiting to happen. Thirty-six rounds weren't enough for him to win a gun battle if Conseco's narco-guerrillas chased them down.

At the street, he gave up on the buttons—three would have to do—and took her hand again. He didn't wait for a break in the traffic. There was no break in traffic in the Calle Uruguay district on Friday night. Taxi drivers honked, and a few people cussed him out in two languages, but they made it across. Half a block farther and he pulled her into the shadows between two buildings.

His heart was racing. Her breath was coming hard and fast. *Geezus*, that had been close, too damn close. Somebody at the DEA in Bogotá needed a freaking heads-up on their security protocols at the hospital, because they'd been breached every which way from Sunday. There was no other way for anyone to have traced him to Panama City, to his own house, except through the name on his hospital file, Peter Alexander Chronopolous.

Cupping her face with his hand, he rested his cheek against her forehead, stealing a couple of seconds to assure himself she was all right. But she wasn't. She was shaking like a leaf.

"Shhh, Nikki. You're safe." Not really, not quite, not yet. But she didn't need to hear the truth right now. She felt like she was going to come apart. She was still in one piece, though, still with him, and that's what counted. He could fix everything else later.

Still holding on to her hand, he turned back toward the street and scanned the area, especially in the direction of the park, looking for anyone out of the ordinary, anyone who might be carrying a weapon, anyone who looked like they were looking for him. When he'd checked the whole area over once, he did it again, reevaluating the scene, checking the new dynamics of the crowd, looking for someone who seemed hyperalert, someone who was doing the same thing he was doing.

"There's...there's blood on my dress," she said from behind him, her voice softly horrified. "I'm sure I didn't...wasn't—"

He turned toward her, his grip inadvertently tightening on her hand, his gaze dropping to the front of her dress.

"Are you hurt?" he said gruffly.

"No...I—no." She sounded confused.

There was a bloody smear at her waist, but she couldn't have run the way she had, for as long as she had—especially in the freakin' little sandals she was wearing—if she'd been wounded, and the material wasn't torn. It was just bloody.

Then it hit him. He'd done that to her. Stabbed the guy, gotten blood on his hands, and then grabbed her. She had blood on the shoulder of her dress, too, a handprint—his. *Geezus.*

"You're okay, Nikki," he said, careful to keep his voice confident and controlled. "You did great. I really appreciate how strong you've been." The encouragement was important, deliberate, the recognition of how well she'd followed his lead. He was incredibly grateful. It all could have gone so much worse—but he wasn't going to think about that.

Her gaze lifted to meet his, and he felt his heart sink. Her eyes were wide, frightened, darkened by the low light and the shadows. She was pale, the tremors in her hand coming from the entire rest of her body.

And he'd done all that to her, too, in record time, without an ounce of intent.

"You killed those men," she said. "The first one . . . you killed him three times."

It was a simple statement, not entirely accurate, but he knew what she meant, and it took the wind out of him. She was in a near state of shock, could hardly catch her breath, and her dress was smeared with some badass *hombre*'s blood who he'd left in a broken heap outside his bathroom door.

Yeah, he'd been pretty jacked up in the house, and try as he might not to, it was all too easy to imagine how the sequence of events and his actions in them must have looked to her—not incredibly skilled and heroic, but absofuckinglutely deranged.

"I only killed him once, Nikki. The rest of it was insurance." Again, he made sure his voice was steady and confident, letting her know he knew what he was doing, no matter how god-awful it must have looked. Ammo was cheap, and her life wasn't, he could have added, but he didn't think that pithy axiom was going to do a damn thing to improve the image of him blowing two guys away at point-blank range, nor did it adequately address half gutting the first guy and breaking his neck.

He was so screwed.

"Insurance?"

"I had to make sure he wouldn't come after us," he explained. "Not him or the man in the other hall."

"But they were already dead."

"Maybe." Probably. But he didn't stay alive on maybe and probably. He stayed alive on head shots. "I know everything happened really fast, but in those kinds of situations, everything always happens fast, especially when there are guns involved. I didn't have a choice, Nikki." The truth was, he'd made his choice about guys like Conseco's a long time ago, and the chances of him losing any sleep over tonight's killings were between slim and none. In the war he was part of, he never doubted where he stood, or what he had to do to hold his ground. That's why he'd joined the Marines. It was why he'd followed his brother into General Buck Grant's black-ops special reconnaissance team. It was why he was part of SDF.

"Guns. I see," she said—but she didn't. He could tell by the hesitation in her voice. She was trying to process what had happened, but there was no way in hell for that to happen in this alley in the next few seconds.

Goddamn. He'd stayed away from Denver for seven months so she wouldn't see the kind of life he'd been leading, wouldn't see the changes that life had made in him, and inside of two minutes, he'd bloody well massacred two guys right in front of her.

He wished it hadn't happened; with all his heart, he wished she hadn't been exposed to that kind of danger, to that kind of brutality; but he couldn't regret the killings. He knew the score. He knew the playing field they were on, and he knew exactly what would have happened to the two of them if he was anything less than what he was: better.

Better than all the guys he'd ever tracked down, better than any guy who'd ever gone up against him—better than the next guy, whoever he was, wherever they met. Kid didn't have to be the best, but he knew with every cell in his body that he *always* had to be better, every single time, without fail. There was only one rule in the warfare he'd been trained for: win or die. For seven months, he'd been living in a world light-years away from Nikki's. It was stark and dangerous and had no room for errors.

Tonight, for whatever reason, she'd stepped into his world, but that didn't change the one rule. It was still win or die.

He checked the street again, then pulled her back onto the sidewalk, into the crowds. They were only a couple of blocks from their destination, a place called the Parrot Bar. The owner of the Parrot had been a friend to J.T. long before he'd been a friend to Kid. A few phone calls, starting with C. Smith in Bogotá and the DEA Panama Country Office right here in the city, should get him what he needed: transportation out of Panama and a plane ride back to the States.

She stumbled, and he caught her more closely to his side.

"I've got you. Don't worry," he said. The DEA had gotten him into this, and the DEA could damn well get him and Nikki out. "I'm taking you someplace safe. Everything is okay."

NO, it wasn't, Nikki thought, half running to keep up with him.

Everything was insane.

Her sandal caught on the uneven sidewalk again, and Kid pulled her tighter, closer.

My god.

My holy, freaking god.

She still couldn't believe what she'd seen, what he'd done. Her heart had stopped when he'd pulled his gun and pointed it straight at her, right after her heart had damn near jumped out of her chest when he'd . . .

Kid, with his knee in the man's back, with the man's head in his hands, the fierce, violent twist that had broken the man's neck. Kid drawing his gun. The deafening double explosion. Kid wiping the bloody knife off on the man's shirt, folding it back on itself and sliding it into his pocket even as he rose to his feet, his other hand still holding the gun steady and aimed.

The utter and absolute focus of Kid's gaze, every move choreographed, everything smooth.

"What did those men want? Wh-what were they doing in your house?" They'd come out of nowhere. One second, she'd been drinking her tea, and the next second, Kid had been in the bathroom hall, slamming a stranger up against the wall and . . .

Kid, striking hard and fast, brutally hard, burying his knife in the man's stomach, jerking the blade upward.

Blood.

Everywhere.

"It was a break-in," he said. "I don't know what they were after, but that kind of stuff happens all—"

"Don't." She jerked free of him, stopping cold. Fury, hot and out of control, flashed through her like wildfire. "Don't you *dare* goddamn lie to me, Kid. You just ki—"

He grabbed her back into his arms so fast, she didn't see it coming. Pulling her against him, he cradled her head close to his chest and leaned down to whisper in her ear. "We're not doing this here, Nikki." It was an order, fiercely given, not a request.

"That was *no* burglary." And she wasn't a fool.

"No, it wasn't." The admission was harsh. "But we have to keep moving. Do you understand?"

At her nod, he started back down the street.

Yes, she understood. She understood he hadn't been nearly as surprised by what had happened as she had been. She understood there were more men behind them, somewhere, looking for them.

The thought was terrifying.

"If you want to talk about something else, that's fine," he said, lightening his hold on her a fraction of a degree, but only the barest fraction. He was holding on to her like her life depended on it—and without a doubt, after what she'd seen, it did. "I know you like to talk when you're upset."

Upset? Sweet Jesus. Her stomach was in a knot so tight she was about ready to throw up, and her nerves were shredded right down to the wires. But sure, she could talk about something else. She needed to talk about something else, anything else—and he knew it. *Damn him.* He wouldn't have forgotten any of her stupid weaknesses, especially the extra-stupid talk-or-meltdown response that seemed to kick in whenever she got shot at, or whenever someone snuck up behind her with a gun, ready to . . . to . . .

"I've got a show tonight in Denver," she blurted out.

"That's great, Nikki," he said, moving quickly, keeping her by his side. "I want to hear all about it, whatever you can think of, every detail."

Good, because that's what he was going to get whether he wanted it or not.

JUAN Conseco looked at the dead bodies of his assassins, both of them slaughtered like helpless lambs. His jaw tightened. They had been two of his best, Hernando Sanchez and Javier Mancos, men who had done his bidding, killed for him for many years. Both had been at the height of their skills, and *el asesino fantasma* had broken them like matchsticks.

He turned away in disgust.

"Peter Chronopolous," he said under his breath, hating the name, hating the man even more. The bastard gringo was making a laughingstock of him.

He remembered the brother, J.T. Chronopolous. He had been held last summer with another U.S. soldier at the rebel camp of the National Revolutionary Forces in northern Colombia. The NRF leader at the time had been as close to a business associate as Juan allowed. Juan had supplied the NRF with weapons, the best money could buy, and the *comandante* had let his soldiers be used as the Conseco family's front line when necessary, quelling peasants who wanted too many pesos for their *coca* leaves, clearing airstrips in the jungle, protecting the cocaine processing labs in the north, and killing or kidnapping politicians who got in the way—the last in the name of the NRF, which left Juan with fewer crimes under his own name and more room to move, especially with the government.

Yes, he remembered the ghost killer's brother. He'd even seen him and the other man, Creed Rivera, the one with the long hair. He could have saved them both, or had them both killed instantly, but instead had suggested to the NRF that one should die a noteworthy death, with photographs for the media. Let the world know not to come to Colombia, and let the other soldier live to take back the tale. The *Norteam-*

ericanos cannot always have it their way, he'd said. They must pay sometimes, pay with violent blood. He was sick of the United States' interference in Colombia, sick of their mercenary soldiers, sick of the foreign oil companies, and sick of a drug policy that allowed foreign planes to destroy his crops.

It had been a petty revenge to have J.T. Chronopolous crucified and butchered. Juan took his real revenge every day, supplying the United States with enough cocaine to make himself one of South America's richest men. He wasn't a cocaine baron. He was a king, and every man, woman, and child who used his product was his subject, whether they were a citizen of the U.S.A. or not. They were his. He owned them all. If his new partnership with the Afghan warlord worked out, his hold on America would be even greater. Damn the United States government. The people were speaking, and they spoke with his white powder up their noses—the fools.

Against all that, the ghost killer was no more than a minor irritation, but a damned persistent one. *El asesino fantasma* had become a hero to Juan's enemies. He'd made a name for himself at the Conseco family's expense, at Juan's expense, and for that he would die. There was no help for it, and no chance of reprieve. No one mocked Juan Conseco's rule; no one killed Juan's family members and lived. If one man got away with it, others might try. Then no one he loved would be safe, and his empire would crumble.

It would be a frozen day in hell before Juan allowed such a disaster to come to pass.

"Drago," he called to his uncle, his right-hand man. "What have you found?"

He'd seen Drago pick something up off the kitchen table. One of the chairs had been overturned when they'd arrived, and his men were currently overturning, upending, and ripping through everything else in the house.

"A woman was here," his uncle answered, handing him a blue-edged piece of paper. "The ghost killer had a woman with him last night. There's lipstick on the cup on the table."

Drago had the eyes of a hawk, and the instincts of an inquisitor. Nothing got by Tío Drago.

"And this?" Juan asked, lifting the paper.

"It's a flyer for an art show tonight in Denver, Colorado. The woman must have been looking at it while she drank her tea."

Juan looked at the flyer. The photograph was of a beautiful young woman with short dark hair in a very short dress standing next to a large painting of an angel. The woman's name was Nicole Alana McKinney, and she was having a show tonight in the United States. Time, date, place—all the information was printed on the flyer, along with a Web address and a short blurb from a Denver newspaper proclaiming her a rising star in the art world.

"Look the artist up on the Internet, check her Web site," he told Drago, handing the paper back to him.

"Maybe the woman here tonight is a friend of this Nicole Alana McKinney."

He walked over to the patio door and looked out on the courtyard. His men had gone through the house and yard and torn them apart, but they'd found no one, not anyone alive anyway. Juan, Drago, and the four soldiers had been waiting in two cars on the street, watching the front of the house, while Sanchez and Mancos had slipped inside. Peter Chronopolous could only have escaped out the back. Juan's men were already in the alley, tracking him down.

They had the bastard on the run.

Him and the woman, Juan realized, his gaze falling on a set of pink suitcases stacked next to each other in the courtyard. The woman drinking the tea must have still been in the house when Sanchez and Mancos had entered.

He looked back over his shoulder, to the kitchen table and the teacup, to the overturned chair, then to where the bodies lay.

She'd been in the middle of the slaughter. She'd seen it all.

A thin smile curved his lips. The ghost killer couldn't have liked that, having his woman be in such danger, having her watch him murder two men.

"Drago," he called, and his uncle came to his side. He gestured toward the suitcases. "He's got the woman with him, and I want her."

Drago was already on his way across the courtyard. He knelt by the suitcases.

A few seconds is all they had left. Staying longer only put them in danger of running into the Panamanian police. *El asesino*'s shots would have been heard all through the neighborhood. His soldiers were already gone and, with a phone call, could be picked up anywhere in the city.

"Bring them," he said, turning on his heel. "We must leave now."

To his surprise, when Drago caught up with him, his uncle was empty-handed.

"*Tío?*" It wasn't like Drago to disobey an order, ever.

"We don't need them," Drago said, handing Juan the poster again. "It's her, the artist. She's the one on the run with the ghost killer. Her initials and a small angel like the one on the flyer are stamped into the leather, *N.A.M.* with a small *c* under the *M*. Taking the luggage will only warn *el asesino* that we are on her trail. Even if they get away, she'll be here tonight." He tapped the flyer.

And wherever they found the girl, they would find Peter Chronopolous, or rather he would find them. Juan would make certain of it.

"*Perfecto,*" he said, his thin smile broadening into a full-fledged grin. Drago was right. Taking the luggage would be a mistake. It would put the ghost killer on his guard and make the woman more difficult to kidnap—and suddenly, having the woman was very important to him. It opened up whole new worlds of possibilities. That she was a well-known artist would

only make his revenge and her death sweeter, and
Peter Chronopolous would witness it all before he
died, a fitting punishment for his crimes against the
Conseco family and a clear warning to everyone else:
The strike of the fer-de-lance was lethal and indis-
criminate. Put yourself in its path, and everyone in
your life became its prey.

Everyone.

CHAPTER

6

❖

Denver, Colorado

SKEETER KNEW SOMEONE was at Toussi's back door before they knocked. It was just a feeling, but those feelings usually turned out to be true, with "usually" running about ninety-eight percent in her favor. Some people thought her ESP was spooky, like her parents, and some people thought it was cool, like Superman and everybody else at 738 Steele Street, the headquarters for SDF and where she lived.

"We've got company," she said, setting aside a screwdriver and looking up at Travis where he was working on the gallery's catwalk. He was finishing up the rigging on the ropes for the triptych they'd suspended in the middle of the room. Each painting was twelve feet high, four feet wide, and totally awesome. The angel's body took up the whole middle piece. His wings were on either side, broken and torn, and he was descending, falling straight to hell, feathers flying, plummeting through a maelstrom—a dark angel. It was still Travis, but this time Nikki had really outdone herself. The movement in the painting was almost tangible, the fall truly frightening. The whole piece pulled at Skeeter, made her want to grab on to the angel and hold him up, or catch him, or do something, anything, to save him.

It was disturbing and involving, both awful to witness and wonderful to behold, and she loved it, the way she loved the new work Nikki was doing with the wildest angels anyone had ever seen. Travis had already hung two of those paintings.

"Not again." She heard him mutter.

"What do you mean, again?"

He levered himself up to look over the iron railing. "The back door hasn't stopped swinging all night long. Are you sure you heard something? I didn't hear anything."

"They haven't knocked yet."

"Then how do you . . . oh, right." Travis was firmly in the "spooky is cool" camp. "Wait a minute. I'll be right down."

"Don't bother," she said, heading for the back door. "I'll get it. It's fine."

"Do you know who it is?" She heard him crossing the catwalk above her.

"No," she admitted. "But the vibe is mellow, nervous but mellow."

"Nervous doesn't work for me," he said, reaching

the stairs and starting down. "Not at three o'clock in the morning."

Normally, nervous didn't work for her, either, but this vibe was different. She reached the door just as the knock came. It wasn't much of a knock, and if she hadn't actually "felt" it first, she wasn't at all sure she would have heard it over the music she and Travis were playing.

She slid off the chain lock, turned the dead bolt key, and opened the door to the alley. A light snow was falling. The alley and the streets were dusted white, the whole city turning cold and silvery.

Skeeter knew an urchin when she saw one because she'd been one—dirty, hungry, small, confused, and cold. That's what happened to kids whose parents fell through the cracks. They ended up homeless on the street and knocking on doors in the middle of the night.

"Hi," she said.

"Hey," the boy answered. He had a coat, but his nose and cheeks were red, and he wasn't wearing a hat or gloves. He looked about twelve. "This is the art place, right?"

"Sure is," she said, stepping aside. "Come on in." Skeeter had a rule—anyone under five feet tall who didn't weigh more than a pile of puppies was not considered a threat, at least not initially.

"No, I . . . hey, I know who you are," the boy said, a big grin coming over his face. "You're SB-three-oh-three."

Skeeter immediately revised her description: dirty,

hungry, small, and cold—but definitely not confused. Of course, she was pretty easy to recognize, with a platinum ponytail down to her butt, Chinese tattoos running down her arm, and her signature ball cap, mirrored aviator sunglasses, and all-around black-leather-and-chain-mail style. She knew it was a Goth cliché, but she also knew she made it look good—damn good.

"That's right. SB-three-oh-three. Who are you?" If she could keep him talking, maybe she could talk him inside.

"Kondo." He had shaggy dark hair, dark eyes, and a freckled nose. "I've seen your hit-ups around town. They're pretty cool." Puffs of vapor came out of his mouth with every word. He had to be freezing, but Skeeter knew better than to try to force him into anything.

"Thanks. Are you sure you don't want to come in? It's kind of cold tonight." Laid back. Playing it cool. That was SB303. The new Skeeter wanted to grab him by the front of his coat and haul him inside. As for the hit-ups he liked, she'd given up writing her name all over the city when Superman had taken her in, but a lot of her graffiti was still on the streets, proclaiming her the vandalism queen of Denver. She even had a few "pieces" out there, as in "masterpieces," works of graffiti art that went beyond throwing up a name.

"Nah. I just gotta give you something," the boy said, digging in his coat pocket until he came up with an envelope. He held it out. "This is for Robin Rulz. Okay?"

"Uh . . . okay." Skeeter looked down at it, her eyebrows arching up toward her hairline. Then she saw the return address and her eyebrows went even further. An envelope for Robin Rulz? From the Castle Import Rug Company? Ho-lee crap.

"They said to drop it off at Tootsie's on Seventeenth," Kondo continued. "So anyway, here it is."

Reluctant as hell, and way against her better judgment, Skeeter reached out and took the envelope from his hand.

"Thanks," the boy said, already backing away from the door. "This is so cool. SB-three-oh-three." Then he was off and running, gone almost before the condensation of his breath had a chance to dissipate.

"SB-three-oh-three?" Travis asked behind her.

At the corner, another small form darted across the alley to join Kondo.

"Skeeter Bang, area code three-oh-three," she said, watching the two kids disappear, still not believing what had just happened, or what she was holding. "I tagged this town about a thousand times. I think I'm still on the cops' top-ten list."

When the boy turned the corner onto the street, she closed the door and turned to face Travis.

"We've got a problem," she said, lifting the envelope. Oh, brother, did they have a problem.

"You better believe it," he said. "That's the fifth envelope to show up tonight, and I don't know anybody named Robin Rulz. How about you?"

"*Five?*" Her eyebrows rose even further. "*Four* other

people have shown up here tonight with envelopes for Robin?"

"Four other kids," he said.

Cripes. The Castle Rats knew Robin Rulz was back in town and living at Toussi's. Or Tootsie's, if you were only twelve and freezing your butt off. How in the heck had she gotten so out of the loop? Steele Street was less than half a mile away. This was her neighborhood, her part of town, and she hadn't known.

"Besides the weather all week, that's one of the reasons I got so far behind with the show," he said. "I've been answering the door all night long."

"Why didn't Jane answer the door?" And pick up her own damn messages, Skeeter wondered. This was unbelievable. Five Castle Rats swarming the gallery.

"She fell asleep about eight o'clock," Travis said, glancing back at the girl— and Skeeter would swear he blushed. "I think she had a long day."

Skeeter had to work to hold back a snort.

"Yeah," she said, "and probably a long night last night. Look, Travis, I—" She stopped in mid-sentence, her whole thought process waylaid by a tsunami-size wave of sudden alertness coming from the other side of the gallery.

She leaned to one side, slanting her gaze over Travis's shoulder, and ran smack dab into a pair of pale green eyes staring back at her, focused, intense . . . disturbingly feral.

Holy cripes.

Jane was awake.

CHAPTER

7

Panama City, Panama

KID WASN'T DRUNK.

He wished like hell that he was, but he wasn't.

"...didn't believe it at first. It really was the most amazing thing, honest to God, for a twenty-year-old fiber artist to be given a commission by the San Diego Tourist Board," Nikki said. "I mean a *real* commission, money, an exhibition, even a full-color poster. A *poster*, for crying out loud—the whole schmear. Did you know the Gay and Lesbian Alliance of Tulsa also commissioned one of his pieces?"

No. Kid hadn't known. But after a half hour of sitting in Rueben's office above the Parrot Bar, listening nonstop to "Nikki talks about Rocky," it was about the only thing he didn't know about her "no, not really" fiancé.

Geezus. Even the word gave him heartburn. It

pissed him off, royally, but man, he had no high ground left in this relationship. Not a foot of it, not until he could get her out of here and safe.

He'd asked for this, though, practically begged for it when they'd been on the street, given her carte blanche, anything to keep her from melting down, and she'd been close, damn close—but that didn't mean he had to like the subject matter that was holding her together.

And he didn't. The one-way conversation had bottomed out for him as soon as "art show tonight at Toussi Gallery," had turned into "art show tonight at Toussi Gallery with Rocky Solano."

But she still had a bloody handprint on her dress, and he was just going to have to tough it out.

"Kid, I need to know what . . . what those men—" She stopped, met his gaze, took a breath in readiness to start again, but he slowly shook his head, *no*, stopping her.

She did have one other subject she wanted to talk about—but he didn't want to talk about it. Ever. Especially in Rueben's with the bar owner coming in and out of the office. The less she knew about Juan Conseco and the two assassins he'd sent to Kid's house tonight, the better.

"But you're hurt," she whispered. "Bleeding."

He shook his head again. He didn't care. They weren't talking about it here.

The look she sent him was full of frustration, and

anger, and sadness—which pretty much summed up how he felt, too.

"Th-the Tulsa commission was so cool," she continued haltingly, abiding by his unspoken rule. "Anyone else might have stuck with the cliché, done the whole rainbow thing, but Rocky took the medium *through* the message, not the other way around, and not *beyond* the message—but *through*. He didn't lose anything in the execution, which for an artist is *so* important. It's a brilliant piece, absolutely brilliant."

Now Kid did know that, because apparently everything Rocky Solano did was brilliant.

"The Tulsa gays just love him."

Of course they did, and he loved her. Loved her because she was doing as he asked. Loved her simply because she was Nikki.

But God, he needed a drink. Badly. He needed two.

Okay. That was a lie. He needed five.

Five shots of premium tequila would almost make this bearable, this sitting across from her and listening to her rattle on and on about the guy she was "no, not really" engaged to marry, and even worse, knowing that because of him, her life had been in danger tonight.

Stone-cold sober, both those facts were killing him.

He wanted her out of Panama.

"Did I tell you Rocky's mother, Marcela, is a potter?"

"Yes," he said, nodding and giving her a small smile.

"Something about the glazes." He reached for his soda and lime.

"Well, she's always been known for her glazes, but over the past year she's created this . . . this—" Her voice suddenly broke, and his gaze instantly narrowed. She covered her face with her hand, her shoulders shaking, absolutely silently, absolutely awfully.

He steeled himself and prayed.

She was struggling, working so hard not to break down and cry, and he was rooting for her. *Goddamn*, he was rooting for her.

After a couple of tense seconds, she dragged in a shaky breath, rallying, pulling herself together. And she started talking again, slowly at first, but letting her words pick up speed.

"Well, it's this . . . this new technique of getting a really cool, utterly translucent layer on her pieces"— she paused for a second, using the back of her hand to wipe at her cheek—"a—a special glaze over the top of the color that you can just *see* right through. I don't know how much you know about pottery and the whole firing process—"

Somewhere between damn little and not much, he could have told her.

"—but what Marcella has discovered, this secret formula of hers, is a revolutionary step, an amazing step, really."

She was amazing. He knew how tough the night had been on him, and he knew it had been a hundred times tougher on her. He knew she had a thousand questions about what had happened, and he knew he was never going to answer a single one.

"It makes every vase, every platter, every piece of work seem to be floating in a rim of light."

He nodded and took another sip of his soda, and let himself wish for just a few seconds that her idea of stress relief was a little more physical.

Okay, a lot more physical, something more along the lines of what they'd been doing four hours ago on his bedroom floor would work real well for him, not that there was any place for making love at Rueben's.

There wasn't.

So forget about it.

He shifted in his seat, took another sip of soda, and tried to take his own advice.

Shit.

"Rocky and his mom did a show together last fall. It was so cool, with these long drapes of soft texture swirling around all these gleaming, hard curves of clay. I think . . . well, really, I think this new glaze thing is going to make her famous."

Rich and famous, Kid thought, like her son.

Rocky Solano was loaded, which was just one more cross for him to bear.

He couldn't see the damn ring with the way she was clutching her purse and had her hands wrapped around the handle, but he remembered every frickin' detail. The diamond had been huge, probably two carats, and it was surrounded by a bunch of colored gems, rubies and emeralds, sapphires, a couple of other precious stones. The whole thing had been very artsy, perfectly Nikki, and had torn his guts out.

"Did I tell you we met through Rocky's dad? Thomas? I already knew his older sister, Lucia. We'd taken a class together at the university, and I knew she had a brother—and a dad, of course—and one day I just sort of ran into Thomas at the photography place where I buy my darkroom stuff, and I don't know who said something first, but then somebody said his name, and it just *struck* me who he was: Thomas Solano. *The* Thomas Solano, and . . ."

He was listening. He swore he was, but she'd gone through these parts of the story before, about the dad and the sister, and how the whole freakin' family was just one famous artist after another. Apparently, there were another couple of sisters and a brother. Somewhere, someone was a lesbian in a long-term, committed relationship, which was *so* important. He'd kind of lost count of some of the other stuff, but he got the picture. Nikki was marrying into One Big Happy Family.

She deserved that. She needed that, and he had damned little to offer in that area. The brother he'd loved was dead, and he didn't think his dad was ever going to recover from the loss. His mother had left a long time ago, when he'd been about eight, to make a half-assed attempt at a Hollywood career that had gone exactly nowhere, and his oldest brother was practically a stranger, living in Ohio, doing some corporate geek job.

He reached for his soda again, discreetly checking his watch, and he let her run on and on and on, because there really wasn't any other option.

He'd had one bit of luck tonight, though. C. Smith had already been on his way to Panama when Kid had called. Their buddy Miguel had been flying him up from Covenas, a town on the coast, and if Miguel's plane had held together, C. Smith should be walking through Rueben's door any minute, and any minute wouldn't be a second too soon. Kid was starting to feel a little sick—lovesick, heartsick, and plain old "I got gut-punched in my stitches and I'm bleeding all over my shirt" sick.

Fuck.

The last report he'd gotten from the DEA guys standing guard down in the bar was that the police and a couple of agents were still at his house and still searching the neighborhood. If by some chance Conseco was in Panama City, they wanted to know it sooner rather than later. There was nothing any of them would like better than to catch the sonuvabitch outside of his fortress in Medellín. Dozens of law enforcement agencies in half a dozen countries would love to be the ones to take Juan Conseco down.

C. Smith wouldn't want to miss the chance, and neither did Kid, but if everything went according to his plan, Smith was going to be hell and gone out of luck.

"...and I guess, well, I guess that's what it comes down to."

Wait a minute. Kid sat up straighter, refocusing his attention on her. She'd actually been leading up to a point for the last half-hour, not just rambling, and he'd missed it? Unfuckingbelievable.

"I mean the two of you are so different. Rocky never could have killed those men, not in a million years," she said, leaning closer, lowering her voice, and breaking the hell out of his rule.

Then Rocky would have been dead, he could have told her, and her right along with him.

"But you did, and I don't know how. I mean I saw the whole thing, and I still don't—"

"Nikki, don't." He shook his head, warning her to stop, but she was having none of it this time.

She leaned even closer. "The killings—what you did, I never knew anyone could be so . . . so . . . *savage*."

Savage.

That was it? Her whole point? That he was a savage and her fiancé wasn't?

He was stunned speechless.

Fortunately, he didn't have time to dwell on her misinformed, misplaced, mis-everything-wrong-about-it freakin' opinion, because someone was coming up the stairs.

Ignoring the pain in his side, and slipping real damn easily back into "savage" mode, he rose from his chair and crossed the room. He had his .45 drawn, racked, and ready to fire before he cleared the desk. Chances were it was one of the DEA guys, but it was the off chance where Kid made his living.

Geezus. Savage.

He should have seen that one coming.

He stationed himself by the door, ready for whatever came down next, but the voice that came from the other side along with a brief knock was thankfully familiar. He lowered his gun and reached for the knob.

THE first thing C. Smith noticed when he entered the office was that Kid was wound tighter than an Arkansas tick. The second thing he noticed was the woman.

She was also the third thing he noticed, and the fourth—*Sweet Jesus.* This was Nikki McKinney? The girl Kid Chaos had left behind in Denver?

His gaze went over her again, strictly professionally, taking in the bloodstains on her dress, the tear tracks on her cheeks, the paleness of her skin—the shape of her legs, the curves of her breasts, and the wild, out-there beauty of her face. She was incredible, a guaranteed, ball-busting heartbreaker.

"Cut it out, Smith," Kid growled. Actually, snarled was more like it.

Smith couldn't help himself—he grinned from ear to ear. Kid had it bad.

He turned back to his partner, and instantly sobered.

"You look like shit," he said, being kind.

"Thanks."

He checked the boy out, saw the last damn thing he wanted to see, and swore under his breath.

"I didn't save your ass in Banco Nuevo so you could bleed to death in Panama City," he said, switching the conversation to Spanish. The girl didn't need to hear this. She looked like the slightest thing could push her over the edge.

"There's a clinic just a couple of miles from here," Kid said, as if that made everything okay.

Bullshit.

"You need a hospital."

"There's a doctor at the clinic, and he's not going anywhere until I get there. Your guys made sure of it."

"Then why the hell aren't you at the clinic?" Smith didn't take kindly to losing partners.

"Because I've been waiting for you to take over the security detail."

Oh, hell. His gaze slid to the woman again.

"No way," he said. The DEA guys downstairs had filled him in on the situation, and he wasn't going to miss out on potentially the biggest bust of the century to babysit some girl—not even a drop-dead-beautiful one.

"You're the only one I trust to get her home. There's a commercial flight out of Tocumen International in two hours. They've guaranteed us two seats, first-class. You came in at Albrook, right?"

"Yeah." But so what? He wasn't the one who needed to get his ass out of Panama.

"Here." Kid pulled a piece of paper out of his pocket. "I've already called."

Smith looked down and read what was on the paper: *738 Steele Street, Denver, Colorado*. A code was scrawled across the bottom.

He knew what it was, Superman's private home address, and home of the Shadow, Dylan Hart, a guy buried so deep, Smith didn't know anyone who had ever worked with him, or anyone who would recognize him if they saw him, except for Kid and the other guys from SDF, a special operations team notorious for their unorthodox methods and high success rate. Seven thirty-eight Steele Street had resurrected General Buck Grant's career. It was where they made guys like Kid Chaos Chronopolous.

"There's a girl at SDF, at the Steele Street address, Skeeter Bang—"

"Skeeter Bang?" he interrupted. "You're kidding, right?"

"No." Kid shook his head. "She runs things for SDF. Make sure she knows to keep Nikki at Steele Street, and tell Nikki to stay put until I get there. I don't want her out of Skeeter's sight until we know for sure who was behind tonight's attack."

Nothing tricky there. It was all standard operating procedure. It just wasn't his SOP, a fact sent doubly home when he glanced at Nikki McKinney.

Okay. This wasn't good.

She'd gotten this look on her face like she was going to burst into tears any second, and he meant *any* second, which was just the sort of thing he took pains to avoid.

Great pains. C. Smith Rydell and crying women were like oil and water. They didn't mix, not even if you shook them, and he'd definitely gotten shook up with a few—more than a few, actually. Certainly enough to know this one didn't want a thing to do with him, enough to know the only person who had a prayer of getting her to Denver without her falling apart was Kid Chaos, the guy she was looking at as if her life depended on it.

He glanced back at Kid, but his partner looked ready to bolt.

Christ.

C. Smith nodded in the girl's direction. "You need to be the one taking her out of here," he said, continuing in Spanish and pocketing the damn piece of paper. Not that he was going to need it. No way in hell.

"No," Kid insisted. "I need to get patched up, go back to the house, see what I can find. These guys are after me, and I need to do something about it."

All true, but Smith wasn't buying it. The look on his face must have said as much.

"Okay," Kid gave in, his voice lowering, even though he stuck with Spanish. "I need a break." He glanced at the woman. "She's . . . she's—"

"Hot," Smith supplied.

"Screw you," Kid said, barely managing a grin, which quickly faded. "She's engaged."

"You told me that weeks ago."

"Yeah, well, things happened tonight."

"So?" Things happened all the time. It was human nature.

"So, regardless of what happened, she was checking out of my place when Conseco's guys showed up."

Oh, now he got it, and it sucked. Big-time. No wonder Kid looked like hell. Nothing took more starch out of a guy than making love to a woman he was crazy about only to have her split in the middle of the night. Man, that hurt.

Kid was tough, as steel-bellied as the next Marine, but he looked about as broke up as the girl. Of course, having two dead guys bleeding all over your kitchen floor and one bleeding out in your garden made for one helluva night. According to the agents downstairs, the transvestite had been clean, no record, no previous arrests, no drug habit—just somebody in the wrong place at the wrong time, and Nikki McKinney had been in the same damn place at the same damn time. If he'd been Kid, he'd want her out of Panama, too, no matter who she was marrying.

But what Kid was asking—*damn*. It was impossible. No way was Smith going to let his night take a nosedive on such a crappy plan.

"I don't do the crying thing," he said, nodding in the girl's direction.

"She'll be okay," Kid was quick to promise—too quick.

"I don't think so, Chico."

"She's just a little blown away right now." Kid

made a small dismissive gesture with his hand, his expression pained. "She's been doing great, but it was, well, it was ugly. About as ugly as it can get. I'm sure the guys filled you in."

"Yeah." They sure as hell had, and he was impressed. Kid had kicked some major ass, but the boy was missing a major point here: Kid was the one with the half-million-dollar bounty on his head, and *he* was the one who needed to get his ass on a plane back to the States.

"Sorry," he said, eyeing the girl again. "But whatever needs to be done, I can guarantee she wants to do it with you, not me."

The office was pretty good-sized, but not big enough to keep Smith from hearing Nikki McKinney let out a little sob, which just proved his point and hardened his resolve. Spending the next nine hours with a crying woman was real close to the top of his "Avoid At All Costs" list, right under untimely death and a desk job.

Kid took a deep breath, swore, then swore again.

"All right," he said, after a couple more long moments. "Sure. Fine. I can take her home. Have them bring a car around to the back door."

"There'll be a Boy Scout badge in it for you," Smith promised, not quite managing a grin.

"Screw—"

"Me. Yeah. I got it the first time," he said under his breath, watching Kid turn back to the desk.

CHAPTER

8

Denver, Colorado

THERE WERE ONLY two things Travis didn't either respect or admire about Skeeter Bang, and those were her sunglasses and her ball cap. The rest of her was extremely hot, extremely tough, extremely smart. Everything about Skeeter Bang was extreme—including her aversion to letting anybody see the scar that ran diagonally across her forehead and through one of her pale blond eyebrows.

It wasn't pretty, but neither was it as disfiguring as she seemed to think, and the ball cap and sunglasses she wore to hide the scar made it damn near impossible to read her sometimes.

Like now.

She'd gone very still, the envelope still in her hand.

Then he felt it, a slow heat crawling up his spine, and he knew why Skeeter had gone so still.

Jane Linden was awake.

Jane.

He didn't dare turn around, not yet. The girl tore him up like none other. He had no explanation for the way he felt about her, kind of wildly, crazily in lust. She didn't seem to know he was on the planet. But a sweet, awful yearning had hit him hard the first time he'd seen her, the first instant, and over the last two weeks, it had only gotten worse.

"Here," he said, extending his hand to Skeeter. "I'll, uh, put it with the other ones."

Four other envelopes had been delivered to the gallery tonight, all of them for someone named Robin Rulz, but nobody named Robin worked for Toussi's. Considering the grubby little group of kids who had been delivering the envelopes, Travis didn't think Robin Rulz actually had a thing to do with Toussi's. The kids had just made a mistake—all five of them, one right after the other, all night long.

Right.

He looked down at the envelope, and sure enough, it had the same return address printed on it as all the others, a business logo for an Oriental rug company just off Speer Boulevard.

"I'll take these back to the Castle Import Rug Company today or tomorrow. They'll probably know who this Robin Rulz is." It was the best idea he had.

"There is no Castle Import Rug Company any-more," Skeeter said, the slight shift of her head telling him she was looking at him now, not the girl. "They were closed down a few years back. The importer, a guy named Greg Stevens, is still doing time in Canon City for felony abuse of child labor laws and trafficking in heroin. The drugs came in his shipments of rugs, and he used a bunch of homeless kids to distribute through downtown, called them the Castle Kids. Overall, he was pretty small-time. He didn't have a lock on the trade, but because of the kids, they put him away with the maximum sentence."

And as quickly as that, the whole mess with the envelopes got a whole lot stickier than Travis ever would have imagined possible up until Nikki's sister, Regan, had gone and fallen in love with Quinn Younger last summer. Since then, every time he turned around, he'd found himself knee-deep in street gangs, derelicts, murder, mayhem, and guys like Quinn, Kid Chaos, and Superman, a.k.a. Christian Hawkins, who took it all in stride.

"So he's in prison, and the kids are still running wild on the streets? Handing out envelopes?" None of this was making any sense, yet.

She shrugged. "The police caught a few of the Castle Kids and handed them over to Social Services. Most of them were never found. They just melted back into the landscape, disappeared on the streets."

"Like the five who showed up here tonight." That much, at least, was damned obvious.

"Yeah. I think so. Robin was one of the kids who never got caught, the oldest, the one who held them together and got them a new gig."

"Doing what?" A new gig didn't sound promising, not for a bunch of former drug dealers, even pint-sized ones.

Behind him, he heard Jane stir in her makeshift bed of chairs, and it took every ounce of control he had not to turn and look at her. It seemed that's all he did these days, look at Jane and fill up with longing like some sixteen-year-old virgin. He both loved it and hated it. Loved the sheer high of wanting her. Hated to think he was never going to get her, but, man, the girl defined the words "hard to catch."

"Petty theft, pickpockets, running a few scams. After they regrouped, they started calling themselves the Castle Rats, which sounded a lot tougher than Castle Kids."

Maybe to a bunch of twelve-year-olds. Castle anything sounded like a video game to him. He looked at the envelope in his hand, then thought to hell with it and tore it open.

"I don't think they're dealing drugs anymore," he said, pulling out a five-dollar bill. "This isn't a night's work of selling anything I've seen on the street."

"No," Skeeter said. "It's not drug money. It's tribute."

"Tribute?" What an odd term, but she sounded damned sure of what she'd said. "For this Robin guy?"

"Robin Rulz isn't a guy."

Travis just stared at her, letting that bit of 411 sink in with all its implications.

"And from the looks of this"—she gestured at the money in his hand—"I'd say the Rats want her back."

Yes. He was getting a nice clear picture now. Former Castle Rat, princess of the underground, and leader of a street gang becomes art gallery shopgirl whose mere presence was enough to turn him into a stumbling idiot. Oh, this was just great.

Damn. Up until last summer, he'd led a pretty sheltered life, a good life, building his cabin up in the canyon and running his sexual imprinting business down in Boulder, sidelining as an EMT, working at a snail's pace on his doctorate, rock climbing on his days off, and modeling naked for Nikki.

A soft sound behind him warned him Jane was rising from the chair, and he braced himself.

There had been no crime in his life, no criminals, no ex-juvenile delinquents trying to make good, though more than a few guys he'd met thought his sexual imprinting business was just a scam to get his hands on a lot of women. It wasn't. He took his techniques very seriously, and he never hooked up with his clients.

"I'll take the envelope, please," Jane said, coming up behind him, proving every word Skeeter had just said, and in two seconds nearly doubling the amount of words she'd spoken to him since he'd shown up at Toussi's two weeks ago and first seen her helping Katya unpack one of Rocky's pieces.

Taking a steadying breath first, and feeling like a fool for needing one, he turned to face her—and damn. Even with all his preparation, all his getting ready, she still made his heart catch—*wild Jane*.

She wasn't classically pretty, not by a long shot. She had a tiny scar along her cheekbone and another one across the bridge of her nose. They were nothing like Skeeter's, just small imperfections that somehow made her more exotic than she already was—which was plenty. Her eyes were almond-shaped and the palest green he'd ever seen, her nose slightly upturned with a dusting of freckles, and her hair was so dark and silky, he'd dreamed of it sliding over his skin for nine nights running—not fantasized, but dreamed. Subconscious. Unbidden. Nine nights in a row.

It was a little crazy. He was so hyperaware of her, sometimes he swore he could feel her breathe.

"Uh . . . sure," he said, handing her the envelope and the money.

She didn't say thank you. She didn't say anything, just stuffed the money in her pocket, glanced at the envelope, then looked back up at him.

That's all it took. He got the message loud and clear: She'd like the rest of them—*please*. He didn't have to go far, just a few feet over to the stairs where he'd put them on a step.

It was the strangest thing. She talked to Katya, Suzi, and the other girls who worked in the gallery, her voice soft and low, slightly husky, but she'd hardly said a word to him, getting by with a nod here, a shake of the head there, a slight shrug for his more open-ended questions. It was like she practiced being quiet and her favorite person to practice on was him. He knew she practiced being invisible. He'd watched her do it, fade into the background, make herself still. About half of the people who came into the gallery never knew she was there, even if she walked right by them. It wasn't just that people didn't always pay attention to their surroundings. It was the way she did it, never approaching anyone directly, always coming up on a person's weaker side or in a blind spot. The other half of the gallery patrons barely noticed her— but not him. He'd actually hurt himself a couple of times, running into stuff because he was so busy noticing her he'd forgotten to watch where he was going.

It hadn't been too embarrassing, though, because she didn't notice him, ever, not even when he was falling on his face. It was the damnedest thing, having someone, especially a woman, be so unaware of him.

He handed the other envelopes over.

"So you're Robin Rulz," he said, thankful his voice didn't crack.

She gave him a quick glance, which very clearly said "yes," then went back to shuffling through the envelopes, turning each one over.

Cripes, he thought, borrowing one of Skeeter's favorite words. Maybe if he stood on his head and juggled flaming swords he could hold her attention for more than a nanosecond.

Then again, maybe not. She didn't seem like the flaming swords type.

Hell.

He watched her flipping through the envelopes and saw that each one had a letter from the alphabet written on the back. He hadn't noticed any letters when he'd handled them, but it looked like she'd expected to find them. She shuffled through the envelopes twice, quickly, shifting the order, her expression growing more and more grim.

When she looked up, it was to Skeeter, not him.

"This won't be a problem. I promise. Tell Superman I'll take care of it. Tell him I would have taken care of it when I first got here, but I thought they'd all gotten picked up when I left. I thought they'd all be in foster homes by now."

"Apparently not," Skeeter said, crossing her arms over her chest and tilting her head to one side, her feet slightly apart.

It was a very considering stance, and Travis couldn't help but wonder what in the world she was considering. If it was kicking ass, it wasn't going to be much of a contest. Skeeter was all long legs, sleek muscles, and mad skills—and Jane wasn't.

Jane was curves.

Soft lips.

Silky.

"You guys never got caught," Skeeter went on. "Ever, none of you, not once, not by anyone. That's what the legend was all about. You pulled more wallets in LoDo in two years than the rest of the city combined, and no one ever laid a hand on you. So why would they all suddenly get picked up?"

Jane just looked at her, her expression unreadable, except for the tension Travis felt coming off her in waves—unreadable to him anyway, but Skeeter seemed to figure it out.

"You called the cops on them yourself."

"Kondo was only ten when I left," Jane said. "And he wasn't the youngest. How old was your crew when you got hurt that night up on Wazee?"

Skeeter stiffened ever so slightly, and Travis went all ears. He'd been trying to get Skeeter's story out of her since the night they'd met, but the girl did not talk about what had happened to her face. It had been violent, that was obvious from the scar, and bloody. He knew from his EMT work that head wounds bled like hell. Jane, however, knew the facts, or at least the rumors.

God, he had led a sheltered life.

"Older than yours," Skeeter said after a long moment. "Old enough to take care of themselves." She turned her attention to him. "The triptych was the last piece, right?"

"Right."

"Then you owe me four hours, and I'll see you tonight at the show."

She was leaving? Just like that?

"But—" he started to say, then stopped. But what? Don't leave me alone with Jane? Hell, all he'd wanted for two weeks was to be left alone with Jane. He'd made more excuses to hang around Toussi's than made sense with his schedule, practically delivering Nikki's pieces for the show one at a time. He'd even started hand-delivering Rocky's work, which had caused the artist to immediately ask "Who's the girl?"

Not much got by Rocky—except Nikki. She'd sure gotten by the guy, or the other way around. Travis didn't know what was going on for sure, and Nikki wasn't talking, no matter how many questions he asked. But she'd stopped crying, and that was a helluva improvement over the last year.

Skeeter had already moved to the alley door and was slipping on her jacket, the fur-lined leather one she'd gotten for Christmas and didn't go anywhere without. He would have offered to walk her to her car, but she would have laughed him off the planet. All Skeeter Bang ever expected out of a guy was for him to watch her back when the bad boys threw down and the shit hit the fan, and she could damn well be depended on to return the favor.

"Okay, then," he said. "Tonight."

"You're done here, too, right?" she asked, but somehow, the way she said it sounded more like an order than a question.

"Finished." He nodded, intrigued. Skeeter had never given him so much as a suggestion about what to do, let alone an order.

"Headed home?"

"Yep," he said, and found himself having to fight a grin at the relieved expression on her face. If it had been anyone other than Skeeter, he would have thought she was showing a little territoriality over him. But this was the infamous Ms. Bang, the same Ms. Bang who had put herself between him and a street gang last summer, and this had all the earmarks of a repeat performance, pure Skeeter as protector. Protecting him from Jane, he supposed, the notorious Robin Rulz, pickpocket extraordinaire and leader of the Lilliputians, all one hundred and ten pounds of her—if that, soaking wet.

Sure the girl undid him, but he wasn't a complete idiot. He could handle himself. He certainly didn't need protection from Jane Linden.

CHAPTER
9

OKAY, NIKKI HAD GOTTEN exactly what she'd wanted so desperately back at the Parrot Bar, Kid going home with her, and she still wasn't happy, far from it. Sitting in an examining room at the clinic, watching a doctor try to put him back together, was tearing her apart.

How could he have let so many bad things happen to him? He was a mess, and from the look on his face, and the tone of the conversation he was having with the doctor—in Spanish, damn him—he didn't have a clue.

The Spanish was deliberate. She knew it. Just like it had been a deliberate choice between him and his friend, C. Smith Rydell, back at the Parrot. But she could have told him that a person didn't always need to know a language to know what in the hell was being said—and back at the Parrot, Kid had been try-ing to dump her on Smith.

Damn him. He'd never seen "meltdown" the way he would have seen "meltdown" if he actually had been able to talk Smith into taking her back to Denver—and Smith had known it. She'd seen the wary glances the other man had thrown her way. Rightly so, but Smith wasn't her concern. Kid was, and looking at him, she knew she had plenty of reason to worry.

How could he possibly think that running out on her all the time was going to solve anything?

And God, he was running. He looked run into the ground, like he'd been running since he'd left last September. It wasn't just the bandages and the blood. It was his body. He'd actually put on weight since she'd seen him last, all of it in muscle, but instead of filling him out, it only made him look harder, less likely to yield—to anything, ever. He'd become the ultimate warrior, frightfully self-sufficient, not need-ing anyone or anything. He looked like Christian Hawkins, and she wouldn't have thought there was another man on earth cut like Superman.

Between the two of them and another SDF opera-tive she'd met, Creed Rivera, they were all perfect savages—absolutely perfect.

It was a new dimension for her, something she had never encountered until she'd photographed Creed. But it was the sheer, uncompromising brutality of tonight's violence that had sent those truths home in a way she was going to be struggling with for a long time.

She'd thought she knew men, inside out, upside down, every which way.

She'd been wrong.

In all her work, she'd missed something vital in the male psyche, something she needed to understand, something she especially needed to understand in Kid.

From where he sat on the examining table, he swore, and the doctor, a man named Varria, apologized profusely. Then Varria gave him another shot with the needle.

She needed to understand it, or she was going to lose him to the wild life—and this time, she feared it would be forever. That she would never get him back.

WELL, this was the last goddamn thing Kid had wanted, to be practically buck-ass naked in front of Nikki, while the clinic doctor poked and prodded and stuck him with needles.

"Does that hurt?" Dr. Varria asked, poking him again with a syringe full of anesthetic.

"No." Kid ground the word out from between his teeth. It stung like hell, and the place where Varria was sticking him looked more like hamburger than a part of his body, but no, it didn't hurt.

Looking at Nikki hurt—so he didn't.

Savage. How could she think such a thing about him?

Then again, how could she not?

"I've never seen stitches get pulled out of the skin like this," Dr. Varria said, peering closely at the wound in his side.

Kid wasn't surprised. Considering that Dr. Varria looked about twenty-two and the diploma on the wall said he'd gone to medical school on an island known for its beaches and piña coladas, he couldn't have seen much.

"Can you sew me back together?"

"*Sí*, *sí*, I'm going to put in a few more sutures than you had, but they're not going to do any good, if you keep getting into fights and getting shot at."

"What?" Nikki asked from behind him, where she was sitting on a chair in the small examining room. "What did he say?" She had refused to stay in the outer office with the two DEA guys escorting them to the airport.

"*Bala*, bullet." Dr. Varria switched to English and pointed out two of Kid's wounds. "Here and here. The injury on your husband's arm has all the characteristics of a stab wound with a dull knife."

Piece of board, Kid could have told him, and he wasn't her husband—not even close.

"But the two major injuries are definitely bullet wounds."

Great, Kid thought. That was just what she needed to know.

He heard her get out of her chair, and his muscles tensed. He'd bet his favorite Porsche that the freaking fiber artist had never been shot, and he most certainly did not want her coming over and staring at his bullet holes—not when she still had blood on her dress.

And not when her suitcases had been packed and stacked in his courtyard, ready to go.

She'd pulled herself together after he'd told her he'd be the one taking her back to Denver, and she seemed to be holding up pretty good, but he didn't like taking chances in that department. As for him, with his butt hanging out, he was already tipping the vulnerability scales.

"A man with such a beautiful wife should take better care of his health, no?" Dr. Varria smiled, all toothy and idiotic, and yeah, Kid knew why. Nikki had that effect on men. She'd slam-dunked Smith, and C. Smith Rydell was a rock when it came to women. He loved them; he was just never in love with any particular one.

Which was just one more reason why Smith should be the guy taking her home.

Goddamn. He sucked in his breath, when Dr. Varria stabbed him again with the needle.

"Absolutely," Nikki said, coming to a stop next to where he was sitting on the edge of the examining table with nothing but a good-size paper towel over his lap. His pants were hanging around his ankles, so the doctor could rebandage his leg. "A man with a wife should take better care of his health. So what happened here?" She lightly touched his right shoulder.

"Another bullet wound," Dr. Varria announced with authority. "Obviously healed."

"And here?" She touched his jaw, and Dr. Varria lifted his head and looked closely at the stitches.

"There's some cauterization, so whatever cut him was very hot." The doc flashed her another toothy smile. "Your husband lives a dangerous life."

"Yes, he does," Nikki said, not sounding any too happy about it, and Kid wondered what she thought she was doing, besides confusing him. "What about these?"

Her fingers landed on the scars marking his upper left arm, and it took everything Kid had not to grab her hand. She wouldn't understand about the scars, but the doctor did. His question proved it, and the fact that he switched back to Spanish to ask it.

"*¿Fueron a propósito?*" Were these on purpose?

The look Kid gave him said it was none of his business and to back off—now.

Varria got the point.

"Knife wound," the doctor said abruptly, turning aside and busying himself with the suturing tray, obviously not wanting any more to do with the dangerous life Kid led.

Perfect, Kid thought. That was just what he needed, a nervous doctor sewing him up. But Varria was right. The scars had been deliberate, and they'd been made with a knife: three horizontal lines incised into his skin in remembrance of a brother who'd borne the same marks.

"You didn't have these last September," Nikki said, tracing the scars—and Kid did grab her hand.

"Don't," he said.

"I've seen these exact markings before, on someone else, and he wouldn't tell me what they meant either."

That got Kid's attention. Only one other person alive had the same scars. They'd been cut into Creed Rivera by the NRF bastards who had butchered J.T.— Creed, who had cut them into Kid's arm over a smoky fire on the side of a mountain in Peru, a legacy of blood and brotherhood.

She was right. He was a savage.

So was Creed, and Nikki had obviously seen the jungle boy without his shirt, maybe without anything, considering that it was Nikki McKinney.

"Don't tell me you painted Creed." Or he was going to go ballistic. First she slept with Rocky Solano, then she stripped the jungle boy down to his skin?

Kid couldn't take it.

"As much of him as I could," she said, doing the exact opposite of what he'd just asked. "Skeeter set up the shoot for me, but Creed wouldn't take his pants off. He just flat-out absolutely refused."

Kid felt a wave of relief wash through him. He should have known he could count on Creed. He'd counted on Creed for everything during those last weeks of their search-and-destroy mission in South America.

"Hawkins did, though," Nikki added. "Everything."

Kid felt Dr. Varria putting in his stitches, the prick and pull of the needle and suture going through his skin. He heard the doctor muttering about the mess he'd made of himself, but he didn't take his eyes off Nikki.

Of course, Christian Hawkins would have taken his clothes off for her. Superman was fearless.

Still . . . still, this was Nikki, and Kid was . . . was—

"He's exquisite, more muscle definition than ten other guys, and the tattoo, my God, have you seen it?"

Of course, he'd seen Superman's tattoo. But didn't she know they had real problems here, and dragging more naked men into the picture wasn't helping?

"He *is* the angel, Kid, the very first."

"Hawkins, an angel," he said bluntly, not buying it for a second. Christian Hawkins had the kind of reputation that would give an angel a heart attack, and he had that reputation in places no angel would ever go, the real hellholes of the world.

"He saved my life, when I was about six, at Rabbit Valley. Snatched me from the jaws of death."

"The jaws of death?" That sounded a bit much, even for Superman.

"A rattlesnake. I didn't realize I'd wandered so close to one, but there it was, tail rattling, and then there was this guy, scooping me up into his arms, and there were feathers all over him, all over his back, down his arms, inked into his skin, but to me they looked real, and the whole moment just flashed onto my brain, being saved by a dark angel."

Honestly, nothing about that bit of information surprised him. He knew all about the bust that had landed Denver's finest crew of car thieves on Doc McKinney's dinosaur digging team in Rabbit Valley, Colorado, and he'd known Nikki had been there that summer with her grandfather. J.T. had been one of the chop-shop boys. As for Hawkins, hell, he'd never mentioned saving a little girl from a rattlesnake, but he wouldn't. Saving people's lives was business as usual for Superman, especially women's lives, and no woman who had ever met Christian Hawkins ever seemed to forget him, apparently even if she was only six years old, but—

"I think that's the dichotomy I'm always working with, Kid, being saved by the dark angel, the darkest angel."

Okay, dichotomy—they'd had this conversation before about the dichotomies in her work, but Kid was stuck in another place right now, and—

"I think that's why I never know if Travis is ascending to heaven or descending to hell."

And now Travis? The glowing wonder-stud, who Kid would have put his money on as the guy Nikki would run off with, not some "civilized" fiber artist, but now that he thought about it, maybe there was a little bit of savage in Travis, too, and—

"So I paint him both ways, but the truth, I believe now, is a lot more complicated."

For all his poking around, Dr. Varria, Kid suddenly realized, had not gotten enough anesthetic into his wound. *Dammit.* And yes, the whole goddamn thing was complicated, a little too complicated for a guy who was getting stabbed with a needle, over and over again, and yet he did have this one point he needed to make.

"*Naked*, Nikki? You photographed Hawkins *naked*?" His head was swimming.

"I do all my models naked, Kid. You knew that from the beginning."

Right. Right, he'd known that, but that wasn't helping matters now, especially with—*shit!*

"You need to numb that up a bit more, Doc," he said between his teeth.

Varria blanched and reached for the syringe.

"My work couldn't possibly be why you never came home," she said, sounding surprised, then unsure. "Or could it?"

"I...I need to lie down." His head really was swimming. There was even a moment when he sort of went blank for a second, and then he was on his back, with Nikki and Dr. Varria hovering over him.

Nikki had ahold of his hand.

He liked that. He liked it a lot, even if he was still so goddamn mad and still feeling as guilty as hell. And yes, he was incredibly grateful she was thinking about something other than what he'd done at the house, *anything* other than what he'd done—but he was still angry about the whole damn situation.

"Kid?" she said, leaning over him, her expression overly worried. "Kid, are you okay?"

"Yeah." He was fine. Too much sex and not enough food, he decided. Too much fighting, too many stitches, and not enough taking it easy like the doctors in Bogotá had told him to do. "Yeah," he said again. "I'm fine."

His head was a fucking mess, but he was fine.

"You were telling me about the three scars you and Creed have on your arms," she said, smoothing her other hand over his brow, suddenly looking so solicitous, he almost grinned. This was the Nikki he'd fallen in love with, a teasing, I'm-so-in-charge-of-my-world Nikki, the take-no-prisoners Nikki who looked into men's souls and took what she wanted.

Yeah, that was Nikki, and he most definitely wasn't in any shape for her to be doing that to him. He wasn't ready for anything even close to that much of an invasion.

Hell, no.

"No, I wasn't," he said, and wished he would just cool out. He didn't like running hot, being on edge inside. Cool, calm, collected, that was him—with everyone and everything except her. "I was telling you not to photograph Hawkins naked, ever again." It was none of his business. He knew that. But she had him flat on his back and was still holding all the cards.

"When you see the painting I did of him, you'll change your mind."

Yeah, he knew that, too. She was an amazing artist, and for a while tonight, when he'd first seen her at the Sandovals', he'd thought she was still his.

Unbidden, his gaze went to her left hand, but the ring wasn't on her finger.

Oh, Christ. Had she lost it at the Parrot? Thrown it out with her tissues or some damn thing?

No. Impossible. His luck couldn't be running that good.

"Where's your ring, Nikki?"

She followed his gaze, and for a moment she looked confused, then stricken. "I . . . I forgot about it. Oh, geez. I didn't think, I mean it's in my luggage, back at the house. I took it off and put it in my jewelry bag when I packed, but in the rush, those men, I don't—"

He tightened his hand on hers in warning, and she fell silent, but looked distraught, which he didn't blame her for, not a bit. The ring had to be worth a fortune. But the important thing, the really so-help-him-God important thing, was that she'd taken the damn thing off and packed it in her luggage.

"You put it in your suitcase?" he asked, his voice very serious, as if buck-ass naked he was conducting some sort of investigation into the missing ring, which of course he would if it proved necessary—but mostly he just wanted to hear that part again.

"Yes, in my big pink suitcase. I took it off, and—" she paused for a moment and her gaze locked onto his. "Yes, Kid," she repeated. "I took it off. After tonight, how could I wear it?"

He didn't know the answer to that, because, frankly, he didn't know how in the hell she'd worn it in the first place.

"We need to talk about this," she said, her voice very solemn. "There are things you need to know."

Or not, he thought, feeling a cold sweat break out on his brow.

Great. This was perfect. Racing heart. Cold sweat. What was next? Hyperventilation?

"I know how angry you are, Kid."

No, she didn't. Not even close.

And excuse me, but was his breath getting a little short?

Fuck.

"Don't worry, Nikki. I'll get the ring back for you," he said. It was a promise—and didn't that just make the whole screwed-up night complete? There he was, filleted like a fish with a paper towel covering his dick, going into panic mode for God only knew what reason, and promising to get back the ring that said she was engaged to marry another man.

He needed his head examined.

A knock sounded on the door, and one of the DEA guys popped in. "Five more minutes, max, if you're going to make that plane."

Kid nodded and completely ignored the guy's quick glance at the paper towel and his shit-eating grin. There was no way in hell they were going to miss that plane, not if he had to finish sewing himself up on the tarmac—and honestly, five more minutes of this situation was about four and a half more than he thought he could take.

CHAPTER

10

Denver, Colorado

TRAVIS WATCHED SKEETER slip out the back door in a flurry of snow and a gust of wind.

Damn. The storm was turning into a blizzard, and getting colder. The temperature had dropped even since the boy, Kondo, had left.

He threw the dead bolt and turned back around only to find Jane looking right at him. For as quiet as she was, she never hesitated to meet his gaze straight on when she wanted to, and twice she'd just about leveled him with an intense sidelong glance from across the gallery. She wasn't quiet because she was shy. Oh, no. She just had nothing to say to him. He'd gotten that message the same way he was getting the message she was sending now, which was "If you're finished for the night, why don't you go home?"

It was amazing, really. He was no mind reader like

Skeeter, but he was starting to feel like one with Jane, or Robin, or whatever she wanted to call herself.

He was also starting to feel a little annoyed with himself and frustrated with the situation, two emotions he usually found useless. The only other girl who had ever blown him off so completely was Skeeter herself. So his batting average with hot, streetwise women was exactly zero. Girls like that were obviously looking for something else, but he'd be damned if he had a clue what. Lots of different kinds of guys came on to Skeeter, from lawyers and FBI agents to gangbangers and downtown hustlers, and he'd watched her shut each of them down every single time.

The same way Jane was shutting him down now, with a look that said he simply didn't register anywhere on her radar.

"Well, I'll just be heading on home now," he said, reaching for his coat where it hung next to hers by the back door.

What the hell, was what he was thinking. He needed to start getting interested in women who were interested in him, instead of driving himself crazy with hot dreams and wild fantasies about Jane Linden.

Jane, who, naturally, didn't say a word. As a matter of fact, she wasn't even looking at him anymore. She'd gone back to shuffling the envelopes, lining them up, and she'd conveniently stationed herself between him and the rest of the gallery, sending another silent message for him to leave by the back door and not let it hit him in the ass on his way out.

Man, oh, man, he'd never seen anybody work the body language the way she did, all of it saying "closed, keep out, no trespassing."

"I'll see you tonight then, at the show."

Oh, Christ. Had he just said that? He couldn't believe he'd just said that. The woman did not want to talk to him, and she didn't give a flying leap if she saw him tonight at the show. What did it take—a neon sign flashing over her head?

He was stuck in perpetual nice-guy mode, and she was all about attitude with a big, silent "A."

He let himself out the door, thank you very much, and closed it solidly behind him. He didn't move away, though, until he heard the dead bolt slide home—just more stupid nice-guy stuff. He was the king of it.

Glancing across the alley, he swore under his breath. His Jeep looked frozen, like a metallic ice cube, cold and heartless, and like maybe it wouldn't get him home tonight.

Great. Just great, he thought, stepping off the stoop. From out of nowhere, a small form darted out from behind him, and his heart jammed up into his throat.

Geezus! He jumped to one side.

The kid was fast, like a streak of lightning, disappearing down the alley and around the corner almost before Travis even registered that he'd been there.

How in the hell hadn't he seen the little bugger? He must have practically stepped on him when he'd come out the door. And sonuvabitch—there was another envelope, lying on top of the snow.

He bent down and picked it up, already knowing what it would say: Castle Import Rug Company, with the words *Robun Rulz* scrawled across the front.

Robun? This one couldn't even spell, and where in the hell did these kids keep coming from? It was damn cold out tonight, almost morning. Shouldn't they still be tucked into their beds or something? Who was taking care of them? Nobody?

He shoved the envelope in his pocket, not about to go back inside. He'd give it to her later, her tribute. It was all starting to bug the hell out of him. Where were all these kids coming from? And why were they running around in the middle of the night?

If he'd thought he could have gotten any kind of answer at all out of Jane, he would have gone back inside and asked for one.

Geezus. He needed to go back to his real life in Boulder and stop getting wound up in all the urban angst of a landscape he didn't understand—street life, pickpockets, girls with crews, girls like Jane, except she wasn't a girl anymore. She'd grown up, gotten a job in an art gallery, and moved on.

He dug the envelope back out of his pocket and looked at it again. *Tribute.*

He'd seen how hard she worked. Toussi's was a big gallery. Besides crating and uncrating pieces for shipment or show, she cleaned the place and worked with Katya in the office. Katya had two other part-time employees and Suzi Toussi, the original owner of the gallery, to help her with the customers, but she was probably going to work Jane into it—unless the girl got involved with the Castle Rats again.

Sure, Christian Hawkins knew what she'd been, but Travis knew what Katya expected her to be, and it didn't include taking tribute from pickpockets.

None of which was his problem, he reminded himself. Jane had kicked him out, after another night of brilliantly ignoring him. He needed to get a clue, and right now wasn't any too soon to start.

By the time he got his frozen piece of crap Jeep running and turned onto Seventeenth Street, he'd decided he was done banging his head against a wall. Then he realized he'd left his backpack. *Dammit.*

Swearing under his breath, he pulled over in front of the gallery. He hated to disturb her, really he did, when she was probably so damn sure she'd finally gotten rid of him, but since he wasn't coming back, he needed his stuff.

At the front door, he pulled out his key to let himself in, a nice cheery "hello" ready to go so he didn't scare the crap out of her, when he noticed her standing in the middle of the gallery, looking up at the triptych.

And looking and looking.

And looking—easily breaking the record for the

longest time she'd ever spent looking at him in real life.

So maybe she liked him naked and going to hell— because that's what was happening in the painting, without a doubt. Nikki was never ambiguous when she tortured him. She made him bleed. She tore him and his wings to shreds. The way she smeared the paint over the super-enlarged photographs she took of him in her studio made him look broken. People found the dark angel paintings disturbing. Some of them disturbed even him, like the triptych. It was especially raw—and Jane couldn't take her eyes off of it, which just fascinated the hell out of him.

He wasn't sure what it meant exactly, but it at least meant she wasn't nearly as oblivious of him as she'd been letting on. He hoped. When he looked at Nikki's work, he saw only what Nikki had created, which wasn't really him. Maybe Jane didn't see him either, but saw only Nikki's creation.

Yeah, that was probably it.

Damn. There was just no way for him to make this work.

He lifted the key to the lock again, then stopped when she moved away from the large paintings to a smaller piece he and Skeeter had hung on the west wall. It was another of him, about six feet in height, more life-size than oversize, an ascending angel Nikki had printed in a creamy sepia and painted over in yellows, gold, and blues. He tended to like the ascending angels better, because at heart he was basically kind of an easygoing, "ascending"-type guy. Not too much angst in his real life, other than not being able to get laid by Jane the way he'd been fantasizing, but that was just regular guy stuff, nothing too life-threatening, no matter how much he wanted it. Or at least that's what he'd been telling himself. The only thing he didn't like about the ascending angels was that Nikki always made him look too good. In real life, he didn't glow, his skin wasn't perfectly smooth, and his face . . . well, his face really wasn't angelic, not the way Nikki made him look.

Not the way Jane looked.

God, she was so wildly different from the other women he knew.

She stepped around one of Rocky's fabric pieces to get closer to the painting, and his gaze slid down her body. Without a doubt, in anybody's book, she had a world-class ass. He tried not to think about it too much, the same way he tried not to think about her breasts too much, because it was hard on him, but for someone who was kind of small everywhere else, she really filled out a sweater.

And here he was, half turned on and freezing his butt off. Typical. He ought to just go home and forget about his pack. There wasn't anything in it he couldn't get by without until Nikki could get it to him.

Slipping the key back in his pocket, he started to turn and go, when she did something that stopped him in his tracks.

She touched the painting, touched him, sliding her fingers over his eyebrows, down his nose, and lingering on his mouth, the tips of her fingers outlining his lips, which pretty much riveted him to the spot.

Painted angel or not, that was his mouth.

Slowly, she traced over his shoulder, following the curve of his muscle down to his arm, then traced the length of his outstretched arm to his hand. One by one, she set her fingertips to his, then pressed her palm flat against the canvas.

She was so close to the painting, he could almost feel her brushing up against him, how the softness of her sweater would feel against his chest, the texture of her jeans against his groin, and suddenly, even with the snow blowing around him, he wasn't cold.

He took a breath and let it out, nice and easy. Ridiculously, this was working for him, the voyeurism of it all, watching her explore him, her hand so small against the lines of his body, her fingers so gently following the curves of muscle and ridges of bone beneath his skin.

She slid her hand to his chest and down his rib cage, continuing her journey, and then, just as things promised to get really damned interesting, she stopped.

It took him a second to realize she was walking away, he'd been so focused on all the possibilities of where her hand was going next. But it wasn't going anywhere.

Damn. If he'd needed any more proof of how hard

up he was, he'd just gotten it. He was so lonely for a girl, it was pitiful, and the one he was lonely for, the one he wanted, was her, the wild one who wouldn't give him the time of day.

He watched her thread a path toward the back of the gallery, but when she got there, instead of heading up the stairs to her apartment, she reached for her coat.

Now what in the hell? he wondered, but not for very long.

Sitting down on the bottom step, she kicked off the heels she'd been wearing, slipped into a pair of boots, and started lacing them up.

He couldn't believe it. She was going somewhere? In the middle of the night, in the middle of a snowstorm, in the middle of lower downtown? Making three of the worst moves he could imagine in one fell swoop?

She'd told Skeeter she would take care of all the loose Castle Rats running around, but he hadn't thought she'd meant tonight, in the cold and the dark and the damned dangerous. It was one thing for Skeeter Bang to cruise the streets alone. He knew she had a switchblade in a sheath on her hip, a Heckler & Koch 9mm holstered at the small of her back, and a reputation that guaranteed she wouldn't need either, not in this part of town. If Jane had a weapon anywhere on her, he sure as hell hadn't seen it, and he'd spent plenty of time checking her out tonight.

So this was perfect—perfectly bad, any way he looked at it.

She slipped into a black hoodie and put her wool coat on over the top. A black knit hat came out of one pocket, a pair of gloves out of the other, all of the gear telling him he was in for a long, cold hike somewhere. *Damn.* He zipped his coat up a little higher, pulled his own hat down lower. She didn't have a car, so it wasn't going to do him any good to fire up his Jeep again, and there was no way in hell for him to let her go out into the city alone, no matter how many little Castle Rats she had waiting for her somewhere.

She'd probably be damn hard to follow, but he didn't see any way around it. The chances of her inviting him along were between slim and none, weighted heavily toward none.

He set off for the corner of the building. Even in his mountain parka, he could feel the cold. He hoped her hoodie and coat were a helluva lot warmer than they looked. At the alley, he waited, his body up against the bricks, until Toussi's back door opened. For a brief moment she was silhouetted in the light, then the door fell closed. A second later he saw her take off, heading away from him, and he started out after her.

And this, he told himself, was what happened to guys who got badass crushes on girls who'd spent their formative years running wild on the streets.

Those guys got curious about where wild girls went in the night, real curious, curious enough to follow them into the darkened alleys and deserted streets of lower downtown at four o'clock in the morning—common sense be damned.

CHAPTER

30,000 feet over the Caribbean Sea

WELL, IF THIS WASN'T the longest goddamn flight Kid had ever taken from Panama, he didn't want to be on the one that was. His side was killing him.

Sure, Dr. Varria had given him a packet of Vicodin, but jacking himself up with narcotics wasn't really an option, not on a commercial flight, not until he had Nikki safely at SDF headquarters on Steele Street in Denver.

Taking a breath, he tried to situate himself differently in his seat, tried to find a position that didn't hurt like hell—and failed. So he raised his hand and signaled the flight attendant for another beer. He'd already had two first-class in-flight breakfasts and was thinking about ordering a third. Eggs and beer, it didn't get any better than that.

Yeah, right.

He glanced at Nikki, sleeping soundly in the seat next to him. Her empty wineglass was on his tray with a bunch of snack wrappers and beer bottles. After the night they'd had, he was glad she'd been able to unwind enough to get some sleep. It was better for her and easier on him.

The DEA guys had stuck with them until liftoff, so the dreaded I-know-how-angry-you-are talk had not taken place, which really was for the best, whether she knew it or not. The wine had done the rest.

He took a long swallow of the beer when it arrived, and then took a deep breath. He had to give her the gold wedding rings. It didn't matter that she'd called him a savage. It didn't matter that she honestly didn't have a clue how pissed off he really was about Rocky Solano, or that he was probably way underestimating how angry she might be with him for not calling her since September.

Okay, that sounded bad. In the jungle, it hadn't seemed so long. In real life, he figured it was long enough to win him the Jerk of the Year award.

Regardless, he'd half killed himself getting the damn rings, and he had to hand them over.

Just not yet.

The timing was bad, even if they felt like a lead weight hanging around his neck.

Yeah, he thought, taking another swallow of beer. This wasn't the place. Being trapped on an airplane with a woman when you gave her the wedding rings you'd taken off her dead parents' bones was probably not a good idea under the best of circumstances. Under the worst of circumstances, which they had, no thanks to him and the goddamn bounty on his head, it was just asking for disaster. Even if the circumstances had been better, Nikki deserved her privacy when she received the rings. He may be a freaking savage, but he did know that.

Yeah, she deserved a lot of things—probably none of them him. And wasn't that the bottom line, the truth as best as he'd been able to see it for months? She deserved better. It was as simple as that, and Nikki being a smart girl, she'd gone and figured it out for herself.

And if he was going to get maudlin, he probably didn't need any more beer.

He set the bottle down and signaled for the flight attendant to clear his tray. With luck, in a few more minutes, the alcohol would kick in and he could get some sleep, too. The cabin was dark, with just a few low lights on toward the front, and the sun hadn't yet started rising over the Caribbean. There were two other first-class passengers two rows back. The rest of the plane wasn't much fuller.

His gaze strayed back to Nikki. He'd bought her a silk T-shirt and a matching skirt in the airport and given her other clothes to the DEA guys. The blood on her dress had been Hernando Sanchez's. The man he'd killed in the hallway had been Javier Mancos. Both bodies had still been in the house when the police had gotten there. Both had been positively identified by the Panamanian police as members of Juan Conseco's organization. The police had picked up another man, too. So far, he'd told them nothing, but Conseco's mark was on him, a tattooed C in the shape of a fer-de-lance, its fangs showing.

Kid was going to be watching his ass for a long, long time.

He started to settle in, when Nikki stirred in her sleep, a frown creasing her brow. Then, suddenly, she jerked awake with a gasp.

He caught her halfway out of her seat and got himself clobbered. Twice. Once with her knee as she twisted around, flailing, and once with her hand across the side of his face. The first injury damn near doubled him over, *shit;* the second woke him up the hard way.

Christ.

"Nikki. Nikki." He grabbed her hands and pulled her close, trying to keep any more damage to a minimum. She was wild-eyed, her body stiff and unyielding. "Nikki, shhhh. It's okay."

"*Kid.*" Her breathing was ragged.

"You're okay, Nikki."

"It was the . . . the gunshots, and . . . the blood everywhere. I was reading, no, having tea, the kitchen was cooler, and . . ." Her voice trailed off, as if she realized she wasn't quite making sense. Then her gaze fell to his cheek, and he felt her soften in his arms. "Oh, Kid, I hit you."

"It's okay, Nikki. I'm fine." And his face was fine. It

was the rest of him that suddenly felt like pure crap again, inside and out. He knew which gunshots had woken her up. His. "You were having a nightmare. That's all." A bloody fucking nightmare about him blowing the hell out of Sanchez and Mancos.

"There was another body, in the garden," she said, a tremor in her voice. "I saw it when we ran through the backyard. I think it was one of the guys who was singing at Sandoval's, a man named Martin."

Oh, Christ. She'd seen the transvestite.

"Those men you killed, I'm pretty sure they'd done something to him, to Martin's face or something." She ran her fingers up into her hair in an absent gesture, her gaze losing some of its focus, as if she was trying to remember—which he really wished she wouldn't do. "It was dark. I couldn't quite see, we were moving so fast, but something was wrong, very wrong. I felt it. When I fell asleep, I could see his face more clearly, and what I saw scared me. Then you were there, and"—she took a shaky breath, her gaze coming back to him—"and for a moment, I didn't know who you were."

More than the wind went out of him at her declaration. Everything went out of him, and he was suddenly, completely drained, especially of his anger.

There was no place for it here tonight, not with her, and there shouldn't have been earlier, either, when the two of them had been lying in bed after making love.

Geezus. He really was the world's biggest jerk.

"It's okay, Nikki," he said, lifting the armrest between their seats. "I saw the body, too." And please, please, please don't want to talk about it.

"You did?"

Hell. She was trembling, and she looked exhausted, with circles under her eyes and her skin pale. There were sleep lines on her cheek, where she'd been resting her head against the edge of her seat.

"Yes. I saw it before I came in the house," he told her. "That's why I was looking for those other guys."

"With a knife."

"Yes, with a knife." And enough stone-cold deliberation to get the job done—and then some. *Shit.*

A heavy sigh went out of her, and he could tell she was still confused by all of it, still about half asleep. What she needed was to be completely asleep. Exhaustion on top of shock was a recipe for disaster.

Settling back against the window, he stretched his legs out and cradled her in his arms, and was incredibly grateful when she didn't say anything else about what he'd done with the knife or question what he was doing now, but just went with it, getting closer, lying down with him. A soft breath went out of her as she relaxed along the length of him, which was exactly where she belonged—cared for, protected.

God, Nikki.

He kissed the top of her head.

Her hair was a mess, of course, silky and wild, black and purple, and she was right. The guy's name had been Martin Chivay.

She relaxed even deeper against him on another sigh, and for just a moment, he thought she'd fallen back asleep.

"Kid?"

"Hmmm?"

"I'm angry, too."

Perfect.

She let out a long yawn and snuggled closer. "Tell me something I don't know about you."

Sure. Great. Anything was better than talking about her anger or poor Martin Chivay.

"I flunked the third grade."

She lifted her head up and looked at him. "You're kidding."

"Nope."

"But you're the smartest guy I know."

Well, if she'd ever wanted to knock him over with a feather, now would be a good time. She lived with a college professor, her grandfather.

"How do you figure?" he asked, truly curious.

She gave a little shrug of the most beautiful shoulders he'd ever seen, before settling back on top of him. "You just know stuff, all kinds of stuff, and you're really aware of everyone and everything around you—way more aware than about ninety-nine percent of the people on the planet."

He was a sniper, he could have told her. He'd been trained to be aware of everything, every sound, every scent, every shadow.

Yawning again, she rested her head back on his

chest. "Tell me more. Talk me back to sleep, Kid, and don't let go of me, just . . . just because."

He wasn't going to let go, no matter how angry they were with each other. This was too perfect, the way it should always be between the two of them.

"I've either skied or boarded every single run at Mary Jane and A-Basin," he said, after thinking a moment. "From the bunny trails to the chutes, and I mean the badass chutes where only the big boys go."

"And the big girls," she murmured.

"What girls? There aren't any girls up in big-boy territory."

She let out a little snort. "They're up there."

"How would you know, Nik?" She didn't ski, or climb, or kayak, or bike, or do too damn much of anything athletic. She ordered out pizza and painted her toenails to look like windows in a house. She sewed her own clothes and painted shooting stars on her legs. She played with makeup and broke his heart on every breath.

"I've seen them on TV, real girls on real mountains. So there."

She painted Hawkins naked.

"I've . . . uh, always wanted to go camping in a yurt," he said. "One of those ski-in and ski-out trips over the divide."

Thank God, Creed had more sense.

"Too cold for me."

"The yurts have stoves."

"Still too cold for me," she said, then, as if to prove

it, snuggled even closer to him. "Tell me a deep dark secret."

No way. His deep dark secrets were classified and guaranteed to give her more nightmares, but there had to be something.

There was.

Geezus, he couldn't believe he was going to go there for her—but he was. *Shit*. He took a deep breath, then let it out.

"I've never seen a porno movie."

That little confession was enough to get him another lift of her head.

"Never?"

"Never."

"You never got together with your high school buddies and snuck a copy of *Donna Does Denver* into the DVD player?"

"Never." Hell, no.

She propped herself up on his chest and gave him a very considering look.

"Why not?" she finally asked.

"Too scared," he said honestly.

She shook her head, obviously not buying it. "You are *so* not afraid of sex, Kid."

"Not sex," he agreed. "Just porno movies."

"This really is a deep dark secret, isn't it?"

He nodded.

"Are you going to tell me why they scare you?"

He'd never told anyone, not even J.T., but yeah, he was going to tell her.

"I was afraid 'Donna,' or 'Trixie,' or 'Charlene,' might turn out to be my mother."

Shock froze her in place for all of five seconds, then she blurted out, "Your *mother* is a porn star?"

"Don't know." He lifted one hand, palm up, with a small shrug. "But that's what Jimmy Pennick told me in the fourth grade, and I guess I was never able to convince myself that he might not be right."

Confusion furrowed her brow. "What would Jimmy Pennick know about it?"

"What everybody did. That my mother left Dad and us boys to go make it big in Hollywood, but as far as any of us has ever been able to tell, she hasn't made anything except a lot of noise about all these producers she knows and all the directors she's worked with. She doesn't have a regular job. We know that. Sometimes she'll call Dad and tell him she's between films and ask for a little cash to tide her over."

"Does he give it to her?"

"Every time."

"Yeah," she said after a long moment. "That does sound a little sketchy, doesn't it?"

"Just sketchy enough that I'm not taking any chances."

"Good call," she agreed.

"So what about you?" he asked, then realized how dumb that sounded. Nicole Alana McKinney didn't have any secrets, let alone any deep dark ones.

Or so he'd thought.

She dropped her gaze, and a little warning bell went off in his head.

"Nikki?"

She didn't say anything, just kept staring at his third shirt button.

Finally, she let out a short breath and started in. "Remember when you asked me why I'd come to Panama?"

"Yes." He wasn't going to like this. He could already tell.

"Well, it wasn't just so I could see you. I came to tell you good-bye."

Good-bye.

The warning bell turned to a silent chill.

"I've been offered a position in Paris for a year, as the artist-in-residence for the Musée de l'Odéon, and I didn't want you to come home and find out that I wasn't there, that I'd left without a word, so I came to see you, to tell you myself. In person."

How incredibly thoughtful. And what an incredible amount of effort she'd put into it, traveling all the way to Panama. About the same amount of effort he was going to have to put into keeping his anger where it belonged—someplace else. Anyplace else.

Fucking Paris?

"What about Rocky Solano?" Really. What about the old fiancé? What did he think about his bird flying the coop?

"Rocky has an apartment on the Left Bank. He's in

and out of Paris quite a bit, so it's no problem for me to stay there."

Of course not.

And it was perfect, exactly what she needed, a sophisticated, artistic, wealthy husband with an apartment on the Left Bank.

Fuck. His apartment was on the South Platte.

Looking down at her where she was lying on his chest, he realized another reason he'd stayed in Colombia for so long: the sheer simplicity of it. There were good guys, like him and C. Smith, and there were bad guys, like Conseco. There were orders, and he followed them. There wasn't a Nicole Alana McKinney in the whole freaking country, no one on the whole damn continent who could turn him inside out with just a glance or a couple of well-chosen words—like "good-bye" and "Paris."

He loved her. That had never changed, not from the first moment he'd seen her, but, *geezus*, he hadn't ever, not from the very beginning, been able to figure out what to do with her. She was amazing, and he was a grunt with a gun, and he hadn't had her back in his keeping four hours before her life had been on the line. Solano was giving her Paris. Kid gave her nightmares.

So great. He'd finally gotten it all straight in his head. He needed to back off. Except there was one little problem with his noble, self-sacrificing plan: It fucking sucked.

Yes, he'd screwed up by not coming home sooner,

and yes, in a lot of ways, she'd be better off with Solano, but neither of those things meant anything compared to the one undeniable truth in the whole mess: She was his—and he wasn't giving her up, even if she had come to Panama to say good-bye.

And if she hadn't fallen sound asleep, sprawled over the top of him, by God, he would have told her.

CHAPTER
12

Denver, Colorado

THIS COULDN'T BE GOOD.

Travis took another step inside the old building where he'd tracked Jane and stopped—and *son-uvabitch*. Behind him, someone else did the same thing, took a step, one squeaky step, and stopped.

Shit.

He'd followed her for almost an hour through the growing storm, freezing his ass off and ducking through alleys, and crossing deserted streets full of closed bars and darkened storefronts to reach a boarded-up theater on Denton Street. Two flights up the back stairs and through a broken door had brought him to this—a hallway with half the linoleum ripped out, a good fourth of the ceiling missing, and somebody behind him in the dark.

Another step sounded back by the stairwell door,

followed by another, but with no squeaking this time, and he ratcheted his alarm down a few notches—quite a few. The steps had been light, not heavy. It was somebody little. Probably a Castle Rat, he figured, since Jane had come here in the first place to find them.

A slight scuffling noise off to his right upped the ante again, but not by much.

Two Rats.

He wasn't worried. He was demoralized. The building was a dump, a helluva place for a bunch of kids to be living. Light from the street lamps outside barely cut through the grime-covered windows. The floorboards creaked. Plaster was crumbled everywhere, and there were wires hanging out of the walls. However much money the Castle Rats had stolen over the years, it hadn't gone into their accommodations.

"Stop *pushing*."

"I'm not pushing."

Three Rats, maybe four.

"*Shhh*."

"*Shhh*, yourself."

Five Rats. Given the six envelopes Jane had gotten tonight, there had to be at least one more somewhere.

Six little kids—he didn't think he was in too much danger, unless one of these wires was live, or he fell through a rotten floorboard.

He started forward again, making a personal note to himself that the next time he decided to chase after an ex-juvenile delinquent in search of her old gang, he needed to bring a flashlight.

Jane had disappeared. He'd lost sight of her when she'd gotten to the top of the stairs and shoved her way through the broken door. But this was the place. He was sure of it. He just wasn't sure what he was doing here—besides being stalked.

His invisible posse was definitely on the move behind him, snagging themselves on the walls, pushing, despite the order not to, squabbling in whispers. Funny thing, though, it was starting to sound like there were more than five of them back there, more than six, way more.

More like a pack of them, scurrying, coming up on three sides, funneling him closer to the set of double doors halfway down the hall. He was headed in that direction anyway, but he'd rather get there without the help.

Coming to a sudden stop, he whipped around and heard them damn near pile up on each other in the dark, trying to stop themselves from getting too close to him, from getting close enough for him to see.

Where in the hell had they all come from so quickly? From out of the woodwork?

Now he knew why they were called Rats.

"Who's the youngest?" he asked, making sure his voice was strong and clear and absolutely ringing with authority.

"Me," a little voice said, and was immediately hushed.

Contact, he thought.

"I'm looking for Robin," he said, his gaze scanning the darkness, picking up bits and pieces of movement all down the hall and in the gutted rooms off to the left.

There were dozens of children. Dozens. Surrounding him, cutting him off from the stairwell and the windows, cutting him off in every direction, except toward the double doors, which was suddenly the last place he wanted to go.

He needed his freaking head examined. He'd walked into this situation completely unprepared. He didn't need a flashlight. He needed riot gear.

"Ro-bin, Ro-bin," a voice said from inside one of the rooms.

The other kids quickly picked up the chant.

"Ro-bin, Ro-bin, Ro-bin."

Oh, Christ. This couldn't be good.

"Ro-bin, Ro-bin."

Too late, he heard the sound of footsteps above him. He glanced up just as someone dropped on him through the broken ceiling and knocked him to the floor.

Then the rest of them swarmed.

so . . . *help . . . me . . . God*—Jane froze on the stage at the front of the Empire Theater, her gaze glued to the unbelievable sight of Travis James being pushed and shoved down the center aisle. The Rats had him tied from top to bottom, like a mummy, his hands bound behind his back, his ankles shackled.

Shackled. The famous Travis James. The sheer horror of it made her feel faint.

He must have followed her, for God only knew what insane reason, and the little buggers had caught him and tied him up with everything they could find, rope, tape, electrical cords, old clothing.

"*Tri-bute. Tri-bute,*" they chanted, marching him along, gagged and blindfolded like some prisoner of war. And it was him, unmistakably. Travis James was the only six-foot, blond-haired, pictures-of-me-sell-for-thousands-of-dollars angel she knew—and he'd been captured by the Castle Rats.

It was enough to give her an instant ulcer. She could actually see her life flashing before her eyes—her new life, the one she'd fought for, the one suddenly in danger of disappearing faster than snowballs in hell.

She was a college girl, for crying out loud, a freshman at Metro State with a GED high school diploma already under her belt. She had a downtown apartment and a downtown job—and a past that simply wouldn't leave her alone.

If anything happened to Nikki McKinney's model, she would never forgive herself, and neither would Katya Hawkins—and something definitely could happen to him. The Rats were children, technically, but they weren't sweet, and they weren't nice, and they had a lot more in common with a pack of hyenas than she was comfortable admitting. She'd made damn sure of it when she'd been Robin Rulz, and she couldn't imagine that things had changed.

"Hey, now, what's this?" the tall boy standing next to her asked, gesturing up the aisle. "Have you gone and gotten yourself a boyfriend, Robin?"

All of seventeen years old and more dangerous than he looked with his shock of dark hair, slender build, and soft brown eyes, Fast Jack Spencer was the one who'd sent the Rats to Toussi's with the envelopes spelling out E-M-P-I-R. She'd gotten the message even without the last E. He hadn't said why he'd set the night in motion yet, but it couldn't possibly be any good for her. No way in hell. Nothing about being back in the Empire was good for her.

But Travis James—*good God*, that disaster was flat on her plate. How could she have been so careless as to let him follow her?

"Boyfriend?" she repeated, at a complete loss. There was no explanation for Nikki McKinney's drop-dead-gorgeous model being in a ratty old theater light-years from the hip bars and studio galleries of lower downtown, absolutely none. It boggled the mind.

The Rats were marching him up the stairs on the far end of the stage, and she instinctively started toward him, trying to think fast. She told herself not to panic, but she knew the situation, which had been sketchy at best, had just taken a real bad turn for the worse.

"Or is he a cop?" Fast Jack asked, following her across the stage.

Well, hell. Between cop and boyfriend, there was no contest. She'd take both.

Undercover vice, she decided, but before she could get the words out, one of the Rats tossed Travis's wallet across the stage to Fast Jack.

"He's no cop, Jack," the boy said.

That only left boyfriend, and while she tried to wrap her mind around those impossible odds, Fast Jack flipped the wallet open.

"He's got forty-seven dollars in here."

"And he's walking out with forty-seven," she said, her jaw setting in a hard line. Bad enough they'd tied him up. She'd be damned if she let them steal from him, too.

"A pair of concert ticket stubs." Jack fanned them out and held them up in the light. "So, did you have a good time at the Violins for Nonviolence in the Home gig?"

"It was off the hook." She started walking a little faster. Travis was struggling, and it was giving her a heart attack.

"Violins for Nonviolence." Jack laughed. "*Jesus*, Robin. Where did you find this guy?"

Under four layers of paint in a photograph hanging on Toussi's west wall, she could have told him. Except at first she hadn't known it was a photograph printed on the canvas. She'd thought the whole piece was a painting, pure Nikki McKinney imagination. She hadn't known the angel was real—until he'd walked into the gallery. By then, idiot that she was, she'd been half in love with him.

Keeping pace with her, Jack quickly went through the rest of the wallet. Behind him, *Fantasia* flickered on the screen, splashing color over the whole bizarre scene. Every night was *Fantasia* night at the Empire. It was the only film they had.

The Rats had taken over the abandoned theater when the rug shop had been shut down, and they'd held on to it despite the odds, fending off four potential gang takeovers and absorbing two rent hikes during Jane's first reign as Robin Rulz. She hadn't planned on a second reign—ever.

But here she was again, and there they all were, the Rats, over a hundred of them, more than ever before, spreading out across the theater, hunkering down in the seats, watching, waiting.

And there *he* was, bound and blindfolded on the stage, the last man on earth she would have ever wanted to see her like this, as a punk pickpocket who'd once been in charge of the scruffiest crew of miniature miscreants to ever hit the streets of Denver.

"Four library cards, all for Travis James," Jack said. "What the fuck does anybody do with four library cards?"

"Goes to the library," she said, reaching over and taking the cards out of his hand. "A lot."

"Hey, he's got an American Express, a plati—"

"Stop it, Jack." She snatched the credit card away

before he could get too excited. "You had it right the first time. We're together. I told him to wait outside, but he must have gotten curious, or worried. He worries about me a lot."

It all came rolling out of her mouth like the God's truth, easy as pie, and if Fast Jack believed for one minute that a guy like Travis James would go out with a street rat, she was going to sell him land in Florida.

But he did believe it.

"You sure as hell could do better than that, Robin, lots better," he said in disgust, tossing her the wallet. She'd claimed him. They weren't going to rob him blind. "Look at him. A bunch of little kids took him down. The guy's no Sandman, that's for damn sure. He's just a lame-ass loser."

She caught the wallet and shoved all Travis's cards back inside. Fast Jack was right, of course. Four library cards. Hell, she could have taken the guy down, but that was the point. He was *not* Sandman, *not* a street fighter. He didn't spend his nights protecting some lousy piece of turf with bravado and a knife, or a gun and his life. His life was worth more than a street corner, or a vacant lot, or a stretch of prime downtown territory.

And she was trying, so help her God, to make her life worth more, too.

"I saw a condom in his wallet," Jack said, grinning.

She did *not* need to know that.

"I saw two."

"Hey!" she shouted, breaking into a slow jog when

one of the bigger kids shoved him into a chair. Someone else pulled out another length of electrical cord
to tie him to it. "Back off. The guy's my friend."

"Her *boyfriend*," Fast Jack added.

Oh, great, Jane thought. That's all the Rats needed
to know.

"*Kiss, kiss, kiss*," the chant changed, with a few
more graphic catcalls thrown in by the older kids.

"I said back off," she repeated, striding through the
small crowd hanging around him. Unless it was Nikki
McKinney doing the tying, she doubted if Travis had
ever been tied to anything, let alone anything as
shabby as one of the Empire's old chairs.

She stepped up close and slipped the blindfold off
his face so he could see her. He needed to know he
wasn't alone in this awful situation.

Or maybe not.

The bluest eyes in the world barely glanced at her
before focusing over her shoulder and flashing bloody
murder at everyone else within bloody murder range.

Yikes. She instinctively stepped back, or at least
tried to, but even with his hands tied behind his back
and with hardly a second to do it in, he'd managed to
reach over and take hold of her coat, and he was
keeping her close with a fierce grip.

It was possible, she conceded with a little frisson of
alarm, that she'd underestimated his street-fighting
inclinations. Looks like he was giving were more than
an invitation for trouble. They were a guarantee, and

the last thing they needed right now was more trouble.

"Sorry you got all tied up, babe," she said, striving for sweetness or a little bit of a coo and at least a semblance of contrition in her voice, and failing. She just didn't have a coo in her. "I'll have you out of this real quick."

But not too quick. That was for damn sure. Not when he was breathing fire and shooting daggers at Fast Jack and the other Rats milling about on the stage.

Bending down to untie his ankles, she decided to keep his arms tied and the gag in place for another minute or so, until he could get a better look at the situation. The man had more degrees than God, like a gazillion of them from the biggest university in the state, and she had absolute faith in his ability to figure out what the odds were against them. Going *mano a mano* with the Rats was not the way out of this mess. This was going to take skill and finesse.

"*Kiss, kiss, kiss,*" the chant continued, bugging the crap out of her. She'd seen the way the women who came into the gallery looked at him. Over the last few weeks, she'd seen dozens of women, literally, gawk and stare and damn near drown in their own drool looking at Nikki McKinney's paintings of him. It wasn't just that his face fit together in all the right ways, or that he was stark naked. There was something in his eyes, the way he looked in the "ascending" paintings, something so open, so easy, so...so...

compassionate, she guessed was the right word, like he cared about you without even knowing you. It wasn't real, of course, but it did make a person want to pour their whole heart out to him.

And she had, kind of, a few times at night, after everyone else had gone home and she'd been alone, just sort of confessed her sins to the golden angel hanging on the west wall, until she'd gotten them all out, the big ones, the little ones, and even the deep dark secret ones she could barely admit to herself.

It was ridiculous, she knew, but she'd felt better for it. Then two weeks ago he'd shown up at the gallery, a real guy, just walked in the back door one afternoon carrying another painting, and she'd damn near died on the spot.

She still hadn't recovered. Logically, she knew he hadn't heard a word she'd said, but in her heart, he knew way too much about her for her to be comfortable doing anything but flat-out ignoring him. Worst of all, and what really made her feel stupid, was that for a short while she'd actually felt absolved, like he'd forgiven her for all her trespasses, this makeshift angel in a painting.

Well, that had all been blown to hell, probably literally, which was no comfort, and here she was, trying to save *his* hundred-thousand-dollar butt—and yeah, she knew that was probably a low estimate.

She pulled at the knots on the old shirt the Rats had used to shackle him, and wondered how in the mother-loving world she'd been so careless as to let him follow her. He never could have done it in the old days. She'd gotten lax, grown soft—grown up.

Another round of catcalls came out of the darkened theater, and she had to work to tamp down her anger. They should have grown up, too. They shouldn't still be here, sending tribute, needing her, wanting her back for whatever reason Fast Jack had dreamed up. A lot of the original crew was gone. Lulu and Ricky were married and living in Colorado Springs. Sandman had been busted and was doing time in the Buena Vista detention facility. Cruzer had contacted her about a year ago. He'd been in Las Vegas, running some games, and he'd wanted her to join him. He would always have a place for her, he'd said. There were half a dozen others who had gotten too old to be Rats and drifted away, looking for bigger scores or a chance at something better.

But for every one who'd left, three had taken their place. Somebody had been recruiting, and that somebody had to be Fast Jack Spencer. He was up to something. Nobody needed a pulling crew of a hundred kids.

With Travis's ankles untied, she rose back to her feet and bent her head close to his. He still had a grip on her coat, was still holding her close.

"I'm not going to let them hurt you, Mr. James," she whispered, reaching for the knots on the clothesline cord they'd used to gag him. "It's okay for you to let go of me."

Apparently, though, it wasn't. He didn't let go. If anything, he pulled her even closer.

Fine, she thought. If it made him feel better to have hold of her coat, she could live with it. He sure wasn't the first.

"I'm going to get you out of here, but you have to let me handle this my way," she continued very softly, for his ears only, working on the knots and having to work ridiculously hard not to just bury her nose in his hair. Nikki's paintings hadn't lied about his hair. It was amazing, thick and silky and a hundred shades of blond, and *geez*, it smelled good, like warm sunshine with a hint of lavender. What guy's hair ever smelled like sunshine and lavender? "If you'll just let me do all the talking, things will be fine." She hoped. "Okay?"

He nodded, and she tilted her head back to glance at his expression to see if it had improved.

It hadn't.

She leaned forward and whispered in his ear one more time. "I'm serious as a heart attack here, Mr. James. I'm going to need cooperation. Just follow my lead. And don't worry about the knife."

When she looked at him again, his eyebrows were drawn together, his gaze narrowed, and she knew that she'd at least gotten his attention.

"He's no fighter. You're right about that, Jack," she said, raising her voice a little so everyone standing around them could hear, and hoping to hell Mr. Travis James was getting the message. "But then that's what he's got me for."

Enough said. She stuck her hand in her pocket and pulled out a knife. It rested lightly in her fingers, the back of the case up against her palm, and with a press of the release, the blade sprung free, razor sharp.

The chant of "*kiss, kiss, kiss*" faltered to a halt, and the kids closest to her stepped back. Even Fast Jack shifted his weight to put a little extra distance between them.

She'd pulled *the* knife, silver and engraved, and every Castle Rat knew the history of the blade—where it had been, what it had done, and who had done it. Robin Rulz.

The Rats weren't going to mess with her, ever. But Travis James was on shaky ground. He was too old—all of twenty-three—too clean, and wearing way too much Abercrombie & Fitch to be anything except the enemy to them, even if he was her "boyfriend." They didn't know he was important. They didn't know he counted, and they sure as hell didn't care that Katya Hawkins would can her butt if she brought him home all roughed up. And Superman—hell, Superman would toss her back to the she-wolves in Phoenix so fast it would make her head swim. The only place worse than the Immaculate Heart School for Young Women was jail, and so help her God, she wasn't going back there, either.

"He was wearing a real nice coat when we left LoDo," she said, carefully sliding the knife under the triple skein of cording wrapped across his mouth.

The coat magically appeared from out of the dark on her left and was dropped in a pile at her feet.

"He had a nice watch, too." She cut through the first cord, keeping the blade away from his face and away from his hair. The knife was wicked sharp. "I can't imagine you guys missed that."

The watch came from her right, lightly tossed onto the coat.

"And a ring, a silver ring he was wearing on his right hand."

It landed next to the watch as she slit the second cord.

"And a gold-and-silver cuff bracelet."

That one started some chatter, some confused whispering on the outskirts of the crowd.

She pulled the knife out from under the last cord, leaving it uncut, and gave them all a steady look. "Come on, guys. There was only one bracelet. Cough it up."

It took a few more seconds, but the bracelet appeared, brought forward by one of the younger kids and carefully set on the coat.

"You don't have to fight for him, Robin," Jack said. "Not here. Not with us."

"No trespass price," she said. Forty-seven dollars wouldn't cover it—not even close—and neither would his nice watch. More often than not a trespass price involved a can of spray paint and maybe somebody's car, or their house, or the place where they worked, or even their body. Or maybe the Rats would

CRAZY KISSES   ◆   177

just take something from the trespasser, like the front wheel of their car, or a piece of their house, or maybe they'd give him an impromptu haircut and spray paint his head. Whatever, it was never lethal, but it was all unacceptable.

Fast Jack agreed with a nod, and satisfied, she turned back to Travis and sliced through the last cord, letting them all fall away.

"*Kiss, kiss, kiss,*" the chant started back up.

Well, she wasn't going to kiss him. Not in this lifetime.

"Cut my hands free," he said, shifting sideways on the chair, his voice low and tight. It wasn't a request.

She looked down and swore under her breath. Underneath the tape and rope and all the other whatnot they'd wrapped around him, they'd used wire on his wrists. His skin had been rubbed raw in places.

"Don't send any more messages to Toussi's," she said to Jack, her own voice pretty damn tight. She started with the tape, pulling it off, then tore away some Silly String they'd sprayed on him. Oh, the little Rats must have thought that was hilarious. "If you want to talk, meet me at Connie's Bagels Sunday morning. Eleven o'clock."

Connie's was neutral ground.

"Sunday morning may be too late," Jack said.

Something in his voice caused her to glance up.

"It's the Parkside Bloods. They're pushing us out. They want the Empire. Raymond says he'll only talk with you."

So that's what this was all about. She should have figured. Well, she didn't want to talk to Raymond the Blood King ever. That part of her life was over. She went back to working on Travis's wrists, cutting through a piece of rope.

Crap. Even the Parkside Bloods knew she was back.

"How in the hell did you last this long, Jack?" Honestly, she was beginning to wonder. "I've been gone for two years. They must have made a play for the Empire before this."

"No. Raymond got busted about the time you disappeared. Peanut took over, but he had his hands full holding off the Locos, but somebody capped Carlos. Baby Duce took over, and the Locos pulled back to the west side, so the Playboys started pushing in from the north side, and when Raymond got out, he started pushing back, and the Empire is getting caught in the middle."

"The last damn place you can afford to be," she said. With the rope gone, she closed her knife and started carefully unwinding the wire from around his wrists, all the while wishing she could sink straight through the floor and just disappear all over again. This was not her life anymore, but Travis James was hearing all of this junk like it was her garbage to sort out—gang crap, turf wars, homies getting killed.

"I know that, but—"

"Then you know how it works." *Dammit.* "The Rats survived because we stayed out of everybody's way, low-key. You take enough to get by, but not so much that somebody wants to take from you. You don't fool with the gangsters or the dealers or their clients. The Rats have always been a small group, strictly hit-and-run. You've got too many, Jack. You're making too much noise." A hundred freaking kids. It was crazy. He was crazy. He had to know all this. "You can't act like a gang, not without being a gang, and the Rats have never had gang firepower. They've never had guns."

"We do now, Robin," a small voice said.

For a second, she was struck dumb. Fast Jack had armed the Rats? It was a death warrant.

She stared at him, speechless, then had to look away.

She couldn't deal with this. Couldn't even look at the kids. She was wearing a blue sweater, dammit, a beautiful blue silk sweater, and had shoes to match. That was her life now. Matching shoes. Not Parkside Bloods and Locos and Carlos getting capped.

"My name is Jane," she said. "Jane Linden. There is no Robin Rulz anymore. I'm not Robin Hood or robbing fools."

"We can't do it without you, Robin," Jack said, almost, but not quite, looking pitifully helpless. He really didn't have it in him to be helpless, not Fast Jack. He was a fighter from way back. They'd done it together, fought against Greg Stevens at Castle Imports.

"Jane," she repeated. "My name is Jane."

"*Jane. Jane. Jane,*" the little Rats started up.

God, they were relentless.

And Travis James was finally free.

She slipped the last loop of wire off his hands and knew she was never going to live this down. Her new life was over, her clean slate muddied all to hell.

He leaned over and scooped up his stuff before rising to his feet and shoving it all in his pocket. He looked like a Nordic god compared to all the grubby gremlins clustered around the chair.

"So what are we doing here?" he asked, taking hold of her hand like it was the most natural thing in the world, like he really was her boyfriend. "Leaving, staying, waiting for Raymond, or kicking a lot of very little ass?"

That set off some giggles—but not from her. *Good God.* He was holding her hand.

"We're . . . uh, leaving," she said, but she didn't know how. She felt a little paralyzed by the hand-holding thing, like her feet wouldn't quite move. And she was simply amazed at his self-control. He was still angry. All the signs were there, the edge in his voice, the tightness of his jaw, the tension in his arm, his stance, but he wasn't giving in to it. He wasn't whacking anybody, or grabbing a kid, or shaking somebody until their teeth rattled, all of which she'd seen more times than she ever wanted to remember.

"You've still got my wallet, right?" He reached down and snagged his coat.

His wallet.

Right.

"In my back pocket," she remembered. She'd put it there after she'd returned his cards.

"Then let's get out of—"

"*Hush*," one of the kids said in a voice tinged with panic, her nose all but twitching as she took up a stand at the edge of the stage. Everyone instantly went still. There was no sound, no milling, no sniffling, only the tinny, muted strains of *Fantasia* echoing through the theater.

Then the warning cry came: "Cops!"

The film was instantly switched off, throwing the whole place into darkness—and as one swarming organism, the Rats ran, melting off the stage, out of the seats, away from the aisles, disappearing, every one, and out of pure, gut-deep instinct, Jane disappeared with them, whisking Travis away with her, across the boards, behind the screen, and into the dark at the back of the stairs.

CHAPTER 13

30,000 feet over the Caribbean Sea

THROUGH THE WINDOW of his private jet, Juan Conseco watched the moonlit clouds course across the sky over the dark ocean below. Beside him, Drago was furious, delivering his polemic in a constant stream of Spanish punctuated by butchered English when he wanted to make a particularly damning point.

"This is insane, *insanity*. Far worse than Panama. You will be naked in the United States, without friends, without protection." His uncle had been stoically unhappy from the moment Juan had decided to make a bold, lightninglike strike at his enemy on his home ground, where *el asesino fantasma* would least expect it.

"We have friends in every city in the United States, Uncle," he corrected Drago's latest mumblings. "In the major cities and the minor ones, in cities on their last gasp of life, cities with new industry and old. We are there, in all of them. You've gotten the name of our Denver connection from our man in Tijuana—¿es verdad? What was it again?"

"Baby Duce." Drago's mouth thinned in disgust.

Juan understood. His uncle didn't like dealing with people at the street level. The regional distributors, the men with money, were as low as he liked to go. But Juan understood there was very little difference between himself and men like Baby Duce, and those differences had more to do with the cut of their clothes than the working of their minds. That understanding gave him an advantage when dealing with the street lords. It was why he had taken over the family business when his father had died. It was why Drago had let him.

"You told Baby Duce what we need?"

"Yes," Drago replied. "There is a club called the Aztec. Very popular, he said. It will be crowded tonight, and it has a basement where we will not be disturbed."

"Good." Besides Drago, Juan had brought three of the other four men who had been with him in Panama City. The fourth man, the one he'd left watching Chronopolous's house, had stupidly gotten himself picked up by the police. There would be no new information coming out of Panama City. If the man was smart, he would hold his tongue, or Juan would hold it for him.

It had been a terrible thing, but he'd had to leave poor Sanchez and Mancos at the mercy of the Panamanian police. With the ghost killer within his grasp, there had been no time to do otherwise. He'd had no choice. Such was the nature of his business. Pray God the bodies would be treated with respect.

He fingered the cross at his throat and said another prayer for his fallen men and for the capture of the hated gringo. The woman was the key now. She would lead him to *el asesino fantasma*. Juan had a thousand ways of getting information out of a woman, and if necessary, he would use them all. Nicole Alana McKinney would be praying for one of her angels to come and save her before he was through.

Denver, Colorado

Agony or idiocy?

That was the question.

One of the little Rats trapped with him in the very small closet under the stairs farted again, and Travis decided on idiocy. That was how he was going to die, sheer idiocy, gassed to death by a ten-year-old with no self-control.

"Robin," a small feminine voice said from right up against his left leg. "Make him stop. I'm gonna be sick."

Yes, sir, that was the only thing missing from this intimate encounter—someone throwing up on his shoes.

"Shut up, Blue," another Rat whispered. "We're s'posed to be hiding, and her name is Jane."

"Jaaaane," Blue whined. "Make him stop."

It was dark and hot and incredibly cramped in the closet, bodies pushing on him from every direction, kids hanging on his clothes, someone actually standing on his right foot. All of which he could have borne, except for Jane being laminated to the front of his body, pushed up next to him so tightly he could feel every curve she had, every breath she took, and the snap on her jeans.

It required pressure to get that close, and he was feeling that, too, intense pressure in all the wrong places.

He was dying.

And she'd called him Mr. James, which was even worse than what the Jack kid had called him, lame-ass loser. Mr. James made him sound like an alien, like he came from another planet, like the only way in hell they could ever get together would be if their worlds accidentally careened out of orbit and crashed into each other... which, when he thought about it, was kind of what had happened tonight, where they'd started off with this huge gap between them, but had ended up in the exact same spot—and he meant exact. If they got any closer, one of them was going to have to change their name.

It was killing him.

Her hair was silky against his neck, and despite what was going on down around his knees, she smelled divine, like heaven. The closet had been a great hiding place for all of two seconds for two people, but it had turned into a torture chamber. He didn't know how many Rats had jammed themselves in on top of him and Jane before somebody had finally gotten the door shut.

"Shhh. All of you," she whispered, then lifted her mouth to his ear. "Boost me up."

Sure. No problem. He'd just bend his knees a little, just slide his face down the side of her neck and over her breasts, and cup his hands for her boot.

No problem—despite the complaints he got for shoving Blue and rearranging everybody else. He couldn't help it. They were packed in like sardines.

No problem at all when Jane's knee ended up in his armpit and her crotch ended up in his face—no problem, but he slipped straight into the twilight zone, his senses flipping on one by one, gearing up for the leap into hyperdrive. It didn't help when he lifted her, and the whole silky length of her midriff slid along his cheek.

Only his years of training saved him, all the time he'd spent studying and working as a certified massage therapist while he'd developed his theories on sexual imprinting. He was used to skin, soft, estrogen-infused skin. Professionally speaking, it was a familiar work surface—for his hands. Of course, that kind of skin against his face conjured up a whole different scenario.

He held his breath, trying not to go nuts, but quickly gave it up. Not breathing was always a strategy doomed to failure.

So he breathed and held her steady against him.

He breathed and let the scent of her skin go to his head. He breathed and felt like he was falling in love, because it had been a long time since he'd been this close to a girl he liked this much.

Above him, she was busy doing something with the wall close to the ceiling. When he heard the scrape of wood against metal and felt a breath of cold air, he realized she'd opened a trapdoor or a ventilation shaft.

"Come on, Rats. Up."

And that was when Travis discovered a new personal talent: He was the perfect shape and size to be a human stepladder.

Who had known?

The Rats swarmed up his body, helped by Jane, who pulled them up one by one, then pushed them through the opening. They used his shoulder as a resting spot and his head as a pushing-off point. He gritted his teeth and bore it, his arms straining, his patience thinning.

Out in the theater, he could hear the police coming up on the stage, the low sound of their voices and the heaviness of their steps hitting the boards. The irony of the situation was not lost on him. He'd never run from the cops in his life. As an EMT, he worked with the police, side by side, saving lives, picking up the pieces. He was one of the good guys, heart and soul. He knew he looked like just another slacker dude, but man, if your heart stopped, he was the guy you wanted showing up fast. If your kid overdosed, he was the guy to call. His best friend from high school, Connor Ford, was a cop, and Connor was going to have a heyday with this story, if Travis could swallow his pride long enough to tell it.

Two beers ought to do the job.

With the last Rat through, five by his count—and he didn't know how five kids had jammed themselves into the tiny closet—Jane boosted herself through the trapdoor and reached down for him.

"Hurry," she whispered, pulling on his shirt. The voices were growing closer.

It was ridiculous, hiding from the cops, but her sense of urgency was contagious, and he found himself reaching for the opening. It wasn't very big, not as big as he'd hoped. He went ahead and shoved his coat through, then grabbed onto the edge of the ventilation shaft and levered himself up. It was a tight squeeze, and between him pushing and her pulling, they ended up tangled together in a pile inside a place infinitely smaller than the closet.

"Weisman, get over here and put your shoulder to this," one of the cops said, rattling the closet door. "I think I heard something."

Jane went motionless beneath him, her hands still clutching his shirt, her breath in his ear.

"What's wrong with *your* shoulder?" Weisman wanted to know.

"Just get over here."

Travis took a breath and told himself to move off of her. It was the right thing to do, as opposed to trying to absorb her through his pores, which was not the right thing to do. But when he rolled to his side, he ran into somebody else, somebody much smaller.

"Hey, get your own spot," the much smaller somebody whispered, elbowing him in the ribs.

Geezus. He winced and rolled back on top of Jane. Bunch of freaking little heathens—he didn't know whether to throttle them, put them all in time-out, or pay them.

He heard one of the Rats take off crawling up ahead, scrambling through the shaft, the sound of their shoes scraping on metal.

"Wait your turn," came a whispered order a few seconds later, also from just up ahead.

"What's taking so long," somebody complained.

"Jeeter's stuck."

Travis knew which kid had to be Jeeter, Rat number two on the human chain that had crawled up him, the big Rat. Jeeter weighed about a ton and a half, and if he was stuck, they were all stuck. Logjam, pure and simple. Nobody was going anywhere.

He swore silently, praying he wouldn't embarrass himself, which was really going to ruin his night, when suddenly, it dawned on him that the universe might be trying to tell him something. Being plastered up close and personal to Jane twice in less than five minutes couldn't possibly be just a cosmic roll of the dice. It was karma. It was fate.

It was going to make him do something stupid, if he wasn't careful.

"Kiss, kiss, kiss," came a small voice, very softly, from somewhere on the other side of Jane.

Yeah. That was it. The stupid thing he was in danger of doing. She already had to think he was a total idiot. Making a move on her just because his face was buried in the curve of her neck and her mouth was just inches away would be totally juvenile.

"Sounds like rats to me," the cop named Weisman said. "These old places are full of them." He put his shoulder to the door with a solid thump. "You want to tell me what we're doing here again?"

Totally juvenile, Travis decided—but he couldn't help himself. Every time she exhaled in his ear, his temperature rose ten degrees, and he was damn close to critical meltdown, because this was Jane beneath him, molded to his body—wild Jane with the wary green eyes who watched everybody within a thirty-foot radius and held them all at bay, Jane who never spoke to anyone except Katya or Suzi, Jane who could disappear in plain sight, blending in, being still, being oblique, so subtle, so smooth.

Jane who simply fascinated him with her feral gaze and sidelong glances, with the way she moved.

Jane whose hand had drifted over his painted angel's body and made him wonder if she was actually seeing him, thinking about him.

"We're making Lieutenant Bradley happy," cop number one said. "And if we find something, it'll make her even happier. We've fielded over half a dozen complaints on the Empire over the last couple of months, but we never find anything."

"What kind of complaints?" Weisman hit the door again with a solid, board-cracking thump.

Damn. He needed to stop thinking about Jane and start worrying about the cops. If Jeeter didn't get his butt through whatever opening he was stuck in, Travis was going to get his ass busted. He was last in the Rat line. It was his cheese hanging out in the wind.

Which brought him to another, sudden, blinding realization: He didn't have anything left to lose. This was it. The whole screwed-up night was heading toward a dead end faster than a Mack truck with no brakes.

Hell, inside of five minutes, he'd probably be in police custody, while all the Rats would be home free. He'd be starting his rap sheet and heading downtown, and they'd be back watching *Fantasia* and tying up some other unsuspecting fool.

"*Kiss, kiss,*" came the little voice again, and Travis stopped fighting it. This was going to happen. Jane had to be thinking about it, too. The Rats had been chanting "kiss" since they'd dragged him up on the stage.

Kiss . . . he'd know soon enough if she wasn't interested. He'd know instantly.

Turning his face deeper into her neck, he let his nose slide through the silky strands of her hair and brush against her skin. Her breath caught softly in her throat, which was a good sign, and she didn't pull out her silver switchblade and gut him, which gave him a ridiculous amount of confidence.

"Trucks pulling up in the middle of the night, unloading stuff. Kids running around at all hours. I don't know," the cop was saying. "I've been here three times, and we've come away empty-handed every time."

"You talk to the owner?" Weisman gave the door another hit, but Travis hardly cared. He was sinking into Jane, into the scent and softness of her, opening his mouth on her cheek, sliding his hand up into her hair, holding her—filling himself up with her. He grazed her jawline with his teeth, and a shiver went through her. He slid his nose down the side of hers, and her hands tightened on his shoulders, which was such a perfect turn-on, to have her holding onto him.

"Louise Nash, yeah," the cop said. "She's been renting it out to a guy in Phoenix for the last four years, a Nick Daley, who we haven't been able to find. Apparently, he's trying to turn the place into a venue for concerts, but hasn't been able to pull together any backers. That's her story, anyway."

"The place is a dump," Weisman said, hitting the door again. "I wouldn't put my money in it."

That caused the first cop to laugh. "You don't have any money."

"Yeah, yeah." Weisman gave the door one more hit and burst through with a muttered curse.

Travis's time was up.

"*Jane*," he whispered her name, then covered her mouth with his own.

Her lips were incredibly soft, her breath catching in her throat again, but her body didn't melt into his. Just the opposite, in fact. She stiffened up. It was pure fight, flight, or freeze like a bunny in the headlights, and she'd gone the bunny route—definitely. He could feel it in her heartbeat, in the silent thrum of energy suddenly holding her so still beneath him. He didn't blame her, not really. She was compromised. He was on top, and there was no mistaking what he wanted. Out-and-out telling him no would have been one thing, but her breathing was shallow, as if she was feeling the same thrill coursing through him, and she was still holding on to him like her life depended on it, so he went ahead and kissed her. He breathed her in and teased her, rubbing his lips over the corner of her mouth so very, very gently, and he whispered her name again.

"*Jane*." Beautiful, wild Jane . . . *open for me*.

And finally, she did, her lips parting on a ragged sigh he felt all the way down to his groin, a sigh of surrender. He didn't hesitate. He slid his tongue inside, into soft, wet heat, into the sensual seduction of her mouth—into serious trouble.

He'd wanted to kiss her. God, how he'd wanted to kiss her, and he'd known it would be good, but he hadn't known it would make wanting the rest of her instantly so much worse.

He should have expected it. He'd been kind of

crazed of late, and all because of her. He'd let his imagination get way out of hand, but maybe so had she. When he buried his hand deeper into her hair, she pressed her body closer to his. When he slanted his mouth across hers, she moved with him, making the kiss hotter, deeper, giving herself up and all but turning him inside out.

Geezus. She was the angel.

He should have done this days ago. He'd needed this days ago, to be with her, physically, to make contact. The dreams he'd had about her had been so surreal, jungle dreams, hot dreams, with smooth skin and wet mouths, dark caves and secret places, and her hair flowing over him like a river of silk. The kind of dreams where he woke up in a sweat, his body aching. He'd lost sleep. He'd lost his appetite—and now, if he wasn't careful, he was going to lose his head and forget that the Empire was crawling with cops and Rats, that they weren't alone, and that no matter how good the kiss was, it wasn't going to go nearly far enough to satisfy him—not in this ventilation shaft.

But after waiting so long to get this close to her, he needed something. Something more than a kiss. He gathered her more tightly to him, loving the feel of her in his arms, the melting heat of her body lying along the length of his, the shape of her. She made another soft, surrendering sound in her throat, her arms sliding up around his neck, her hands tunneling up into his hair, and every functioning brain cell he had left dissolved into pure instinct and sensation. His knee went between hers. His hand went under her sweater, sliding up over silky skin. It all felt so good, and there was absolutely nowhere to go with it, not when they were crammed inside a tin can with five kids. He shouldn't even be kissing her the way he was. He knew it. She knew it, and between the two of them knowing so damn much the kiss slowed to a stop, until the only thing moving between them was their breath—their lips touching, their hearts racing.

And then it was all over.

"Hey, I got one." A large hand clamped down around his ankle. "Weisman, help me out here."

Another set of hands grabbed on to his other leg and started pulling.

Travis quickly jammed his feet against the two-by-fours framing the shaft opening. He wasn't ready to go, not yet, not like this, and the cops wouldn't have the leverage to get him out, not until he let them.

"Come on, buddy. Come on out of there."

The Rats were moving around him and up ahead, moving away. Jeeter must have finally gotten through.

But Jane wasn't moving. She was still with him.

A beam of light bounced around the inside of the ventilation shaft, throwing enough illumination to reveal her face. One look, and he was just about done in all over again.

The Rats needed a few more seconds to get away, but she looked like she was going to need days. Her mouth was soft, her cheeks flushed, and he could tell from her eyes that she was still just a little bit lost in that wonderland where they'd been.

He didn't blame her. He would have stayed there, too, for days, right along with her, except he had two bruising hulks trying to drag him back into the closet.

Sonuvabitch. This was all so stupid, he couldn't believe it.

She had to go, and she had to go now.

He slid his hand down to her waist and gave her a push.

"*Go*," he whispered, trying as best he could to get her out from under him. The Rats were abandoning ship, and she needed to be with them.

When she was finally free, she hesitated, then cupped his cheek with her hand and kissed him, her lips brushing across his not just once, but twice. In the next instant, she was gone, silently. Unlike the little Rats, she didn't scramble, or scurry, or even make a sound. She simply moved and disappeared.

He was tempted to follow her. Damn tempted. Chances were he could shake off Weisman and Company and catch her on the other side of wherever it was the shaft led. But chances were Weisman and Co. would follow, too, and the gig would be up.

Better to finish it now, he decided. Let Jane and the Rats go and throw the cops off their trail. Besides, how bad could it be getting busted?

BAD enough, he thought two hours later. Especially with Skeeter scowling at him.

"Arrested," she said for about the fourth time, like she just couldn't believe it was true. "Arrested running wild with . . . with—"

"Uh, let's not go there, Skeeter." He'd told the cops exactly nothing, and he'd like to keep it that way.

"You said you were going home." She was looming over him where he was sitting at Weisman's desk, her foot tapping. "You said you were done for the night."

"I don't need a lecture, babe. That's why I called Connor." With only one phone call, he'd thought he'd better get another policeman on his side, and he'd known Skeeter would chew him up.

"Your cop friend?"

"Uh-huh." He nodded and looked up at her. "So who called you?"

"Who do you think?"

Jane. Despite the current crappiness of his situation, he couldn't help but give in to a grin.

"What did she say?"

"That she was real sorry, but the night had gotten a little complicated, and maybe I should haul my ass down to the police station and bail your ass out."

"It wasn't her fault."

Skeeter let out a disbelieving snort. "At least you've still got your hair. She said the Rats tied you up."

Great. That was just the sort of information he wanted everybody to have—that he'd been bush-whacked by a bunch of juvenile delinquents.

"There were a lot of them."

"They spray paint you anywhere?" One of her pale blond eyebrows arched above her sunglasses.

"No." *Geezus*. Spray paint and hair—those were three words he didn't want to hear together, not with any Rats attached.

Connor and Weisman were in the lieutenant's office, a woman named Loretta Bradley, trying to negotiate his release. So far, he hadn't been slapped with anything but a misdemeanor for trespassing. As far as he could tell, it really wasn't what he'd done that was holding things up, but where he'd been caught doing it. Lieutenant Bradley had a lot of questions about the Empire, none of which he'd answered very helpfully. He'd been keeping the night's events on the down low, sliding around the facts, which had worked out pretty well up until Connor had arrived and explained that he wasn't the skater-boy vagrant he appeared to be. On his own, with his long hair and no wallet, he hadn't bothered to correct the impression he'd given of being someone who'd maybe had a little too much to drink earlier in the night and had crawled into a ventilation shaft inside a closet behind the stairs in an abandoned theater on the wrong side of town to sleep it off.

Okay. Maybe the cops hadn't bought his story, but he hadn't exactly done anything wrong, either. Being inside a building with an open lock on its back door that was owned by a woman who didn't have a clue who she'd rented it out to wasn't the crime of the century.

Skeeter's outfit was the crime of the century. There wasn't a guy in the squad room who hadn't checked her out twice and was maneuvering around for a third pass.

"Did you get dressed up just for me?" he asked. She'd left the gallery wearing a pair of cutoff jeans over black wool tights with a black sweatshirt. She'd shown up at the precinct dressed to kill in thigh-high boots with lug soles, a black leather miniskirt with a chain mail belt, and a pink angora sweater.

With her long platinum ponytail and killer body, she looked good enough to eat and like she'd hurt going down. Just the sort of thing to turn on a bunch of guys, any bunch of guys.

"These aren't the Feds. These are the local cops, and it's not a bad idea to put your best foot forward when you're dealing with them," she said with an absolutely straight face.

Especially if your best foot was in sky-high patent leather, he thought, and your sweater was fuzzy, pink, and tight. This whole pink thing was new with her, and he couldn't help but wonder if Skeeter had the hots for somebody. He'd sure as hell like to know who. He'd love to know what kind of guy it took to spring her trap. Probably some cruiser down on the Sixteenth Street Mall with a purple Mohawk and enough tattoos to qualify as a piece of living art.

"Some of these cops remember me as SB-three-oh-three," she went on. "I just wanted to make sure they knew I'd grown up."

Travis wisely kept his thoughts to himself, but the words "grown up to be a Goth hooker" came to mind, though not quite as strongly as "grown up to be a comic book superhero," because hookers did not have Skeeter's muscle definition, which was awesome. Not juiced, just sleek and cool looking, like she'd worked for it. And not many people on any career track had her perfect, baby-soft skin. Nobody looked like Skeeter Bang in real life—except Skeeter Bang. She was damn cute from the neck up, her tough-girl sunglasses perched on a button nose, but man, from the neck down, she was pure kick-ass gorgeous.

So if there was a guy who'd flipped her switch, where was he? Travis wondered. He'd never seen her hang out with anyone who didn't work for SDF or who wasn't somehow connected with 738 Steele Street.

He didn't wonder for long, though. The door to Lieutenant Bradley's office was opening.

Connor and the other two cops came out first, with Connor not looking very happy, and for the first time, Travis started to get a little nervous. He rose to his feet. If Connor couldn't get him out of here, who could?

Lieutenant Bradley followed the men out, busy looking through some papers, the expression on her face unreadable—until Connor and the cops stumbled to a stop in front of her and almost caused a pileup. Then she looked damned annoyed.

"Watch yourself, Weisman," she barked, glancing up. Her attention, like everyone else's, quickly went to Skeeter, who was impossible to miss, the pink queen of punk amidst a sea of police department blue.

This is it, he thought. Weisman couldn't get his jaw off the floor, and the other cop wasn't in any better shape. He was doomed. They were going to lock him up and throw away the key. The Rats had been right to run.

"Skeeter?" the lieutenant said. She was a tall woman, big-boned, her nose a little too large for her face. Even so, she wasn't unattractive with her reddish hair and golden brown eyes—but she was damned imposing.

Beside him, Skeeter turned around, toward the group.

"Hey, Loretta," she said, sounding genuinely pleased and more than a little relieved.

"So this Mr. James is one of yours?" the lieutenant asked, nodding in his direction.

"Yes, ma'am."

The lieutenant gave Weisman, Connor, and the other cop another very annoyed look. Connor didn't seem to notice. He was too busy grinning like a fool at Skeeter.

"Gentlemen, we're done here. This incident is officially off the books as of now." She turned to him.

"Mr. James, you're free to go." Her gaze shifted to Skeeter. "Have Christian or Dylan give me a call."

"Yes, ma'am," Skeeter said, almost to the woman's back. The lieutenant hadn't wasted any time in burying her nose in her papers and heading back to her office.

Travis was nonplussed. That was it? Skeeter shows up, claims him, and he's out?

"You know Lieutenant Bradley?" he asked her.

"We're like this," Skeeter said, holding up her hand with two of her fingers crossed.

"Yeah. Travis and I are the same way," Connor said, stepping forward with his hand out. "Hi. I'm Connor Ford, the guy who *couldn't* get him out of here."

Skeeter took his hand. "Skeeter Bang."

"Nice to meet you, Skeeter." Connor was still grinning, his gray eyes sparkling with mischief and more interest than Travis knew was going to get him anywhere. He had sandy blond hair and a broad, open face. "Travis showed me some of the *oekaki* sketches you drew of him. I thought they were great."

Which was all wonderful, Travis was sure, but this wasn't the time to be gushing about art, or hitting on a girl. He wanted the hell out of there.

He put his hand to Skeeter's back and gently but firmly directed her toward the door.

"You like manga?" she asked Connor, her feet thankfully moving in the right direction. Manga was the Japanese comic book art she did. Skeeter had given Travis some of the unfinished drawings she'd done of him, her *oekaki*, and he'd framed them and hung them in his cabin. In contrast, he hadn't hung a single one of the angels Nikki had given him over the years. For Skeeter, he played a character, Kenshi the Avenger. It was fun, even though he didn't think she had the character quite right, or that he was the right model for the job. Nikki, on the other hand, had everything right, sometimes painfully right. She knew him, every square inch of him. She stripped him to the bone with every angel she painted, and there was no mistaking that they were *his* bones. It wasn't something he wanted to face over breakfast.

"Love it. Are you doing *dojinshi?*" Connor asked Skeeter, referring to the unofficial comics made by fans. "Or are you with a publisher?"

"No publisher," she said, her smile warming with every Japanese word he spoke. "Not yet. But I've got a really cool story arc I'm working on called *Star Drifter.*"

Oh, brother, Travis thought. Once Skeeter started in on *Star Drifter*, it took an act of God to get her to stop.

"Great title." Connor kept even with her, stride for stride, letting Travis hustle them all out the door. It was a bum's rush, with all three of them the bums. "I'd love to see some more of your stuff. Are you showing anything at Toussi's?"

"No. This whole week is just Nikki McKinney and Rocky Solano."

"Rocky Solano, yeah, I know him," Connor said.

"Met him at Nikki's a couple of times. He's an interesting . . . uh, guy. It's amazing what some people can do with yarn and a couple pieces of string."

"Yeah, right," Skeeter said, letting out a laugh.

Connor's grin broadened again, and then they were out the door, into the cold air and weak sunlight of a late March dawn without a precinct cop in sight.

"Arrested? *Geezus*, Travis," Connor said as soon as they cleared the door, his tone as disbelieving as Skeeter's had been earlier. "You've never been arrested in your life. So do you want to tell me what you were doing such a damn good job of not telling Lieutenant Bradley? And why do you have a size five tennis shoe tread mark on your left cheek?"

A tread mark. Crap. Travis used his sleeve to wipe it off. That had to look at least as stupid as it sounded. Damn Rats.

"Buy me a cup of coffee, and I'll tell you anything you want to hear." He gave his cheek another swipe. "Add breakfast, and I'll tell you the truth."

Damn, it felt good to be out of the police building.

"Don't forget I'm a cop, okay?" Connor said, completely serious. "I don't want to have to arrest you myself."

"Nothing illegal happened tonight, Connor. Strange, maybe, but not illegal."

"So how about you start with the strange thing that happened to your wallet," his friend said. "Like it disappearing. Did you get rolled or what?"

"Rolled hard," he admitted. "By a pack of Rats. Skeeter, are you coming to breakfast? Connor's buying."

"Wouldn't miss it," she said, and Connor's grin returned in full force.

"We can talk about *Star Drifter*," he said to her, then turned his attention back to Travis. "Rats, huh?"

"Lots of Rats, dozens of them, and a wild urban jungle girl named Jane."

"Of course, there'd be a girl," Connor said. "Was she hot?"

Travis smiled. Jane had kissed him, and it didn't matter that he'd been rolled, robbed, and arrested. It didn't matter that the only thing she'd ever called him to his face was Mr. James, or that badass Raymond wanted her old turf and Fast Jack wanted her back.

She'd kissed him, *really* kissed him—and that was all that mattered. He could handle the rest of it.

"Oh, yeah. She's hot," he said. "*Dangerously* hot."

CHAPTER
15

"THEY TORE THE PLACE apart, Kid. You've got nothing left but the walls."

Kid stood in his kitchen at Steele Street, phone to his ear, listening to C. Smith describe the mess Conseco's men had made of his house in Panama. Nikki was sitting on the floor at his coffee table next to the windows, drawing on paper she'd taken out of his printer while she waited for him to make the coffee.

She'd slept like a baby the whole way home, hardly bothering to wake up even for the plane change in Dallas. She'd been exhausted, but was definitely back on board now, scribbling away with a pencil.

"Sorry, Chico, but you really need to sell your little tropical bungalow." Smith's tone was flat-out serious.

"It's way too far south of the border, way too close to Colombia, and man, it's been com-pro-mised. You've got enough blood on the floors to qualify as a House of Horror."

"Screw—"

"Me. Yeah. I got it, but I mean it."

Kid finished pouring water in the coffeepot and switched it on.

God, it was good to be home, even if he had kind of forgotten how much stuff he'd crammed into the place. His loft looked like a sporting goods store that had gone berserk. The ceilings were fifteen feet— plenty high enough for him to have installed a climbing wall on the north end and racks for his gear on the south end. He had two kayaks propped up in one corner and three bikes housed behind the couch. Snowboards and skis went on the racks, along with his ropes and rappelling gear. Backpacks and sleeping bags went anywhere and everywhere.

"I know a woman here in Panama City and—"

"You know more than one woman in Panama City," Kid interrupted, remembering the last time the two of them had taken R&R. The weekend had gotten pretty wild, but he'd managed to come out of it without getting engaged to anyone.

C. Smith let out a short laugh. "Yeah, well, this one sells real estate, and I could give her a call for you."

"Sure. Give her a call."

It was time to let go, probably time to let go of a lot of things. Never J.T. His brother would be with him until the day he died. He just didn't want that day coming any sooner than necessary, and that meant staying out of South America for a while.

Goddamn, what a helluva night. He could still hardly believe how quickly Conseco's men had found him.

"Maybe you could quit that fringe group you work with and come on over to the DEA," Smith was saying. "You could take my old job in Afghanistan. You'd love it. Beautiful country, lots of wide open spaces, plenty of action, and it beats the hell out of Iraq."

"I'll pass." He'd done some time in Afghanistan with the Marine Corps. It wasn't any worse than a lot of places he'd been, but he liked working at SDF. "Besides, if the intel we found at that airstrip on the Putumayo pans out, Conseco could be waiting for me in Afghanistan as easily as Colombia."

"Good point."

"Did you call Rosa and tell her not to come in?" He didn't want his Panamanian housekeeper anywhere near the house, not while it was such a hot spot for trouble.

"Yes. Our guys took the bodies to the morgue, but the rest of the mess is going to be here a while longer, especially the one you made with Sanchez and Mancos. That's going to take paint, Chico. Maybe a sander. Definitely some plaster."

"What about Conseco?"

"We're going over every inch of the place, trying to confirm whether or not the big boss was actually here. The man they picked up with the fer-de-lance tattoo is backpedalling like crazy on his original story, but a few of the things he said earlier have checked out. A privately owned Learjet did set down at Albrook late last night, and the plane does match the description that we have of Conseco's."

"What about my neighbors? Are you getting anything out of the interviews?" Kid wasn't pinning many hopes on it.

"A big zero. Nobody saw anything. Of course, I gotta tell ya, everyone I've talked to around here today has been as hungover as hell. What is this part of town? Party central?"

"Absolutely." It's what J.T. had loved about where he'd lived in Panama City. The privacy of the properties, the friendliness of the neighbors, and the wildness of the parties. "What about Nikki's suitcases?"

"Still under house arrest—hot pink, mock croc, with her initials stamped into the leather, and I don't like that."

Kid's brow furrowed. He didn't like it either. "Are you sure about the initials?" He didn't remember any initials.

"It's subtle, but they are definitely there, along with a small angel stamped in next to the letters."

"Did you find anything else that might identify her?"

"No, but that doesn't mean Conseco's guys didn't. I noticed she had her purse at the Parrot, and I'm hoping you can tell me that her passport and plane ticket and all that kind of stuff was inside and not lying around somewhere in the house."

"Yeah. She had it all with her." But he still wasn't happy about the damn initials. "See if you can get her luggage released as soon as possible, and just have the suitcases sent here." The coffee stopped dripping, and Kid poured Nikki a cup.

"I'll do what I can. How's she holding up?"

"Pretty good." Actually even better than that, he thought, watching her rise from the floor and pad across the loft toward the bathroom. There'd been no more nightmares while they'd been in the air, and she hadn't mentioned the incident at the house since they'd landed. She'd just been so damn glad to be home. He felt safer, too, like now maybe they could talk reasonably, like a couple of adults—instead of like one adult and one insanely jealous asshole.

Right.

"Great," Smith said. "I'll check back in with you later. Sooner, if we come up with anything."

"Thanks." Kid hung up the phone and started over toward the table with Nikki's cup of coffee.

Paris was at the top of his agenda this afternoon, right under the same heading where he'd put Rocky Solano, in what he was hoping would become her out-box. Her in-box only had one item, him, and after all the thinking he'd done on the plane, he was fairly confident of his ability to get her around to his side.

No matter what, he was the man she'd made love with last night. They'd been electric together, an instantaneous firestorm. A connection like that had to mean something. It had to mean a lot.

It sure as hell meant a lot to him.

His confidence in his mission stayed high all the way across the room, right up until he leaned over the table to set down her coffee and took a glance at what she'd been doing with her pencil and paper.

Then his heart stopped—for all of a second. Then two.

Savagery. Brutal. Unadulterated.

Kid was looking right at it, and it looked exactly like him. It *was* him. Nikki was too brilliant of an artist not to have depicted him exactly as he'd been— deadly, his face contorted with fury, every muscle in his body tight with lethal intent. She'd drawn him with Hernando Sanchez's head in his hands, his knee in Sanchez's back, and blood all over the floor. It was unmistakable.

It was also a helluva thing to have to look at, a helluva thing for her to have remembered in such excruciatingly accurate detail.

It was enough to make him sweat.

He picked up the top drawing.

Geezus. Was this the nightmare that had woken her up? Him?

His gaze went over the bold harsh lines and the subtle shading of the sketch, and he felt something turn over in his chest.

Fuck. Even he didn't want to see himself with his war face on.

He let the paper drop back on the table with the others and stood for a minute, looking around his loft, taking it all in, trying to breathe. It had been months since he'd been home, but nothing had changed. Skeeter made sure of things like that. No matter how long their missions might last, no matter how far away the job might take them, the SDF guys came home to the place they'd left. With very little warning, Skeeter would have food in the fridge, the heat turned up, fresh sheets on the bed, half a dozen morning papers stacked on the counter, and towels warming in the bathroom.

The trip home from Panama had taken a good portion of the day, and late afternoon light was slanting in through the huge wall of windows facing out toward the city. Kid was a morning person. When he'd first started working for SDF, he'd shared J.T.'s loft for convenience's sake. He'd kept it because of the morning light.

On a clear day, the sun broke across the straight edge of the eastern horizon like a blade. Night was always drawn up from the ground like a veil.

He checked his watch. She had only a couple of hours before her show opened at Toussi's, a couple of hours before her real life started back up again—the life that up until last night had not included a guy with a half-a-million-dollar bounty on his head.

He'd promised to run her up to Boulder, to her

house, so she could get some clothes, but someone else would have to do that now.

He let his attention fall back to the drawings, his gaze going over each one. Where necessary, he pushed a paper aside to better see the sketch beneath.

She was so good.

They were all variations on the same theme: Peter Chronopolous the Destroyer, and carnage, lots of motherfucking carnage.

The ones where he'd shot Mancos the first time weren't quite as bad as the rest. She'd left the guy's corpse out of her point-blank view of him firing the .45, and instead given that grisly thing a few pages of its own, all of them as incredible as anything she'd drawn of Sanchez.

Goddamn. She shouldn't have seen the aftermath of the head shots. He'd been so careful, so fucking split-second careful with both of them.

But somehow she'd seen it all, drawn it all, and nobody was better. Even with just a regular number two pencil, he could tell the difference between a shard of skull on the floor and a splatter of brains on the wall. He didn't know how she'd done it, made the difference so incredibly clear, and he wished like hell that she hadn't.

Fuck.

Just thinking about her seeing the killings made him feel a little faint. That he'd burned those images into her memory banks made him sick.

Geezus. Nothing was ever easy—and nothing was going to change. He was a marked man, with his life forfeit every single day. He'd thought he could leave *el asesino fantasma* in South America.

He'd been wrong. A half a million dollars changed everything.

He heard her start the shower in the bathroom, and he knew he had to make a choice. He could go in there with her and pick up where they'd left off in his bed. She'd welcome him. He knew it. She'd slept on him all night long on the plane and kept close to him all day, her hand sometimes reaching out just to touch him, just to make sure he was still by her side.

So yeah, he could go in there.

Or he could grow up.

He couldn't change what he'd done. He *wouldn't* change it. But the choices he'd made had come with a price, and there was no decision about whether or not it would be paid. The price was Nikki, and the deal had been closed. What happened next between them wasn't about who she'd slept with, or who she hadn't slept with. It wasn't about sex, or even about love. More than anything else, it was about Paris. It was about her life, her whole life. His path was set. She was just starting out on hers. She was young and talented, and the world was just waiting to lay itself at her feet.

And that's what he wanted for her, even more than he wanted her for himself. Twelve hours ago, he would have said that was impossible. On the plane, he'd decided beyond a doubt that there was nothing he wanted more than to have her for himself.

He'd been wrong.

This was easy.

Leaving everything on the table, he walked back into the kitchen and picked up the phone.

"Skeeter," he said, when she picked up. "Where are you?"

"Down on the firing range, shooting with Travis. Where the hell are you?"

Perfect. He'd known Skeeter and Nikki's model had become good friends over the last year, and there was probably no one Nikki would be happier to see than Travis.

Well, maybe her "no, not really" fiancé, but he didn't think Rocky Solano was anywhere in the building—which, for as easy as this was for him to do, was a damn good thing. He was walking away from her, yes, but he had no intention of actually handing her over to some other guy. Given the "no, not really" situation, he figured Rocky was probably already hell-and-gone out of the running.

"I just got home. I've got Nikki with me. We've had an interesting night. Left three dead guys in the house in Panama. I want you to come up here and debrief her, get the facts, let her tell you everything. Bring Travis with you. I'm sure she'll be glad to see him."

"Juan Conseco's guys?" Skeeter asked.

"Two were Conseco's, the third guy was one they

did." He knew she wasn't supposed to have had access to the Top Secret file of the work he was doing for the DEA, but he also knew Skeeter.

"Whoa, Kid. Congratulations."

"Thanks." He was good at his job. Damn good.

CHAPTER 16

NIKKI STOOD IN THE MIDDLE of the Toussi Gallery, among the hundreds of people who had come to the opening, saying hello and shaking hands with a smile plastered on her face while her insides seethed.

Kid had run out on her.

Again.

Without a word.

Less than twenty-four hours after telling her how much he loved her, how he couldn't live without her, after making love to her all damn night long, he'd run out on her—and that was unforgivable.

When she got her hands on him, she was going to throttle him, and by God, she was going to get her hands on him, if she had to chase him all the way back to South America. Being taller, heavier, bigger, faster, and stronger wasn't going to save him. No way in hell. She didn't care that he had more guns than God and years of combat experience. She was taking the boy down—hard. To the mat.

"You're going to hurt yourself," Travis said by her side. "Either that or your face is going to crack in two. I mean it, Nikki. You need to breathe yourself through this, or you're going to do some permanent damage. Let go of the anger."

He'd been telling her that for the last two hours, and her answer hadn't changed.

"No." On this point, she was absolutely adamant. "I'm not letting go of anything, least of all Peter goddamn Kid Chaos Chronopolous. He can't do this to me."

"He already did."

The look she gave him would have leveled a lesser man.

Travis didn't flinch, not so much as a twitch.

"Rocky's been looking for you," he said.

Of course he had, and she should have been looking for him, too. Instead, she was idiotically looking for Kid, because everything inside her said he couldn't possibly have left her, the facts be damned.

"If the engagement is over, you need to tell the guy," Travis said, giving her more helpful and totally unnecessary advice.

"He knows," she said. "He knew before I left, and after our phone call this afternoon, I don't think he can have any doubts."

"So you already gave him the ring back?" he said, gesturing at her left hand.

"No."

"Well, the ring has to go back, babe."

Of course the ring had to go back, the incredible, one-of-a-kind, Rocky Solano-designed masterpiece. She'd tried to return it before she'd left Denver to go to Panama, but Rocky had asked her to keep it until she got back, until she'd had a chance to find this Kid Chaos guy and figure out how she felt.

Well, she'd found the Kid Chaos guy all right, and figured out exactly how she felt, in spades, and the ring was going back. She was planning on it, couldn't wait to do it, except for one little problem.

"I don't have it."

Travis shot her a wary glance. "Don't tell me you lost a thirty-thousand-dollar ring."

"I didn't lose it, exactly. I just don't have it."

"Why not?"

"It's still in Panama. In my luggage."

"In the house with all the dead guys." It wasn't a question. It was a declaration of exasperation.

"Yes."

"Well, that's a helluva place for it to be. Do you think maybe you should reconsider Rocky's offer? I don't think he gets many dead guys at his house."

She knew what he meant. He'd been tight-jawed when he'd seen the sketches she'd done on the coffee table and seen the kind of danger she'd been in. She had an awful feeling Kid might have had the same reaction to her drawings, that it had all come back at him, and that's why he'd left.

But all she could do was shake her head. "You know how it is between Rocky and me."

"I know you haven't slept with him, if that's what you mean."

"He wanted that to change."

"And that's when you hightailed your butt to Panama. So what in the hell were you thinking in the first place when you said you'd marry him?"

"That he was brilliant," she said, not having to think for even an instant. She'd known exactly why she'd said yes to Rocky. "That he was beautiful, good, and fine, and that he cared for me. That we could build a life together."

"And that you were never going to see Kid again."

"Yes," she admitted. "That, too."

"These guys Kid killed," Travis said. "Skeeter thinks they were after him, like after him for money or revenge or something."

She nodded.

"And you said there were more guys chasing you, when you and Kid ran from the house."

She nodded again.

"*Geezus*, Nikki. Just how much trouble do you think we're talking about here?"

"Plenty."

"Did it ever occur to you to cut your losses and just—"

Travis kept talking, but suddenly, Nikki was only

half listening. Her attention had been drawn to the gallery's front door and the man walking through it. With all the people milling about and crossing the room between them, she only caught glimpses of him, but even the merest glimpse was enough to flood her with relief.

Kid.

He'd come—and she knew the only loss she wasn't willing to risk, ever, was him.

KID stood just inside the doorway of Toussi's, looking at all the people who had come for the show, watching the crowd, and trying not to be completely blown away by Rocky Solano's "fiber art."

Geezus.

Fiber artist his ass.

If Rocky Solano was a "fiber artist," Kid was a Boy Scout.

Fiber engineer, was more like it. Or fiber architect. Or even fiber freaking magician.

The work was incredible. Towering. Great swaths of intricately woven material hung suspended from twisted forms of iron and steel, cast bronze, and copper pipe, ten to fifteen feet high.

When he'd left his apartment, he hadn't planned on coming to the gallery, or at least not coming inside; at least, that was the story he was sticking with even if he was the only one buying it. Because against his better judgment, the gallery is where he'd ended up. His instincts had said "follow," when Skeeter and Nikki had left Steele Street for Toussi's.

So he had.

And of course, Skeeter had known. She'd picked up his tail about half a block from home.

"Glad you could make it," she said, coming to a stop next to him, grinning.

"It's not that I didn't trust you to do the job."

"Yeah, I know," she said, her gaze quartering the gallery. "There's a helluva lot of people here tonight."

Over four hundred by his estimation, enough to give the fire marshal apoplexy.

"How did the debriefing go?" he asked.

"She pretty much filled me in, gave me as much as she had, and let me just say that you made a helluva impact with your Rambo impression."

He ignored that.

"Head shots, Kid?"

And he ignored that.

"A little jacked up, were we?"

"Eat worms, Baby Bang." He wasn't going to talk about it.

"Well, just so you know, I don't think the head shots upset her nearly as much as coming out of the shower and finding out that you'd handed her over to me."

That was good to know, kind of a relief, but he wasn't going to talk about that, either.

"You said he was a fiber artist, Skeeter, like he

wove baskets or something." That's what he wanted to talk about.

She shrugged. "You're seeing some of his best stuff. 'Arma-X-Geddon' over there." She pointed to a piece on his left. " 'Slave-2-Queen' next to it. See how they're all about strength and subtlety, holding fast and letting go, will and acquiescence?"

He slanted her a curious glance, then went back to the art. Yeah. He saw it all right—all the soft/hard, weak/strong, stiff/flowing stuff, and it was all nothing short of freaking amazing.

Hell.

Worse than hell, all of Solano's work was some-how really sexy, sensual, like the curve of Nikki's hip, which Kid swore he could see in the black iron and blue silk piece Skeeter had called "Slave-2-Queen," and he couldn't help but wonder if Nikki had posed for her fiancé naked, which just made his gut churn.

He wasn't fucking going to live through this. He could tell. But maybe he could live through the rest of this minute, and then he'd just hope for the best on the next.

He'd made the right decision. He knew that—but being right was getting harder.

His gaze lifted up the length of the giant piece in front of him. Hugely thick, knotted yarns as big as his arm and saturated with color hung between a pair of gleaming copper spikes. Other pieces were draped with the finest woven linens and silks. Some were no more than strings of fiber, all of them with an eye to weight and form, to the "hand" of the cloth and the qualities of the metal. He wasn't an idiot. He could see what was right in front of him, and he couldn't compete with what he was seeing, which led him to the million-dollar question: What had Nikki been thinking last night?

"You could have told me he was a freaking genius." Not that he would have liked hearing it.

"He's a freaking genius fiber artist."

"And a metalworker."

"And he's headed this way."

Shit. That's all he needed, and it was exactly why he'd planned on staying outside. He had not wanted to get within a hundred feet of the guy Nikki had thought she was going to marry, the guy whose apartment she was moving into in Paris, whether she married him or not.

Skeeter started to move, and he grabbed on to the back of her belt so fast, she grimaced.

"Uh . . . wedgie alert there, Kid."

He didn't doubt it. She was wearing skintight leather pants.

"You're not going anywhere," he ground out. "So don't even think it. You and me, we're like Siamese twins, until he's gone."

From where he'd waited outside for a few minutes, he'd seen Nikki get whisked away when she'd entered the gallery, and though he'd glimpsed her here and there, on the move, it wasn't easy keeping her in view. The crowd wasn't like anything he'd ever seen in

Denver. It was like Friday night at Rico and Luis Sandoval's, except on steroids, and maybe hallucinogenic mushrooms. From what he'd picked up in the few minutes he'd been there, half the people were from L.A. and half were from New York and the other half were from Denver, with about a third mixed in from Chicago.

"Where is he?" Of the hundreds of people in the gallery, none of them seemed to be heading toward him and Skeeter. Everyone was milling.

"He's behind 'Undressed Destruction' now. He's the one those other people are following."

Kid did see a group of about seven people winding their way through the crowd on a collision course with Nikki, which was leading them in the general direction of the front door, but no one in particular seemed to be doing the leading.

"He's got a white stripe in his hair," she added helpfully.

Of course Solano would have a stripe in his hair, Kid thought, still not seeing the guy. Didn't everybody here have a stripe in their hair, except him?

"The one in the white shirt and the indigo blue watered silk tie."

Nada. Kid couldn't see him. Nothing—and in this crowd, someone in a shirt and tie should be easy to spot. It's what he'd worn with his black suit, very professional, very bodyguardlike, and that was what he'd told himself his job was tonight.

He knew what Conseco wanted, and it wasn't girls

with mock-croc pink luggage, and yet he'd felt compelled to come tonight, to watch over her. Call it seven months of justifiable paranoia, or lovesick stupidity, but he hadn't been able to stay away. Later, he'd promised himself, he would let her go, after the party. If she left with her "no, not really" fiancé, Solano, he'd go throw himself off the nearest bridge, then crawl out of the river and go home and get mind-bendingly drunk. And if she didn't go with Solano, he'd send her home to Boulder with Travis, back to her grandfather's house. The writing was on the wall, right along with Sanchez and Mancos's blood: She was better off without him, and it wasn't something he was going to allow himself to forget, because he knew what Conseco did want: Peter Chronopolous, the gringo who'd gotten shot outside Banco Nuevo and been admitted to the Bogotá hospital, the guy he'd tracked to Panama City. Conseco wanted *el asesino fantasma*.

"I still don't see him, Skeeter."

"Well . . . uh. He's—" her voice trailed off.

Kid glanced over and caught the look she was giving him through her sunglasses, and yes, he could read her like a book, shades or no shades, and she looked guilty as hell. Skeeter Bang didn't have any secrets from him, not even the one about her being in love with their boss, Dylan Hart, which was about as big a road to nowhere as he could imagine—and his love life was in shreds.

"He's the...uh, guy in the wheelchair," she finished.

Wheelchair?

Sonuvabitch.

The crowd opened up, and there he was, Rocky Solano. Kid was riveted to the spot, his hand tightening on Skeeter's belt until she squeaked.

He felt a twinge of remorse, but there was no way in hell for him to let go of her. He couldn't even lighten his grip. Holding on to her was the only thing holding him together, and she deserved to squeak, dammit. There were about a thousand things she hadn't bothered to tell him, and the goddamn wheelchair was only one of them. Maybe one of the least of them, he thought, getting a good look at the guy.

Rocky Solano, *geezus*, a cripple. He'd imagined a big guy, somebody with some heft to him, maybe somebody whose ass he could kick. But the freaking genius fiber artist looked like Nikki, amazingly like Nikki. He was slight of frame despite the broadness of his shoulders, dark-haired, and—no shit—more than half pretty. The features of his face were harder edged than Nikki's, his jaw wider, his mouth thinner, but the resemblance was still damned disconcerting. They were both beautiful, gray-eyed and silky-haired, about half fey, insanely talented, and the absolute center of attention.

Soul mates.

The guy had a few years on her, but the white stripe in his hair wasn't from age, and it wasn't from out of a bottle. It wasn't an affection. It was an anomaly, like the man himself, a guy who could weave silk *and* torch steel.

But couldn't walk.

How could Skeeter not have told him that?

Rocky finally made it through the crowd to Nikki and pulled her into his lap. A small cheer went up, and Kid felt instantly sick, hating what he was seeing. When Rocky tilted her back and kissed her, everything inside Kid went cold. The chattering of the crowd grew unbearable, the angles of all the lights, the crush of people.

Mine. He wanted to shout it, to startle the sonuvabitch into letting go of her, to tell him he couldn't touch her like that.

Mine. Every cell in his body echoed with the need implied in that one word. It ran through his blood, entered with his breath and would not leave him, no matter how much logic and common sense he used trying to bend it to his will—*mine*.

The kiss slid off her cheek. By accident or design, he couldn't tell and didn't care. Momentary disappointment crossed Solano's face, but Kid didn't give a damn if the guy was disappointed or not. All he cared about was the sense of loss threatening to overwhelm him. Nikki was his and somebody else had her, another man, and it sure as hell didn't matter that the other man was in a wheelchair. Kid knew what he would do to her, if he was paralyzed from the waist down. He would still make her his, still hold her close.

Still find a thousand ways to make love to her with his mouth, with his hands, with his heart.

His hand fell from Skeeter's waist.

"I'll be outside," he managed to say, surprising himself. He wanted to howl, and his voice sounded almost normal. "I need some air."

He needed more than air, but when he stepped outside, it did help, enough to get him to the alley. He took a few steps down the darkened way and leaned back against the building, letting his head fall back, pressing his body against the bricks.

Impossibly, for a moment, he missed the jungle, the deep rain forests of Colombia where he'd spent most of the last seven months, the nearly intolerable heat, the heavy humidity, the utter silence of midafternoon. Then reason reasserted itself. What he missed was the sense of purpose he'd had in the jungle, the certainty of what he was doing, but every single day, he'd missed Nikki.

He let out a weary breath and pushed off the building. *Fuck*. He had to find a way to do this, to let her go. It seemed impossible, like cutting out his heart and walking away. She was that dear to him. All he had to do was close his eyes, and he could almost smell her—the sweet mix of woman, and musk, and paint that was pure Nikki. The way she tasted when he had his mouth between her legs, his tongue sliding over her, so incredibly soft, so sweet when she came. How was he supposed to live without that? He could share her smiles and the sound of her voice. He could share the five earrings in one ear and the three in the other and those damn short skirts she loved to wear, but not the way she arched into him when he had his mouth on her breasts and ran kisses down her belly, not the way they smelled together when they'd made love for hours and the sweat was cooling on their skin, not the way she tasted then. That was private, sacrosanct, only between them. It was primal, the way he breathed her in. It knotted around his gut and sunk its talons into his psyche.

So much for growing up and doing what was right. It sucked.

He dragged his hand back through his hair. He needed his head examined, to have left her for so long. Unfortunately, in his line of work, there was a whole battery of people lined up, ready and eager to do the job a little more thoroughly than he was willing to allow. For the most part, he handled his own demons, the glaring exception being the last time he'd been in Toussi's. He'd died in Nikki's arms that night, soaked her with his agony and tears, his heart cracking wide open. It had been the most unimaginable, god awful feeling ever. It had been the night he'd brought J.T.'s bones home.

Only Nikki could have saved him that night.

But she sure as hell couldn't save him tonight, not when she was sitting in Rocky Solano's lap.

Geezus. Just take a breath, he told himself, *then take another. Look around. Get your bearings.*

The day had been warm, melting the previous

night's snow and leaving the streets wet. A warm wind was still blowing, the nice weather bringing a lot of people out for a Saturday night in LoDo.

Kid watched the couples and mixed groups of men and women pass by the mouth of the alley. There were a lot of clubs in LoDo, a lot of bars and restaurants within walking distance of each other.

As he watched, a small form darted across Seventeenth Street, and for a second or two, when the boy reached the other side, there was a tangle-up with a group of college-aged men. The young men laughed, picking him up off the sidewalk, brushing him off, and setting him aside with cheerful advice for him to watch where he was going, look both ways, and keep his feet under him—and then the child took off, heading up the street.

One wallet at least, Kid thought, maybe two. The boy had been quick, exceptionally skilled, but Kid had seen the pull. Under other circumstances, he would have grabbed the pickpocket, retrieved the wallet, and saved the day.

But tonight, it was going to take everything he had to save himself.

He glanced back down the alley the other way, to the far end, and to his surprise, saw another boy getting himself picked up and brushed off. This time it was an older man providing the service and getting fleeced.

Geez. LoDo was hot tonight.

He started back toward Toussi's, knowing he had

to tough it out and do the right thing. Going home wasn't an option. He didn't know why not, but it wasn't. Nikki was with her friends now, with her fiancé. She didn't need him—and yet his gut feeling was to stay and see the night through to the end, no matter how awful it got, no matter how much it hurt. So he was staying.

Back on the street, he glanced up toward the intersection, his attention drawn by a sudden bunching up of people at the light, waiting for the walk signal. When the light changed, the first boy, joined by two girls, crossed against the crowd, weaving their way through the Saturday night partiers. Kid caught two pulls, maybe three, before everyone got across the street to their respective sides.

He looked down Seventeenth the other way, toward Wynkoop and Union Station and saw three more kids, one tall and older, and two pretty damn little to be out on the streets, hanging around.

LoDo was not only hot tonight, he thought, it was crawling with pickpockets. They were everywhere, coming out of the alleys, working the streets, and disappearing again, like a pack of rats.

It was true, he'd been out of town for a while, but he'd grown up in Denver, and he'd never seen the likes. Then he saw something at least as noteworthy, if a hundred times more common than half a dozen kids stealing wallets. Two gangstas piled out of a black Escalade parked in the lot on the corner and got into another black Escalade that had stopped on the street. From the amount of movement Kid saw through the briefly opened door, he guessed there were at least three, maybe four other guys already in the second luxury SUV.

Somebody's gang was on the move.

He checked the first Escalade, and sure enough, there were still two guys inside. *Waiting for what?* he wondered. A few things came to mind, all of them criminal, none of them his business. This wasn't his trouble, the underside of nightlife in LoDo, pickpockets and gangbangers. Still, he'd tell Suzi to warn her guests to be careful tonight. The streets weren't safe.

CHAPTER 17

TROUBLE.

Jane was looking it straight in the eye, into two of them actually, and those eyes were brown, set into a thin, little face covered in freckles.

Kondo squirmed under her unrelenting gaze, undoubtedly getting her message that he was in the wrong place at the wrong time. He didn't belong at Toussi's. Neither did trouble's side dish—the girl named Blue. They knew it. She knew it, and Suzi Toussi knew it.

"This isn't a day-care center," the older woman said, censure lifting one artfully shaped eyebrow.

"Yes, ma'am." Jane had known last night was the beginning of the end, and damn Fast Jack, he'd just had to go and prove her right.

Up until five minutes ago, the gallery showing had

been going great. To her surprise, Travis James had shown up, looking none the worse for wear, but she was still avoiding him, which hadn't proved too difficult.

She let out a short breath and glanced around the room. She'd never seen such a crush. There had been huge sales, lots of them, for both Nikki and Rocky. Katya was still in L.A., meeting with her partner, Alex Zheng, but Jane didn't mind working with Suzi, the original owner of the gallery, not usually. Tonight was proving to be the exception. Suzi knew everybody, no matter which coast they were from, and she knew how to keep the party going and the caterers doing their job.

Unfortunately, as of five minutes ago, she also knew Fast Jack Spencer, who had shown up at Toussi's back door with Blue and Kondo in hand—and left them.

"And you are not a babysitter," Suzi admonished, not at all happy with the turn of events.

"No, ma'am," Jane said. It was one of the hardest things she'd had to learn in the last two years, the "yes ma'am, no ma'am" business, but she'd had a very patient teacher, Sister Theresa Ann—patient like a steel trap and just as unforgiving.

"I want you to put them in a corner somewhere, and warn them not to touch *anything*."

"Yes, ma'am."

Suzi Toussi was elegant, always richly turned out, tonight in a perfectly gorgeous emerald green dress.

Her clothes were conservative and expensive, in direct contrast to her preference in art and men, which veered toward cutting edge and outrageous. Her auburn hair was blunt cut to her chin, the deep reddish brown underscored with blond highlights, the whole of it somehow matching the color of her eyes.

She intimidated the hell out of Jane, with good reason. Suzi ran a tight ship, and there was nothing tight about having a couple of gangly street urchins dropped into the middle of a high art gallery showing. To his credit, Fast Jack had cleaned them up and tricked them out in decent clothes, but Suzi hadn't been born yesterday, and she'd no sooner bought Jack's story about "cousins just happening to be in the neighborhood," and "the little ones wanting to see Jane," than she would have bought a velvet Elvis.

"And would you watch the back door for Yves? He's bringing more *escabeche* and crab canapés. They're mad for the *escabeche* tonight."

"Yes, ma'am." But Suzi wasn't throwing them all out on their butts, and for that, Jane was truly grateful.

"Also tell him we're running low on the Merlot."

"Yes, ma'am."

"*Escabeche* and Merlot," Suzi mused, turning away. "Who would have guessed?"

Not Jane. She didn't drink wine, ever, or beer, or anything else, and the *escabeche* everyone was so mad for looked and smelled like tuna fish to her—expensive, large-flaked, marinated tuna fish, but still tuna fish, of which she'd eaten a boatload in her younger years, plenty of it straight out of the can.

She looked down at Blue and Kondo, then glanced around the gallery again, pulling herself together. This mess, this trouble, wasn't their fault.

"There are a lot of people here tonight," she said. When she looked back at the children, they nodded, attentive, their faces solemn. "Under normal circumstances, we would pick them clean."

Another nod.

"But these are not normal circumstances."

They both shook their heads.

"Some of these people are very rich, all of them have money in their pockets, and in their wallets, and in their purses, and we aren't going to take any of it. Not a dime. Not a single credit card."

Blue's brow furrowed beneath a thick fringe of blond bangs. She was ten years old, disarming, quick-fingered, and suddenly confused. Jane was sure she'd expected to work the room for all it was worth, and it looked to be worth a lot.

Kondo looked equally confused. He was twelve and desperately needed a haircut. The brown mop of curls on his head was going in about a thousand different directions. His freckles stood out on his thin, pale face, making Jane wonder if he was getting enough to eat.

She bit back a curse, silently damning Fast Jack.

For two years, she hadn't had to worry about children eating, and she resented like hell that Jack was trying to dump it all back in her lap—all the hunger, and the danger, all the scraped knees, lost gloves, and runny noses, all the bruised faces, and once, the broken bones of one of those Rats who had juggled their lives between the Empire and their capital-S-screwed-up families, coming and going as best suited their survival needs of the moment, or the day, or the week.

She'd run with the wildest of them, seen more than she ever should have, at ages when impressions became scars, street life at its worst, teenage whores, drug addicts, and the certifiably insane. They'd all left their mark.

Then one night she'd lifted Superman's wallet, and her life had changed.

"You see the tables with the food?" she said, pointing to a cleared area not too far from the back door, then looking back at them.

Both kids nodded again.

"Go ahead and get a plate and fill it up with whatever you want. No one will mind." Rats were always hungry. There had been times when Jane had wondered if the whole world was hungry. "My apartment is on the fifth floor. That's where I want you to go. That's where I want you to stay."

This was not the "Do Not Touch" speech Suzi would have expected. Jane knew the older woman had meant for her to tell the kids not to touch the artwork, not to break anything, but that was unnecessary, a waste of time. Rats didn't break things, ever.

They touched, lifted, held—all in the blink of an eye. They did not drop. They did not mess around. If something wouldn't fit inside a coat or into a pocket, they ignored it, saving their light, sticky fingers for something they could spend or fence, always looking for value. No sense in getting sent up to juvie for a cheap piece of junk or a damn candy bar, she'd told them over and over, drilling it into them, the way her mother had drilled it into her. Make your moves count, she'd said, and then taught them how, the same way her mother had taught her how.

She'd been so proud of the Rats when they'd been hers. But they weren't hers anymore, and she didn't want them back, so help her God. She didn't even know Blue.

She didn't want to know Blue.

The two children left for the buffet table, and Jane headed toward the back door to watch for Yves and the *escabeche*. But all she found was Fast Jack, lingering in the alley, three more kids in tow.

This, she decided, was turning into a nightmare.

"What's going on, Jack?" She wasn't happy, and she made no effort to hide it. She didn't like being used, and Jack was a user, always looking for an angle, always looking out for himself.

"Raymond. He's here." Jack didn't look any happier than she felt, and he looked a whole lot more nervous, which should have been impossible. She felt like a cat in the middle of a dog pack.

"What do you mean here?"

"*Here*," he said more forcefully, taking a step forward, making a short cutting motion with his right hand. He was holding a young teenaged boy by the scruff of his jacket with his other. "Out front, out back, on every side, everywhere, *here*. He's making his play, Robin. I've got to get the kids off the street. They can't go up against the Parkside Bloods."

Jane just looked at him. Was he insane? The Rats against the Parkside Bloods? That was like sending a puppy out to fight a Rottweiler.

"I can take fucking Raymond," the boy said, and Jane's disbelieving gaze slid to him. He was all of a hundred and ten pounds, maybe. The two girls with him weren't any bigger, or any older. Raymond, she remembered clearly, topped the scale at two-twenty. It was his personal tag—220.

Two hundred and twenty pounds of pure serious mean packed around a seriously sly, conniving, self-serving, highly intelligent brain, and the Parkside Bloods had guns.

So did Jack, she noticed, alarmed. When he turned to the side, she could see the butt end of a pistol sticking out of his jacket pocket.

"And what are you doing here, Jack?" *Do not hyperventilate*, she told herself. *Take control of the situation. Make it work for you.*

"It's Saturday night, Robin," he said as if the fact spoke for itself. "We were working our way into lower downtown. Then I noticed we had Bloods on our tail."

He was lying. It was written all over his face.

"I haven't seen anybody working LoDo since I've been back, and that's been over two months."

"Robin—"

"Jane." She cut him off, her hand tightening into a fist at her side. There was no taking control of this situation, not with guns, and Bloods, and Jack lying with every word he said.

"Jane," he conceded, glancing over his shoulder. "Look, Jane, I . . . I've got some things going at the Empire. We're making money now, real money, and Raymond wants in—or actually, what he wants is me out. But if you were there, it would be different."

"What kind of things?"

"High-end merchandise," Jack said cryptically.

"Drugs?" That would be the last straw for her. She and Jack had been that route at Castle Import.

"Play stations," the boy Jack was holding clarified. "Laptops, digital everything, HD televisions, big ones."

A slight, self-conscious grin curved across Jack's face. "I've got over a hundred thousand dollars of the stuff at the theater right now, Jane, hidden under the stage. Retail, of course, but there's still plenty of profit in it for down the line, when we unload it all."

Jane blinked, then blinked again. A hundred thousand dollars? For the Rats?

"I . . ." She started to say something, then couldn't figure out what it had been. She was stunned, and terrified for him.

"It's the big picture, Jane. No more scrounging. I

didn't have time to show you, but we've done a lot of work on the Empire. The theater is still a dump, I know, but we've cleaned up the rest of it. We've got whole rooms upstairs now, call them Rat's Nests. Get it?" His grin broadened. "I've got kids coming to me all the time. They want to be Rats. You're right, Jane. I've got too many. The whole thing is getting too big. I need you. Especially tonight. Let me stash my crew at your place. We can't let Raymond get to them."

No, "we" couldn't. Jane didn't think Raymond would actually kill one of them. The Rats didn't exactly qualify as a rival gang. But he could do other things to them. Things she didn't want to think about.

Jack was a different story.

"He'll kill you for that kind of money." It was the truth. "Hell, Jack. He'd kill me for that kind of money. The truce I had with Raymond wasn't solid. When things didn't look so good, I just laid low, kept the Rats home for a couple of weeks."

"We're just doing what you said, Jane. Old Nick Daley? That's what we're doing. Nicking people daily." It had been their joke, using slang for thieving to make up a name for the lease. The woman who owned the Empire was a nutcase. As long as she got her money every month, Jane doubted if she'd know if it was Raymond or Fast Jack shelling it out.

"My apartment is on the fifth floor," she said, regretting every word, but she didn't have a choice, not in this. "They can stay there. You, too, Jack."

"No." Jack shook his head, then answered his cell

phone when it rang in his pocket. "Yeah. Right. Stay put. I'll come to you." He flipped the phone shut, looking back to Jane. "I've got four more out there, and Raymond has his fleet of black Escalades out all over LoDo, looking for Rats. I've got to go get them."

Two years ago, that would have been her job, to go get scared Rats. She knew where they'd be, inside one of LoDo's many bars, by the front door, trying to blend in and not get kicked out, or in one of the restaurants, pretending to be with a couple or a group waiting for a table. They'd avoid the alleys. If there was a cop car, and they were scared enough, they'd be sitting on its bumper, staying out in the open. Rats knew what lurked in the dark, and they knew their size and age put them at a terrible disadvantage. They knew how vulnerable they were, and they knew the Parkside Bloods.

They had reason to be scared tonight.

Jane felt a chill go up her spine, even though the weather was warm. In that one way, she'd been spoiled rotten at the Immaculate Heart School for Young Women. For the first time in her life, she'd been safe, completely and totally safe.

Now she was back in the world, and Raymond the Blood King was cruising the streets, looking for kids like she'd once been, and maybe, God forbid, looking for her.

The chill she'd felt congealed into real fear, and suddenly, she wished she had a gun.

Jack couldn't keep her safe, no way. He'd be lucky to save his own butt.

Skeeter Bang had a gun. Jane had seen it in a holster at the small of her back last night, under her sweatshirt. Apparently, Skeeter worked with Superman now, and though she hadn't figured out exactly what it was Christian Hawkins did, she knew it had something to do with law enforcement, and maybe the military.

He could get her a piece, but she doubted if he would.

Oh, yes. Life was definitely taking a dive at light speed. Guns and Rats at Toussi's in the middle of an art show, with all of Katya's most important clients in attendance. For one fleeting instant, she considered calling the cops.

And what? she wondered in the next instant. Tell them Fast Jack Spencer was in over his head with a hundred thousand dollars' worth of electronics to unload, and Raymond of the Parkside Bloods was out to steal his stolen merchandise?

No. That wasn't her best bet. Fast Jack would scrape through. The same way she'd scraped through last night. Travis James had made it out of the Empire without his head being shaved. Everything had been okay. He hadn't been hurt—only arrested.

Oh, right, Jane, she thought. He had to be angry about the arrest. Maybe angry enough to have called Katya. Maybe she was already on the way out of her cushy new life and just didn't know it yet.

But that kiss.

She'd played it over and over in her mind, every nuance. How it had felt to hold him, the softness of his lips, the boldness of his tongue. It had been so achingly sweet. She'd felt cherished—but that had all been before the cops had dragged him away.

Skeeter had saved him, though. Skeeter Bang could probably save anybody—the thought came into Jane's mind and stuck. Denver's most notorious tagger would know how to work both sides of this mess, and Jane had seen her talking to a tall, dark-haired man just a little while ago.

"What's your cell phone number?" Jack asked, catching her attention. "I'll call you, let you know when to let them go."

"You'll have to call the gallery. I don't have a cell phone." And no one to call. She'd met a few people at school, but mostly she'd been keeping to herself, laying low—for all the good it had done her.

She needed help. She couldn't do this street-gang princess thing anymore, skating on the edge by the seat of her pants, always expecting disaster and seldom being disappointed.

Jack looked surprised for a second. "No cell phone? I'll give you one. We've got about a hundred in storage, camera phones. You'll love it. I can even put you on our family plan."

The Rats had a family plan—Jane had to keep from rolling her eyes. And a hundred thousand dollars' worth of camera phones, laptops, and HDTVs hidden in the Empire. God, how things had changed.

"So give me the gallery's number," he said.

She gave it to him and watched him enter it into his phone's database.

Perfect. Now Toussi's could look forward to getting phone calls from one of the city's better thieves. What most amazed her about the whole situation was how she'd been blindsided by it. Somewhere, somehow, over the last two years, she'd started to believe her life had taken an irreversible change for the better.

The more fool she.

The catering van pulled into the far end of the alley, and Jack released the boy with a small shove toward the door.

"Thanks, Rob—" he caught himself and grinned. "Thanks, Jane. I'll give you a call."

She almost told him to take care of himself, but that would have been a waste of breath. The one thing Jack was good at was taking care of himself.

FROM the backseat of a rented Cadillac, Juan Conseco watched the city slide past the car windows. He'd been to Denver once before, as a young man with his father, God rest his soul. It didn't seem so very different from then, gray and brown, snow shoved up into piles here and there, the trees bare, a few buildings of interest. There were more people on the streets at night than he remembered, which he considered an improvement.

His entrance into the United States had gone smoothly, which still had not allayed Drago's fears. The deed had truly been no more difficult than moving thirty metric tons of cocaine into the country, which he did on a regular basis, a fair portion coming to Denver every month. It had been a long day, with two plane changes, instead of the truck route his merchandise usually took, but the journey had landed him in Denver in plenty of time to take in a gallery opening.

Nicole Alana McKinney's Web site had showcased the artist's upcoming events, like tonight's showing at the Toussi Gallery, where the angel artist herself, it had promised, would be in attendance—*Come meet Nikki McKinney!*

Indeed.

Toussi's Web site had given him the map showing its location, and the rest had fallen into place.

God truly was on his side in this, smoothing the way—a point Tío Drago had yet to appreciate, though it was his son they were out to avenge, and Diego, and now Sanchez and Mancos.

Cell phones, the Internet, wireless networks, onboard navigation systems—technology streamlined his business from the fields to distribution. It helped him maneuver his product and his men for the greatest efficiency and profit. It helped him outmaneuver the police and the narcotics agents on two continents, and tonight it had cleared a path for kidnapping and murder, a brutal double murder on American soil so the message would be clear. Nicole McKinney and Peter Chronopolous would not live out the night. Kidnapping the woman was the key. *El asesino* had already proved he could win *mano a mano*. Juan had to make it in his best interest not to win—and then he would kill the woman anyway.

"Benito," he said to his driver, ignoring Drago's endless mutterings. "How far are we from the gallery?"

"A few miles only, Don Conseco."

Tío Drago had been right on the plane, of course. It was insanity for him to have left Colombia—but this gringo . . .

His hand tightened into a fist. This gringo's crimes had been personal affronts and needed to be dealt with personally. It wasn't just for poor Ruperto and Diego, though their deaths had been hard. Nor was it simply the theft at the airstrip on the Rio Putumayo, though that was bound to cost him dearly. It was the man's daring, killing Ruperto at breakfast, Diego in Juan's own home. Such daring could only be met with even greater daring, the kind of daring that had propelled Juan to the top of the deadliest game in the world.

On this playing field, Juan was king. He would prove it again tonight, when the legend known as *el asesino fantasma* died by his hand.

CHAPTER 18

Nikki slipped off Rocky's lap, brushed a haphazard kiss across his forehead, and made her escape to the buffet—not that she was going to eat. Her stomach was one giant knot of tension, and it was starting to turn in on itself.

Rocky had waylaid her, and she'd lost Kid. One minute, he'd been by the front door, and the next he'd been gone.

Dammit. He couldn't have left, not after actually showing up at the gallery, not without at least talking to her. My God, they'd practically died last night.

She made it all the way to the buffet tables, working the room, shaking hands, making chitchat and checking faces without catching sight of him anywhere. She hated admitting it, but her heart was going to break if he'd left. She could already feel the tightness building in her chest, the first flutter of panic.

He *couldn't* have left.

"Hi," someone said.

She turned her head, following the voice, then had to look down.

"Hi." She was standing next to a young girl who was trying to fit a half dozen shrimp on a plate already piled sky high.

"I like your hair," the girl said. "The purple parts are cool. Did you see the angels?"

Nikki found herself smiling, despite the lump growing in her throat. "Thank you, and yes, I've seen the angels. I painted them."

The girl's eyes widened, bright blue and peeking out from under blond bangs.

"All of them? Even the yellow ones?"

"Yep. Even the yellow ones. Do you like them?"

"I like the yellow ones," the girl said around a mouthful of shrimp. There hadn't been a place on the plate, so she was eating them, stuffing them in one right after another.

"What's your name?"

"Blue."

"Wow. That's a great name," Nikki said. "I always wanted to be named after a color."

The girl beamed. "Which one?"

"Well, two, actually. Violet Green. I thought that would be a really cool name."

"It is cool." In went another shrimp.

The crowd shifted, Nikki looked up, and when she looked back, the girl was gone.

It was a little spooky, how fast she'd disappeared, but then it was a strange night all the way around. There were more people in the gallery than she'd ever seen, now including her first child sighting ever in Toussi's, a skinny little moppet named Blue.

Oops. Make that two. A curly-haired boy with freckles darted out from behind the buffet and disappeared into the crowd, also carrying a plate of food that defied the laws of physics.

A pained sigh lodged in her throat. Everybody was disappearing into the over-capacity crowd. Rocky was a huge draw, and since her *Esquire* cover, she'd become a lot better known as well. Thus the crush—with more people arriving all the time.

A cool drift of fresh air drew her attention to the rear of the gallery, where the back door opened and Katya's newest employee, a very quiet, strangely arresting girl named Jane Linden, walked in with the caterer and—of all things—three more kids, teenagers this time.

The girl had a fascinating face, a lot of angles and curves; very distinctive, almond-shaped, feral green eyes; and the silkiest, straightest, sable-colored hair Nikki had ever seen. She was beautiful in a unique way. Intriguing, and Nikki had wanted to photograph and paint her with Travis since the first time she'd seen her—painted angels together, two light-infused beings on the same canvas. She'd seen it in her mind, how all the wings would curve, the shape of Jane's shoulder. She knew Travis so well, the planes and angles of his body, every muscle, how the light caught the colors of his hair and shaped his cheekbones. It would be exciting to work with someone new, and a challenge for Travis, too, to bring someone else into his space.

Nikki made another sweep of the room with her gaze.

Gallery openings were usually fairly sedate affairs, at least in Denver, but this one was going over the top, way over, becoming a real crush. It wasn't just that so many of Rocky's avant-garde friends had flown in. It was that there were so many of everybody "in," Katya's regular clients, a lot of local artists, society people who supported the arts, especially when a senator's daughter was involved, and Katya was certainly that. She'd lost sight of Rocky in the crowd, too, but she wasn't worried about him. He always had a posse of people ready and willing to do his bidding.

Rocky and his posse—it was part of his charm, to be welcomed into his inner circle, taken in and coddled. He was kind, and wryly funny, and in a lot of ways, undemanding, a lot of important ways.

But it was Kid she wanted. Kid she needed, and he was gone, nowhere to be found

Damn. Damn. And double freaking damn. She should have grabbed him on her way by the kitchen this afternoon in his apartment and dragged him into the shower with her. Naked, she seemed to hold his interest just fine. Honestly, naked seemed to be the *only* way she held his attention.

She needed to remember that, remember it and use it.

Her hand came up to her chest, to ease the sudden ache there. Hindsight was so perfect, but what she wanted now, what she needed now . . . was the man standing in the shadows on the far side of the room, the man looking up at the paintings hanging from the catwalk.

Kid. Relief flooded through her, weakening her knees. She gripped the edge of the table for a moment, then started across the gallery.

THERE was a reason Kid had not wanted Nikki to paint Christian Hawkins naked—and he was looking right at it. All eighteen inches of it. Of course, the painting Nikki had done of Superman was super-size, over twelve feet high, but still, it was a pretty damn big dick.

Geezus. He really hadn't needed to know that.

And what Nikki had done with Hawkins's tattoo, taking it all the way to his groin, bringing it around low on his hips in two openwork, stylized lines and giving him a real "caged cock" look. He hoped to hell she hadn't actually drawn that on Superman's body. But knowing Nikki, hell.

The painting was still exactly what she'd promised, though—beyond his ability to regret, dark and fierce, ruthless, beautiful. Christian Hawkins was no Travis James. There wasn't an angelic cell in his whole body, and not even giving him wings could change the fact. What had changed was the concept of "angel."

Hawkins wasn't ascending to heaven or descending to hell. He was the angel who brought hell with him. It was in his eyes. It was in every hard line of his body, in every "wound" she'd inflicted on him. He was the dark angel, the darkest, skirting the edge of demonic intent, but not crossing over—not yet.

And Nikki was a genius to have made it all so absolutely clear with nothing more than a photographic image painted over on a piece of canvas.

Rocky Solano had nothing on her in the brilliance department. She more than held her own.

Next to the painting of Hawkins was a triptych of Travis descending, and man, the boy was going to hell fast. So fast, it almost gave Kid vertigo. More than one person stopped and raised their hand a bit as if to catch him—talk about "interactive art." Nikki had surpassed herself with the piece. The triptych also made it clear why Travis was her favorite model. Kid didn't think it would matter how many times she painted Hawkins, she would always get the dark angel, and if she'd found any "feminine mystique" in Christian Hawkins, Kid would eat his socks.

Travis was more of a chameleon, able to change as circumstances required, able to express a whole host of emotions, from the glory of victory to the utter exhaustion of battles lost, but hard fought.

Definitely hard fought, Kid thought, looking at the triptych and for the first time wondering how much damage the broken angel had inflicted on the demon who had beaten him and banished him to hell.

Curious, he looked around the gallery, picking out other "descending angel" paintings, and slowly coming to the realization that he'd had the paintings all wrong. Completely wrong. They weren't of defeat. The doomed angel had given up nothing, conceded nothing. He'd fought to the death, claiming his victory in valor when triumph was beyond his reach.

The truth struck Kid hard. He'd seen victory in death before, half a dozen times in half a dozen places around the world, in combat. He didn't know where or how Travis had come to his understanding, but he had to give it to the guy for getting it right. There was more to Nikki's angel than he'd thought, maybe a whole lot more.

Then his gaze fell on the last painting hanging from the catwalk, the one most in the shadows, and he suddenly knew that in some unsuspecting way, he'd underestimated Nikki, too.

Kid wasn't the first savage she'd seen, and not the first she'd drawn. Before him, there'd been Creed.

God. Even half clothed and in wings, the jungle boy was no less than what he always was—wild, fierce by nature, not by intellect, and deadly by design.

And the demon who had vanquished Travis? It hadn't gotten by Creed. The beast hung broken and lifeless from the jungle boy's hand, his fist closed around the scruff of the monster's thick neck, his fingers digging deep through the skin to clutch broken vertebrae and torn muscle.

Shit. Creed made Kid look civilized. Whatever expression Nikki had caught on his face when he'd broken Sanchez's neck, he at least had not been snarling, his teeth bared, and there had been no blood on his mouth.

There was on Creed's.

Geezus. What the fuck kind of angels were these? Demon-eating angels?

Nikki had never done work like this before, and he hated to be the one to tell her, but he didn't think anyone was going to buy a painting of a bloody-mouthed angel who ate monsters.

Then he saw the sold tag on the bottom of the frame.

I'll be damned. That was the last thing he'd expected.

Okay, second to last, he quickly revised, catching sight of Nikki headed in his direction.

He braced himself. His makeshift plan for the night had not included actual face time with her. His plan had been to watch her from afar and count on Skeeter to take care of any close work. He wasn't up for close work with Nikki, but if she was coming over, and she definitely was, they were going to be pretty damn close, about two feet apart max, if that, in this crowd.

So he braced himself, because he had too much

pride to run. He just hoped to hell she wasn't coming over because she wanted him to meet Rocky. She could have saved herself the trip. He wasn't doing it. No way. No how. He did not want to talk to the man whose "no, not really" fiancé he'd been making love to less than twenty-four hours ago. He'd at least figured that out in the alley.

Twenty feet and closing.

Ridiculously, and despite his pride, he found himself backing up, until he was up against the wall, or rather, a door.

No. Correction, he realized. It wasn't *a* door. It was *the* door. The door to the oversize closet where she'd saved his life the last time he'd been in this freaking art gallery. The coincidence literally flabbergasted him. She could have cornered him anywhere, but no, the fates, which he didn't even believe in, had decreed that he face this next little ordeal of emotional angst with his back up against the door of the room where she'd gone down on him for the first time.

He hated to be such a guy about it, but the truth was, sex defined a lot of the more memorable moments of his life—especially sex like they'd had in the closet. *Geezus*, he'd lost it that night.

Ten feet. She'd entered the red zone.

And she looked good enough to eat, all curves and sparkle and flash. Her hair stuck out all over just so. Earrings shone in glittery arcs down both of her ears.

And the dress. Her dress was what happened when

"business formal" met Nicole Alana McKinney. It became "business sensual." Black, with a thousand little buttons all the way down the front, the dress was cut like a suit jacket, but the material was light, kind of airy and shimmering. It moved with her, sliding across her hips when she walked, catching the light in a way that made it almost silver at times, and typical Nikki, it barely covered her butt. Add the black stiletto heels with straps that wrapped around and around her ankles, and suddenly not-very-tall Nikki looked like she had legs that went on forever.

Where in the hell did she find clothes like that? Clothes that always looked like they'd be fun to take off—and her clothes were lots of fun to take off, sweet little nothing scraps of a guy's fantasy. Even her "business" dress would ball up to fit in his hand. And last night, hell—pink satin panties, the soft cotton of a bikini top, and all the shush and sparkle of a sequined miniskirt. He'd loved taking those off her— which flat-out broke his heart. Her clothes weren't his to take off, not anymore, all the little wild things she wore.

Up until he'd met her, he hadn't dated a woman who didn't own a parka and wear it most of the time. Cargo pants, T-shirts, hiking boots, ski gear, bike shorts—when he thought back over his previous girlfriends, there was a lot of sports equipment in the memories.

But he'd fallen for her, the girlie-girl time bomb with diamond studs and silver hoops in her ears, with eyeliner, and shadow, and sooty mascara, with artfully blushed cheekbones, and glossy lipstick on her mouth.

Eight feet, and he knew he was doomed.

Five feet, and she didn't stop.

Two feet, and he was pressed so solidly back against the door, he felt like the world's biggest fool.

Then she was standing next to him, so close he couldn't tell if she was actually touching him or not, until someone jostled her from behind. Suddenly, she was smack up against him, all over, all at once, landing softly on his chest and grabbing on to him for balance.

He caught her with both arms.

Absofuckinglutely zero feet. Less than zero.

Dammit.

"I—are you okay?" He couldn't believe this.

"No," she said, her hands pressed against the front of his shirt. Then she laughed, but it sounded nervous, and she shook her head. "No, I'm not okay."

He tightened his hold on her, something in her voice setting off his warning signals. "What happened?"

A hundred things flashed through his mind, too many of them with Conseco's face attached, which startled the hell out of him. Is that why he'd come back, instead of leaving from the alley? Deep down inside, did he really think Conseco could have seen a matched set of hot pink, mock-croc luggage in Panama City and figured out that out of all the millions and millions of people in the world, Nikki

McKinney from Boulder, Colorado, was having an art show on Saturday night in Denver?

It didn't make sense.

But the nagging sense of unease was still there. It hadn't left him all day. He'd missed something. Something subtle. He knew it, but he couldn't figure out what it was.

That's why he'd stayed.

"Just that you . . . *oh*." The sound came out of her suddenly, on a little breath of surprise when her hand accidentally brushed against his shoulder holster. "You're armed."

She looked up, and his heart flipped over in his chest. She was so damn beautiful. He'd never seen a face like hers, so perfectly shaped, every feature delicate, balanced, divine. She'd explained it to him once, very matter-of-factly. It was the angles, she'd said, the golden triangles, pleasing proportions to the human eye. Her face was made up of them. She'd measured them out on a photograph once. Travis had a lot of these golden triangles, too.

But not him. Oh, no, she'd assured him. His face was far more interesting, far more beautiful. The exception that broke the rule.

Well, it probably broke something. He'd give her that much.

"Doubly armed," she continued, peeking under his jacket. "At an art show."

He let out a short breath.

Yes, he had two guns in a double shoulder holster.

His .45 on the right, and his 9mm on the left. No special reason. He'd just felt like he needed plenty of firepower to face the night, whatever the hell that meant. Even he didn't know. Like she said, he was at an art show, not in a combat zone.

And the thirty-round magazine for the Glock 9mm he'd put in the trunk of his car? Hell, a banana clip on a semiautomatic pistol was so crazy, so much overkill, he thought he better keep that little fact to himself.

Obviously, whatever edge he'd fallen off of in Colombia, he still hadn't quite crawled back on top of it.

"It's okay," he said. Okay for him. Some of the people in Toussi's might have a problem with it, if they found out.

Tough. He was licensed.

"It's always like this for you, isn't it? The guns, I mean, your whole life."

"Yes." What could he say? He was never unarmed, and he didn't see that changing any time soon.

A sigh escaped her. "Kid, those men, the ones last night, they were there because of you, weren't they, not to rob the house, or, well, anything like that." It wasn't a question, and he wasn't going to lie to her, not now that they were safely out of Panama.

"Yes."

She withdrew her hands from the front of his shirt, her gaze falling to the floor. "Were they there to kill you? Like they did Martin?"

CRAZY KISSES ◆ 263

Now here was where a lie would come in handy, he thought, but he couldn't bring himself to use one.

"You know the job, Nikki."

"No." She shook her head. "No, I don't. You told me you were a bodyguard, but that doesn't quite cover it, does it? And as far as the rest of what you all do, nobody tells me anything, not even Regan, not even since Quinn started flying for SDF again."

Nikki's sister, Regan, had married one of the original chop-shop boys, Quinn Younger. Quinn had taken some time off after the wedding, laid low, stayed out of the line of fire, but when Dylan needed him in Indonesia, Quinn came back on board. Kid hadn't been surprised. Quinn had been living on the edge and running the streets since he'd been thirteen. A guy just didn't up and walk away from that kind of adrenaline.

"Everything SDF does is either classified or doesn't officially exist," he told her truthfully, knowing it wasn't much, but not having anything else to give her. Those were just the facts. "There isn't much I do that I can talk about."

"You killed those men last night. We could talk about that."

She hadn't lifted her head, which worked for him. He didn't want her to see the look she'd put on his face, but *fuck*, he wasn't going there, not even for her.

Angry, he turned to leave, but she held him with just the touch of her hand.

"I'd never imagined anything like what you did."

No, he didn't suppose she had, but he really didn't want to hear it. He'd seen it on his coffee table, thank you very much.

"Creed talked about how good you are, and then last night, when I saw for myself . . . well, I never saw anyone move so fast, think so fast. You were faster than them, Kid, stronger than the first guy."

"More savage." It was a cheap shot, but he took it anyway.

"Yes," she said unequivocally, lifting her gaze and meeting his square on.

Great. This was just what he wanted to hear.

"Creed wouldn't have talked about the mission." No way in hell.

"He didn't," she admitted. "But he did tell me how glad he was to have J.T.'s brother at his back when he returned to South America, and that you'd found the men you'd been looking for. I figured out on my own what you probably did to them."

He narrowed his gaze at her. No, he decided. Impossible. There was no way for her to have figured out what he and Creed had done to the NRF rebels they'd tracked down in Peru.

"No, you didn't." He shook his head. No matter what she'd dreamed up, it wouldn't have been the truth.

"Look at the painting, Kid. The only thing I imagined was what the demon looked like. The rest of it is all Creed. It was in his eyes. I saw it in his body. Everything in him changed when I asked him to tell me about Colombia."

He hated to think it, that she'd *known* anything, but when he shifted his attention back to the demon-eating angel, he was forced to admit that she might have seen the truth. Nikki McKinney didn't miss much when she had a guy under her lights, and the jungle boy did not have much subterfuge in him. For anyone who knew him, it was written all over his face, what a freaking savage he could be.

"Kid," she said softly, her hand coming back to rest on his chest. "You told me what the Colombians did to J.T. You told me Creed was there with him, and I *cannot* imagine that the man in my painting did not repay them in kind, the way you did last night. You need to talk to me, Kid."

No. Not about this, he didn't. Not ever.

"I want to understand."

"I get paid to do a job, Nikki, a job I'm trained to do, a job that I don't think plays very well in this crowd." He didn't have to look around to know he didn't fit in here tonight, not with her friends or her life. "I'm sorry about what happened in Panama, really sorry, and I should have told you that before I—" he stopped short, suddenly unsure of what he'd meant to say next.

But she wasn't unsure.

Her hand went back to her side. "Before you dumped me on Skeeter and ran out on me again."

No. That wasn't what he'd been about to say. Something along those lines, maybe. Or maybe he'd meant to say something more along the lines of—

"You're the one who got up in the middle of the night and packed your bags."

The minute the words were out, he knew he'd nailed them. Yes, sir, that's *exactly* what he'd been meaning to say to her all day long. He just hadn't meant to ever actually say it.

Her gaze locked onto his. "Now we're getting somewhere."

"No, we're not." Not anywhere he was willing to go.

Three women negotiated their way past them, chatting excitedly, holding their wineglasses high, and Nikki pressed herself closer to him.

Perfect.

"Damn," she said under her breath. "Come on."

He felt her reach around him for the doorknob to the closet, and a little trickle of fear coursed down his spine. She couldn't be serious. She couldn't possibly be planning on dragging him into the closet. He didn't want to be within a thousand feet of the damn closet, which was why, he was sure, it took her all of ten seconds to get him in there, instead of the reluctant, against-his-will thirty it should have.

She closed the door behind them and threw the lock, which only upped his alarm.

"I need to tell you about Rocky and me."

Then he really was changing his mind about being in the closet. He didn't want to hear another damn thing about her freaking fiancé, and by God, he was going to tell her. All he needed to do was get the words out of his suddenly very dry throat.

CHAPTER 19

"YOU'VE GOT RATS all over your buffet," Travis said, coming up behind Jane and whispering in her ear. It wasn't the sort of thing anybody would want advertised, even these kinds of Rats. There had been three ravenous teenagers piling their plates high when he'd walked by, and he'd recognized two of them from last night. Plus, he'd just wanted to whisper in her ear.

Jane started, whirling around and practically ending up in his arms. He was that close, but not close enough to suit him, not after having held her, even if it had been in a ventilation shaft.

God, the kiss they'd shared had been so hot. It was all he'd been able to think about all day.

"So how did everything turn out last night?" he asked. "You got home okay, right? I came by about eight this morning, but you didn't answer."

"I was still asleep at eight. It was . . . a long night." Her gaze slid away, which he tried not to let bother him, but it did, just a little. The last thing he wanted, please, was to end up back at square one with her.

Last night had been a turning point in their relationship, from not being anywhere near one, to a kiss. That wasn't the sort of ground he was willing to give up.

"Thanks for calling Skeeter. She's the one who finally sprung me."

"I know. I called her today to make sure you were okay. I'm so sorry about what happened."

"Don't be. It wasn't your fault I followed you."

She shrugged, as if she wasn't quite as sure as he was about what was whose fault. Then she went and proved it.

"Trouble seems to be following me around a lot lately. If you want to stay out of it, you might want to stay away from me."

She was dead serious. He could tell by the tone of her voice and the nonchalant way she tried to downplay the warning. No unnecessary drama for the urban jungle queen. Just the facts. Ignore them at your peril.

He did.

"Actually, I was hoping we *could* spend some time together. Do stuff. Talk." He ducked his head to get a better look at her. "Kiss."

To his relief, she blushed. She wasn't completely immune to him, and she hadn't forgotten their kiss.

"Suzi was asking for you," she said, changing the subject. "And Nikki is here, but I haven't seen her since, well..." She looked around the gallery, her voice trailing off.

"Since?" he prompted, curious now. The last time he'd seen Nikki, she'd been in Rocky's lap.

"Well, since she and this guy disappeared into the storage closet. People are asking for her. A lot of them came just to meet her, and Rocky, of course."

Travis straightened up, curious. Nikki didn't disappear with just anybody.

"What did this guy look like?"

"Tall, short dark hair, serious." She slanted him a small grin, which he was glad to see. "Seriously cute. Not like anyone else here. Watchful. Extremely aware. Maybe some kind of bodyguard. Does Nikki have a bodyguard?"

"If she did, that would be the guy. Kid Chaos Chronopolous," Travis said, not knowing for sure what to think. He knew the more time those two spent together, the better off they were going to be, but not if Kid was a marked man. Skeeter was afraid he was, complete with a bounty on his head, which didn't freak her out nearly as much as it did him. SDF wasn't a social club, she'd told him, then offered to take him up on the firing range again tomorrow.

For a dyed-in-the-wool pacifist, he was amazed how much he liked shooting, amazed at how much he liked all the stuff Skeeter showed him when she wasn't busy drawing him, all the hand-to-hand combat and tactical pistol techniques, how to call the wind for a rifle shot at a thousand meters. Cool stuff, deadly stuff, the kind of stuff that Nikki had witnessed firsthand last night.

Man, he'd lived his life on the soft side. That was for damn sure. He doubted if a bunch of twelve-year-olds could have tied up Kid Chaos, which was something he'd been thinking about all day, ever since he'd seen those sketches and asked the age-old guy question: Could he have done what Kid had done?

Could he have saved Nikki from those men?

Could he have saved himself?

The verdict was still out, but he was hoping the answer was going to be "not yet," rather than "no."

Skeeter could have done it. He knew that much. The girl had mad, mad skills.

"Does Nikki need a bodyguard?" Jane asked. The question had a real curiosity behind it, almost like a professional curiosity—this from a girl who ran wild on the streets of Denver alone in the middle of the night with a silver switchblade in her pocket.

"Maybe." And he hated even thinking it.

Someone jostled him from behind, and at the same time, a man walked between them and stopped, completely unaware that he was literally in the middle of their conversation.

Travis grinned at her over the guy's shoulder, and for a second, she grinned back. Then the man moved on, and her smile faded.

She was definitely nervous around him, and not in a good way, he didn't think.

"There are way too many people in the gallery tonight," she said, looking around, scanning the crowd.

Travis followed her gaze. She had a point.

There were a lot of people in Toussi's, some of them on the strange side, but in truth, nothing wilder or more outlandish than at a few of the parties he and Nikki had gone to in New York and L.A.

"Yeah, there's a lot," he agreed.

"Raymond is here. Outside," she said, then gave a small shrug, as if the news wasn't as awful as it sounded. "That's why the Rats are inside. They're scared."

"Are you?" He remembered Fast Jack talking about Raymond, the gang leader he wanted Jane to meet with tomorrow at Connie's Bagels.

"No. Concerned," she said. "But I wouldn't mind if there was some professional muscle around."

Travis brought his gaze back to her. Something told him she was more than "concerned." He remembered one night on the street when he'd wished he'd had some professional muscle around.

"If it's Kid with Nikki, he's about as professional as it gets, and he'll be armed."

"Skeeter Bang carries a pistol, too," she said. "I noticed the other night, and she's here." She was still scanning the crowd, checking things out—avoiding his gaze.

Yeah, and Skeeter could kick butt, but if the night

had reached a point where Jane thought she needed Kid and Skeeter to kick butt, it was time for a reality check.

"Katya and Suzi usually have a rent-a-cop at these things. Do you want me to go find him?"

"And what? Tell him there are Parkside Bloods cruising LoDo in black Escalades?" She let out a little snort. "There are always Parkside Bloods in black Escalades on the streets. The cops probably know where they are better than I do."

She had the most amazing way of making him feel like an idiot and incredibly naïve about how her life worked, with Rats and Raymond and street gangs.

"I have a friend, a cop in Boulder. I could call him if you like, tell him what's going on. He won't ask for incriminating details, but he can tell us what he thinks."

She didn't say anything, just shrugged again, which left the field wide open for him to compound his idiocy.

"Or would you rather I minded my own business and left you alone?" He truly didn't know. She'd kissed him, yeah, but that was just one kiss, one moment of acknowledging his existence out of weeks of completely ignoring him. Maybe, for that one moment, she'd thought he was somebody else, somebody who ran from the cops and hid in old buildings, somebody living on the edge of danger, though he hadn't found Weisman to be all that dangerous.

"No, I don't think we should call your friend," she finally said. "The cops and I—well..." She let her sentence die unfinished, but he got the gist of it. What he had to offer didn't have any worth in her world, and if he'd just get a clue, he could figure that out.

It frustrated him, this culture gap that seemed to open up and swallow him with damning regularity every time he tried to get close to her.

"Jane, I don't go around bullying children, or trying to shake down old people on the street, and I have never once in my life hit someone with violent intent, but that doesn't mean I can't understand the problem you have here or that I can't help you with it. I may be a regular, boring, nice guy, but guys like me make good friends."

Her gaze finally shifted to meet his. "You've never hit anybody? Ever?" She sounded dumbstruck by the concept.

Well, now he'd gone and done it, he thought, confessed all his sins and shocked her with his lack of depravity. *Christ.* Didn't she know any regular, nice guys? Or were all the guys in her life Fast Jack hustlers and capped homies? He hoped not. She deserved better. He knew she wanted better for herself, or she wouldn't be here tonight, trying to do her job, trying to fit in. She'd be out on the street, running with the Rats and trying to stay out of Raymond's clutches.

God, he hated the image that conjured up.

"Never," he admitted, then added fuel to the flames. "The Violins for Nonviolence in the Home concert Jack found the ticket stubs to in my wallet? I was one of the sponsors of the event. No kidding. I give money to people to promote not hitting each other. Crazy, huh? I mean, you've seen my car. I'm not exactly rolling in cash like this guy Raymond who you're telling me has a whole bunch of Cadillac Escalades so he can drive around in luxury while he terrorizes little kids."

"Raymond isn't my friend. He's more like an enemy."

"And I'm so boring, I don't even have an enemy."

"You're lucky."

"I'm lonely." It was the truth, and he couldn't stand there looking at her, wanting her, and losing something he'd never even had without telling her. She'd kissed him, and all those fantasies that haunted his nights had paled in comparison to the reality of holding her in his arms. "I've been lonely since the first time I saw you, Jane. It's crazy, I know, but it's the truth."

And how was that for laying his guts out on the line? He'd never done that before. He was usually a little smoother, not much, but a little.

"Last night," she started, then paused, trying to continue holding his gaze and failing. "The kiss, it was nice."

Nice?

He was doomed. He'd just confessed his undying fascination with her, and she'd dismissed his kiss as nice.

"But if you knew me better," she continued, "you

wouldn't have done it." She paused again, her color deepening with embarrassment. "If you knew me at all, you'd wish you hadn't."

Talk about laying your guts out on the line. Every instinct he had told him she'd just made a confession far worse than his. She'd just left out the facts.

"Skeeter told me all about the drug dealing," he said. "The whole Castle Rat thing when you were a kid."

"But I bet she didn't tell you about the man I killed."

Uh, no.

For a moment, all he could do was stare at her.

"It's why I got sent up," she said. "Hawkins knows. He's the one who got my conviction reduced for self-defense. He's the one who arranged for me to do my time at the Immaculate Heart School for Young Women in Phoenix."

"You killed a man." He was dumbstruck.

"Me and Sandman, yeah." Her gaze never left the floor.

He remembered Fast Jack talking about Sandman.

"It *was* self-defense, a situation kind of like tonight, with too many Rats on the street and the gangbangers looking for trouble. They grabbed one of my kids, and by the time Sandman and I got him back, the gang guy was dead."

She came to a halt and glanced up, and he knew it was his turn to say something—preferably something full of understanding and compassion.

But he was blown away for a second, and in the next second, she'd taken a step back.

"Jane." He reached for her, feeling guilty as hell, but she stepped backward again, eluding him.

"You're not a regular guy, Travis, not even close." Something behind him caught her eye, her gaze flickering in that direction. When her attention returned to him, her expression was even more distressed than before. "You're so much of everything beyond regular, it scares me," she said, then turned and fled.

He watched her leave, completely nonplussed. Raymond was outside, dogging the streets for Rats, and she was afraid of him, a part-time emergency medical technician and sometimes nude male model? Well, that put him in his place. He was about to go after her, but someone caught his sleeve.

He turned around. *Dammit*. She could have warned him. But it was too late now. He was trapped.

"You're Travis James, aren't you?" the woman who had hold of his arm said. "I told my friends it was you."

Her friends comprised a group of seven other women, a daunting group of well-dressed thirty-something professional women with a certain look in their eyes that told him they'd spent a little too much time looking at him naked.

He smiled on the outside, and swore on the inside, and wished like hell that he'd run off with Jane.

NIKKI had turned him to butter.

Kid had made a half-assed attempt to talk her into going back into the gallery and getting out of the closet, but instead, she'd sat him down in the chair and started rattling on about the massage techniques Travis used in his sexual imprinting business, and about how he looked a little pale and could probably use a little massage—whatever the hell that meant. He really didn't have a clue. All he knew for sure was that she'd put her hands on the back of his neck and shoulders and turned him to butter.

Which wasn't such a bad consistency to be, he realized, when she dropped her bombshell.

"I never slept with Rocky," she said. "We never had sex."

The closet hadn't changed much. There was still a desk, a chair, a rack of clothes, and some paintings stacked against the wall, all of it crammed into a small space with a window facing onto the alley. Light from the street lamps on Seventeenth dimly lit the interior.

"No sex," he said bluntly, getting a little of that "head-swimming" feeling he'd had last night again.

"I'm not going to tell you I didn't kiss him, because I did, but—"

"No sex." He hated to get stuck in one spot, but that couldn't be right. "The guy asked you to *marry* him, Nikki."

"I know he did, but—well, it's been kind of a whirlwind since I met him, all the parties, L.A., New

York, and he was in Paris for a while, and well, we just never got together."

Geezus, she'd just turned him completely around again.

"Excuse me, but if I remember this correctly, it took us about all of five seconds flat to get together last night."

Hell, more like two seconds, but who was counting?

He was, dammit. Two seconds and she'd been his, walking away from the poker table, holding on to his hand.

"Are you telling me the guy hasn't had five seconds?" He didn't believe it.

Her fingers stilled on the back of his neck.

"He's in a wheelchair, Kid," she said, sounding slightly exasperated.

"And if I was in a wheelchair, I would have my hand up your skirt so fast, it...it..." It would make her head swim, the same way his was swimming—in a big old pool of "no way in hell."

How could the guy love her enough to marry her, and not love her like that?

"Sometimes he's in pain," she said, starting up again with the neck massage.

And he hadn't been in pain last night? Hell, he was still in pain—patched up, sewn together, and Band-Aided.

"It isn't going to work," he said.

"Not if you're going to get all tense. Try to relax your shoulders."

Screw his shoulders. "I mean the whole he's-in-pain Rocky thing. The whole goddamn engagement thing. Unless he's going to be in pain forever, he's going to want to make love to you, and when he does, I'm going to want to—" What? he wondered, stopping and asking himself the question of the hour. What was he going to do? Kick Rocky Solano's ass?

Not very bloody damned likely.

"You're getting all tense again."

"You have to call it off."

"I did."

"No, I mean right now, tonight." He was *not* going to stand by and let her marry the freaking genius fiber artist, or anybody else, for that damn matter.

"I did."

"*Geezus*, Nikki. You're in love with me, not him, and I think it's time we just faced the facts and tried to—"

She'd called it off.

"When?" he asked, turning in the chair so he could see her.

"The night he decided he was feeling good enough to take our relationship to the next level, so to speak. The next day, I was on a plane to Panama."

Good. That was very good.

"So why were you wearing his ring last night?" The damn thing had damn near given him a heart attack when he'd finally noticed it.

"Sandovals' is a pretty flashy crowd," she said. "Especially when Rico and Luis declare it a Carnival night. So out came the sequins and the tiaras and Rocky's ring."

Of course. He could have figured that one out for himself, if he'd been in a logical frame of mind. But his logic was never on the same page as his feelings for Nikki. Hell, he couldn't even get logic and Nikki in the same book.

"You should have given it back the night you called it off. That's the way I would have wanted it, a clean break." Bullshit. He wouldn't have wanted any "break" at all, and he bet old Rocky hadn't, either.

"I tried," she said, leaning forward and resting her knee on the chair, and giving him all sorts of ideas that did not in any way fit in with his plan to grow up and let her have Paris. "But he wanted me to keep it, until I had a chance to see you and find out how I felt."

A pitiful, last-ditch effort, but Kid didn't blame the guy. He would have tried every trick he had to keep her, too.

"So how do you feel?" he asked, trying not to sound too goddamn insecure.

"I don't know, Kid," she said, climbing into his lap and basically confusing the hell out of him. Settling in, she looped her arms around his neck. "I'm feeling a little hot. What about you?"

Definitely hot.

Dangerously hot.

"Do you want to see something?" she asked.

Hell, yeah, he nodded, pretty much riveted in place by the possibilities of what she might do. When she lifted her hand to the top of her dress and released the first button, his Let Her Go To Paris plan started to smoke.

One by one, the buttons came undone under his gaze, until her dress fell partway open.

"Wow," was the first thing to come out of his mouth, then, "You've got cleavage." Nikki never had cleavage. Her breasts were small, sweet, perfect, but there wasn't enough of them to make cleavage.

"Do you like it? It's a push-up demibra."

A freaking hot push-up demibra, cherry red lace with black satin ribbons.

He couldn't help himself, he ran his fingers over the little mounds of her breasts, and Paris went up in flames. He'd never seen them like this, all pushed together and a little wobbly. It made him hot all over. "I love it, Nikki. It's so sexy."

"I wore it for you," she said. "I was going to have Skeeter let me back into your apartment after the show, and wait for you in your bed wearing nothing but my undies."

He looked up at her. All the time he'd been thinking he'd lost her, that he was going to walk away for good, she'd been arranging herself into a cherry red push-up demibra for him?

Geez, he was a clueless sonuvabitch.

But he knew what to do with Nicole Alana

McKinney—what he never should have stopped doing, not for seven long and lonely months.

Reaching up, he slid his hand around the back of her neck and drew her mouth down to his. He kissed her softly at first, then more deeply, letting his tongue play inside her mouth, letting the taste and feel of her get him hard.

And she kissed him back, her hands in his hair, holding him. Her tongue slid across his teeth, exploring his palate, invading him on every front, and he gave himself over to it—soft lips crushed against his, her breath on his skin, the taste of her in his mouth. They kissed forever, deliberately, erotically, until he was drugged with the sensation of her body moving against his, pressing him back into the chair. She consumed him, kiss after kiss, until he was so hard he couldn't think and all he wanted was to be inside her.

Nikki.

She was his, every cell, every sigh. Her thoughts of love—his. Her thoughts of sex, those sweet, dark yearnings that had her unbuckling his belt and lowering his zipper—all his.

Paris could wait, and those damn packed hot pink, mock-croc suitcases—they could all wait.

He slipped out of his shoulder holster, then lifted his hips and helped her get rid of his pants. When she sat back down, she was straddling him again. It was such a perfect tease, being half naked with Nikki in his lap, the way she grazed his lips with her teeth, gently biting him, licking him with her tongue and moving back inside his mouth, and all the while she was kissing him, she was stroking him.

He was floating in carnal bliss, the sweet weight of her holding him in place, her hand small, exciting, and so much less predictable than his own.

"*Geez*, Nikki. Don't, yes . . . ah, God." She was incredible this way, destroying him with soft, wet, deep kisses, the exquisite friction of her palm, and the lazy trailing of her fingers going around him, over the top of him, all over him.

Suddenly, he needed to see her naked—her shoulders and breasts and between her legs, where she was practically riding him, the naked curve of her hip. He needed to see it all.

He started unbuttoning the rest of her dress, then gave up. There were about a hundred and eighty thousand buttons, all of them too tiny to grip. "Can this come off over the top of your head?"

"Yes, I think."

"Lift your arms."

They struggled for a minute, with him pulling the dress up, and her trying to shimmy out from under it. Finally, it came off, and he let it fall into the pile of his clothes.

The first thing he noticed was what else she was wearing.

"Matching panties," she said, lifting her hips a little so he could see.

"Heartbreaking." He didn't know what else to say. It was a miracle he could get even the one word out.

"My panties break your heart?"

"Oh, honey. They're breaking everything I've got." Slain, by a matching bra-and-panty set. "Take them off."

She stood up, still wearing the killer stilettos, and God, he wondered if it was possible for anything to be more erotic. Then she slipped the panties down her legs and stepped out of them.

Equal parts lust and love welled up in his chest and literally dropped him to his knees. She was so incredibly pretty there.

He pulled her to him, kissing the soft skin of her belly, the silky length of her thighs, the even silkier, softer place between her thighs. He buried his face in her dark curls, then buried his tongue even farther, finding the sweet place that made her melt.

And he stayed there, played there, teased her until he thought he'd die, everything else becoming so elemental. The way she gave it all up for him, her knees weakening, her hands coming to rest on his shoulders, the taste of her, the lovely female scent of her. It all made him drunk.

When she came, it was with a soft moan and her body shuddering against his mouth. It was with him stroking her deep inside with his fingers and her silken contractions rippling over him.

He licked her until she pulled away, trembling. Then he lifted her up and lay down with her on the desk. His lips were still warm with her heat, still tasted of her, when he kissed her. This is love, he thought, to be able to feel a kiss in the marrow of your bones.

Slowly, he pushed into her, lifting his head to watch her face. Her eyes were dreamy, the tip of her tongue tracing her upper lip. She sighed, and he brought his mouth back down to hers, letting her breath infuse him with a light sweetness. It was unlike anything he'd ever known except when he was inside her, a part of her, their heat and bodies joined.

It wasn't sex. It was sacrifice, and he gave himself willingly. When she took him, he felt taken, absolved.

"Kid, please," she whispered, and he thrust—*flesh of my flesh, my pleasure for your own.* It was so sweet. A soft sound escaped her and her head went back, her throat arching.

She'd told him once what it felt like to have him inside her, the aching tenderness, the heavy fullness that opened a whole new dimension inside her body, how intensely lovely it was to have him moving in and out of her, how the rhythm he set and the way he changed it was like a journey where she never knew what would be around the next bend.

How he never disappointed her.

And not tonight, either. Her body was growing taut beneath him, so slick and heated and wanton, her breath coming in pants. He was on his forearms on either side of her, his hands in her hair, his thoughts dissolving into mindless sensation and need, desperate, compelling need, and his cock—oh, God. He bent his head to look down between them, to where he was sliding in and out of her, a driving heat. His cock was rock hard, his belly tight, his chest, his thighs, his balls, tight.

"*Kid*," she gasped his name. "*Please . . . oh.*"

He pulled the cup down on her cherry red lace bra and took her breast into his mouth, laving her nipple with his tongue, warming her skin, and when he sucked, she came undone.

A cry left her lips, and sharp, sweet pleasure shot through him, gathering instantaneous force. He rocked into her, pumping hard and deep, his teeth gritted, his body rigid—then release, even sweeter. *Fuck.* It was heaven, pouring out of him, all consuming . . . transcending.

"Oh, my god, Kid," she said a couple of minutes later, her body lying limp next to his.

Oh, my god was right. He pulled her closer to his side of the desk.

"Are we going to do that again?"

"Yeah," he said, and dragged his hand back through his hair, trying to catch his breath, trying to ground himself. Then he kissed her shoulder and her cheek. A grin teased his lips. "Yeah. We ought to have another go. Just give me a minute."

The minute passed, and then another, before he felt her laughing.

"What?" He looked down at her face.

"We couldn't do it again in another hundred minutes."

He grinned. "I don't know, Nikki. You're pretty inspiring."

"Nobody's that inspiring."

"Oh, yeah?"

Her eyes widened slightly. "You're kidding."

He shook his head, and she looked down between them.

"Oh, my god, Kid."

Oh, my god was right. No woman had ever done this to him, done it so quickly. No one except her.

CHAPTER

20

JUAN CONSECO had Benito circle the block around the Toussi Gallery three times, slowly. There was an alley, and that was good. They cruised it twice, locating the gallery's back door, which had been propped open for the caterer.

God truly was on Juan's side in this mission.

There were hundreds of people in the gallery, and that, too, was good. No one would notice them, at least not overly much. From what he'd seen, the mix of gallery-goers was eclectic, people from all walks of life. He and Benito and Sergio could hunt without fear. No one would recognize them or remember them. No one was expecting a heinous crime.

"Benito, go ahead and let us out at the front of the gallery, then park in the alley. Don Drago, Sergio, and I will go in and find the woman. Simón," he said, turning toward the other man in the backseat. "You stay here with Benito, see if you can find something in the trunk to tie her up with. When we locate her, I'll call. Come in then, and we will give Señorita McKinney a proper escort out."

"*Sí*, Don Conseco."

The plan was simple, Juan's favorite kind. The simpler, the better. Nicole Alana McKinney was no high-ranking judge or wary newspaper reporter. She wasn't a manager for one of the big oil companies. There would be no ransom. She had no worth, except as bait to bring him the ghost killer.

Juan didn't know how long that would take. Perhaps days, depending on where the man was, but the time didn't matter. They weren't going to wait for him in Denver. As soon as their plane was ready and their escape route planned, they would head back to Colombia. Let *el asesino fantasma* come to him there.

Drago had already made a number of phone calls, setting the wheels in motion for their return trip. Juan had no intention of getting arrested by some low-end border guard or immigration agent who hadn't been paid to look the other way. Using the same route to get out of the country that they'd used to get in was a bit risky. The less recent activity on the airstrips they used the better.

Benito pulled the Cadillac to a stop at the gallery's front door, and the three men got out. As Juan had predicted, no one took undue notice of three more men entering the crowd of people in Toussi's.

Finding Nicole Alana McKinney in the same huge crowd, though, proved to be annoyingly difficult. With only a black-and-white photograph on a flyer to go by, it took far longer than he had planned, a good forty minutes, but when Tío Drago gave him the sign, Juan's hopes rose, and when he saw the girl Drago had picked out by the buffet tables, he knew there had been no mistake.

He took his phone out of his pocket and called Simón in.

Unbeknownst to her, Nicole Alana McKinney's life had just become forfeit. With luck, she wouldn't live out the night. If it took longer to bring *el asesino* to his side, the only change would be that the girl would wish she hadn't lived out the night—and she would be wishing it with all her heart. Juan could guarantee it. Within the next few minutes, without doubt, her life would become a living hell.

He was going to see to it personally.

SHIT. Fast Jack ducked into the alley behind Toussi's, running flat-out. He'd had to leave the last two kids who had called him where they were. But they should be safe now, because fat-ass Raymond was after him.

Right on his butt in his big black Escalade.

Shit. He skidded to a stop behind a Dumpster and tried to get his bearings. There were two options: the caterer's truck was a big white van with the back doors open and its interior lights on full blast. But hell, if he could see all the way to the guy's croissants, he figured Raymond could, too.

Toussi's was his other option, but hell, there was a for-real gangster at the back door, an uptown barrio badass. Jack knew one when he saw one, and he knew better than to mess with one, especially with the guy packing a piece and looking like he was on the look-out for trouble.

As Jack huddled there, sweating it out, trying to cut his losses, option number one disappeared. The caterer came out Toussi's back door, all but jumped when he saw barrio boy, then got in his big van and drove off—with the doors banging and the lights still on. He was no fool.

But Jack was, getting himself stuck between a rock and a hard place like this. *Damn.*

He peeked around the Dumpster, and *fucking-A,* Raymond was cruising in with his brights on, looking for Jack-knew-who.

He looked back to barrio boy, and noticed a black Cadillac had been parked in front of the caterer's van. Its trunk was open.

Bad idea, Jack, he told himself, and knew it to be true.

The sound of a phone ringing almost had him wetting his pants, but it was the gangster's. Jack watched him answer the phone, then turn, open the back door of Toussi's, and look inside.

Instinct, more than reason, propelled Jack down

the alley like a shot, keeping close to the wall, and before he had time to talk himself out of it, he was in the trunk, scrambling under a piece of cardboard, a tangled pile of rope, and a pair of jumper cables.

NIKKI had gone for a cup of coffee and a soda, after Kid had assured her she didn't look like she'd been put through a blender twice. Once was fine, a look she actually cultivated, but twice was merely an unkempt mess, she'd said.

What he hadn't told her is that they both probably looked like they'd fucked themselves goofy—because they had.

A big grin split his face. He couldn't help it. He and Nikki couldn't possibly keep surprising each other forever, but they'd sure done it tonight. Did other people make love like this? he wondered. What did Nikki call it? Crazy-wild-monkey sex?

Crazy-wild-monkey-on-fire sex was more like it.

He finished strapping on his shoulder holster, his grin broadening even more. She was his down to the red polish on her toenails. All his.

And he still hadn't told her about the rings. *Damn.* He really needed to do that.

And he really needed to find his other shoe. That's why she'd gone to get the drinks off the buffet instead of him. She still had two shoes.

They had found a light switch for the closet, over

by the window of all places, but the bulb was dim.
Even so, when he got down on the floor to look
around, he was able to finally spot his shoe. Somehow,
it had gotten jammed into the swivel gear on the
chair.

He worked it free, put it on, and tied it up, then
noticed something else on the floor: a pile of blue flyers, about half a ream of them. Flyers, he guessed, that
hadn't been handed out.

He shrugged into his jacket and checked both guns
to make sure they were riding right and not showing.
Everything was fine. He was good to go—but his gaze
was drawn back to the flyers. A black-and-white photograph, the blue edge of the paper.

He'd seen one somewhere.

Probably in Toussi's front window, he figured, but
he went ahead and bent down to pick one up.

The minute he had one in his hand, a bad feeling
went through him. A very bad feeling. He *had* seen
one of the flyers before. The same shade of blue on
the paper, the large square of a black-and-white photograph covering the top half.

He lifted it up to the light to read it, and everything inside him went cold. Nicole Alana McKinney,
it said, was having a showing at Toussi Gallery, and
the photo was of her. The time, date, and place—Denver, Colorado—were printed at the bottom of the
flyer along with her Web address.

Like a strobe, a series of images flashed across his

brain: his kitchen table in Panama City; her purse and a blue-edged flyer lying next to a half-empty cup of tea; Nikki in the chair; Javier Mancos coming up behind her; Hernando Sanchez dead beneath him.

Smith had said there'd been nothing to identify her in the house—but that damn poster had been in the house when he and Nikki had left, and the identification was undeniable, absolutely solid. *Fuck*. Her photograph was right on the goddamn thing.

He was running out the door even as the images were still forming, even as he was trying to make sense of them.

NIKKI had been doing a pretty good job of juggling a lukewarm cup of coffee, a soda, and a small plate of shrimp, until somebody bumped her elbow.

Dammit. The shrimp went flying, and she lost half the cup of coffee, fortunately not on her dress, which she still wasn't sure didn't look like it had been ridden hard and put away wet.

She was debating whether or not to try to go back for more shrimp, when somebody else shoved up against her.

The crowd tonight was simply amazing, and amazingly rude, but also a blessing of sorts. She'd seen over a dozen sold signs on her way over to the buffet.

A man backed into her then, almost knocking her over, the jerk, but there was another guy behind her, so instead of falling, she just sort of bounced off him and managed to stay on her feet and keep what was left of her drinks in their cups.

Still, it was disconcerting, because suddenly there were three men, instead of two, and she was definitely getting shoved.

"Good God," she all but yelled. "There's plenty of food. There's no need to—" She looked up from the coffee and soda, and the rest of the words died on her lips. The men were foreign, Hispanic, and looked frightfully like the two men Kid had killed—rough-edged, even in their suits, and empty-eyed.

She wasn't normally paranoid, but the men unnerved her, especially the way they were gathered around her, especially after last night. While she was wondering what it all meant, somebody grabbed her arm from behind, grabbed it hard. The soda fell to the floor.

Fear shot through her. She tried to shake free, but whoever had a hold of her tightened his grip. Then a large hand clamped over her mouth, and the men closed in around her. Suddenly, she was being half carried between all of them.

And no one was noticing. There was a lot of jostling around the buffet table by everybody. She kicked and squirmed, but the men just tightened their ranks, closing her off from the rest of the crowd.

She doubled her efforts. There wasn't much time. She'd been close to the back door to begin with, and

she could tell that was where they were taking her—
out the back door, into the alley.

Oh, God. Oh, God.

When the cool night air hit her face, she knew it
was all too late.

She'd been kidnapped.

CHAPTER

21

A LOT OF commotion outside brought Fast Jack's ears up like a terrier's. He peeked out the back of the trunk, through the small crack he'd left. Raymond was still halfway down the alley, his SUV parked in the shadows next to the Dumpster, nearly invisible in the darkness, but Jack could tell it was there, waiting.

The commotion, though, was going on at the side of the car nearest Toussi's back door. He couldn't see what was happening, and he really didn't care what the excitement was all about, as long as it wasn't going to include the trunk.

Suddenly, a scream rent the air, a woman's scream at very close quarters, sending a chill down his spine before it abruptly stopped. Too abruptly. Somebody had shut her up damn near instantly, and Jack started to get an idea of maybe what was going down. Like maybe somebody was taking a woman out of the art gallery against her will—and he was in the getaway car.

He couldn't believe his frickin' luck. He'd gotten himself into the middle of a kidnapping, that was for damn sure. One minute, everything had been fine—okay, not so fine—with stupid Raymond wondering where in the hell he'd gotten off to, and the next minute he had to wonder where in the hell he was going. The trunk of the Cadillac might not have been his best choice after all.

But it had been the best available choice, he reminded himself. And how could he have known somebody was going to drag a screaming woman into the car?

But please, not into the trunk.

Somebody rattled off a stream of angry Spanish. Somebody else answered, contrite, and the next thing he knew, the trunk was slammed shut.

Well, not exactly shut. Jack was having a bad night, but he was no idiot. He'd used the jumper cables and his knife to rig the trunk not to lock, but still to close enough to keep the inside warning light from going off.

He'd been in plenty of tight spots before, and a couple of times, he'd been in the trunk of a car.

The doors closed with more slams, and the Cadillac took off, sedately, like a Cadillac should.

But the car behind it took off with a squeal and the gunning roar of a big engine.

He peeked back out the crack he'd left in the trunk. *Geezus.* Raymond was following the Cadillac.

Geezus. This sucked. This sucked unbelievably.

So now what? he wondered.

He didn't have to wonder long. His options were pretty damn slim and narrowed down to doing nothing. Bailing out of the trunk with Raymond on his ass would be counterproductive and probably leave him greased on the road.

So there was nothing to do but stay put and hope for the best.

Hell, that had been too much of his life, holding on and hoping for the best. When he'd finally gotten it together to make the best happen for himself, Raymond had started horning in on the Empire.

He settled into the trunk, getting comfortable, and hoping Raymond got tired of the game before they got to wherever they were going. If Raymond caught him in the trunk, it wasn't going to be pretty.

The car was nice, though, all class, a smooth, quiet ride—so quiet, Jack could hear the conversation going on inside. He couldn't understand it; the kidnappers only spoke Spanish. But he could hear it, and Jack was one fine listener in any language. If he was going to be stuck in this trunk all the way to Phoenix or something, the quicker he figured it out, the better off he'd be. He wanted to get away from Raymond, sure, but he didn't want to leave Denver. His big deal was going down in three days, if he could hold Raymond off that long, and once he unloaded all the merchandise out of the Empire, he had plans, big plans.

California plans. Beaches, bikinis, and babes. That was the life for him.

Something said inside the car caught his attention like a slap on the face, bringing him front and center and fully focused. He listened more intently, hoping whatever it was he'd thought he'd heard and recognized would be said again.

It was, and a big grin curved his mouth.

Oh, this was perfect.

Club Azteca is what he'd heard, the Aztec Club, which just happened to belong to Raymond's sworn enemies, the Locos.

No matter what else, the night had been damned interesting, and it was only going to get better—or a whole helluva lot worse.

Robin Rulz would have loved it.

Maybe Jane would, too, and damn, she really needed to know about the kidnapped woman. Someone stolen out of a fancy place like Toussi's was probably front-page news.

He lifted his butt in the confined space and slipped his cell phone out of his back pocket.

One ring, and somebody at the gallery answered.

"Hey," he whispered. "I need to talk to Jane Linden."

CONSECO had her. Fear unlike anything Kid had ever known gripped his brain and damn near paralyzed him. He leaned against Toussi's back door, holding his aching side, trying to pull himself together. That's all he needed, to split his gut—again.

"What do we do now?" Travis asked, his breath coming short.

They'd both run their hearts out in the last fifteen minutes, trying to stop a disaster that had already escalated beyond their control.

Suzi Toussi had seen the abduction, seen Nikki being hustled out the back door—but the crowd, *geezus*, the crowd had made it impossible for her to be heard, impossible for her to get to Nikki, to raise the alarm, to get anyone's attention. By the time Kid had reached the buffet tables, Nikki had been gone for at least a couple of minutes by Suzi's estimation, and the pandemonium Suzi had generated in those two minutes had only added to the confusion.

Travis had instantly understood what Suzi had struggled to get out between her choking sobs, and he'd been out the door almost before Kid. But there'd been no one in the alley. Nothing on Seventeenth. Travis had taken the south end of the street. Kid had taken the north, looking in every car, slapping them on the hood when the sight of him bearing down on them with a drawn gun hadn't been enough to stop them.

It had been insane. He knew it, like he knew a dozen cop cars were probably headed to Seventeenth and Wynkoop to arrest a pistol-wielding madman in the street. Good. He needed the police.

"We get help," Kid said, as much help as possible. The more people looking for Nikki, the better their chances of finding her.

Jesus Christ. Conseco had her. He didn't have a doubt about who Suzi had seen.

Forcing himself back into action, he pulled the door open. Inside, he heard Skeeter demanding details, information, asking questions of everyone, and trying her damnedest to organize the people who had seen anything from the hundreds who hadn't.

How many men had there been? she asked. *Who had seen what? When? Had anybody seen the car?*

"A black Cadillac pulled into the alley when I was helping the caterer bring in the last of the Merlot," a white-haired man said.

"Three men," a tall, bald man in an expensive suit said. He'd shoved his way forward, sideways through the crowd. "They stood out. I noticed them cruising through the gallery, looking at people's faces, not the paintings, which I thought was a little strange. They were all Hispanic, well dressed."

Suzi was on the phone to the police. "No. I need to talk to Lieutenant Loretta Bradley, now. It's an emergency."

Skeeter would have given her Loretta's name—a good call. They needed someone on their side who understood that they were dealing with SDF, and what that implied about the seriousness of the situation.

It all looked crazy to him, felt crazy. He'd been

holding Nikki in his arms less than twenty minutes ago. She'd been safe—and now . . . *Fuck!*

"Cocaine," he said. No one seemed to hear him, except Skeeter. She turned her gaze on him like a laser.

"Why?" she asked.

Frozen in fear or not, his brain was still working.

"Conseco doesn't have any connections in Denver," he said, his voice raw. "Nothing personal. That only leaves business. He won't know any names, but he can get them. His pipeline empties out here like it does everywhere else. There'll be people in that pipeline, big dealers, the biggest, and they'll bend over backwards to help him."

Skeeter swung her attention back to a girl Kid hadn't noticed before, a girl with silky dark hair and green eyes. "Who do you think moves the most cocaine through Denver? Bloods or Locos?"

"Parkside Bloods," the girl answered without hesitation. "After the Bloods, it'll be Baby Duce and the Locos, then the Playboys."

Travis, Kid noticed, had moved next to the girl's side.

"Yeah," Skeeter said. "Yeah, I agree. It's going to be the Blood King or Baby Duce, then Playboys, and that means we need to cover the River Lounge, the Aztec Club, and that hellhole of a house up off Highway eighty-five. Somebody at one of those places is going to know something."

And Kid was just the guy to get it out of them.

He met Skeeter's eyes. "We're going to have to

split up. Take Travis with you." He turned to the blond-haired man. "Are you up for this?"

"Yes."

The guy's lack of hesitation was all the convincing Kid needed. It was all he could afford.

He pulled his 9mm out from under his left arm and handed it over.

"This gun is loaded. There's a round chambered, and this is the safety." He pointed out the small lever. "Do you know how to use a pistol?"

"Yes." Again, the guy didn't hesitate.

Kid looked to Skeeter, who nodded. It's what he'd expected. Travis had been on the firing range with her this afternoon when he'd called.

"I'll take the River Lounge," he said, hoping the odds were in his favor. "You two take the Aztec. Suzi," he called to the gallery manager, who was still on the phone. "Have you got Lieutenant Bradley yet?"

The woman shook her head no.

Dammit.

"When you get her, tell her we think Juan Conseco, one of the biggest cocaine barons in Colombia, has kidnapped Nikki, and he might be heading to the River Lounge, the Aztec, or the Playboys' crib up on eighty-five. We need her on these places, especially the Playboys' place. Be sure and tell her about the Cadillac, and that it's me they're after. That'll help her put it in perspective."

Kid knew all he had to do was wait and Juan Conseco would get in touch with him. The word would go out to the DEA's Bogotá office, and come here to Toussi's, Conseco's only connections to him, telling him exactly where Nikki was being held, and what he had to do to get her back. But he also knew that every second she was in Conseco's power, she was in more danger than she could possibly conceive. She had an incredible imagination, but she had no idea what Conseco was capable of doing to her.

Kid did—and he wasn't waiting for anything. He was going to bring the whole fucking city down on Conseco's head, hard and fast.

"Let's go, Skeeter." He started to shove his way through the crowd, but stopped when Rocky rolled up.

Oh, geezus. He couldn't do this now, even less than he could have done it an hour ago.

He put out his hand anyway. He didn't know what else to do. "Mr. Solano."

Rocky took hold of his hand. His grip was amazingly strong.

"Kid Chaos, right?" The man looked devastated.

"Yes." He didn't know what else to say.

He started to release the guy's hand, but Rocky gripped him tighter and held his gaze, until it dawned on Kid that the guy probably knew a whole lot more about Kid Chaos Chronopolous than Kid knew about Rocky Solano, despite all Nikki's rambling at the Parrot.

It was odd, weird, being trapped in this awkward, awful moment with her fiancé.

Ex-fiancé, he reminded himself.

"If there's anything I can do," Rocky finally said.

"I'll let you know," Kid promised, feeling the seconds tick away. "I won't come back without her."

If the guy knew anything about him, he'd know he meant it.

Turning away, he headed toward the door with Skeeter and Travis, when the gallery's phone rang on the second line.

Everyone went silent. Kid hadn't expected Conseco to call this soon. It usually took hours. Kidnappers usually wanted to get everybody good and freaked out before they made their demands.

Within one ring, Suzi had switched lines and said hello. After listening for a second, she held it out toward Jane. Her voice trembled. "It's for you. A boy. He says he's in a car with the woman who was taken from Toussi's."

CHAPTER

22

NIKKI WAS SO frightened, she could hardly breathe. The men who had kidnapped her had shoved her into the backseat of a Cadillac and all but piled in on top of her. She was being squeezed from both sides, and one of the bastards had his hand on her knee.

"Nicole Alana McKinney," the bastard with his hand on her knee said with a bright, super-white smile, his voice silky smooth, his accent noticeably foreign. "I am Juan Conseco. I have gone to a great deal of trouble to find you. Do you know why?"

She shook her head, too terrified to speak, which she wouldn't have dreamed possible. Motor-mouth McKinney always blabbered when she was scared—but she was beyond scared, well into the fear-knows-no-bounds zone. The car was moving fast, heading west, over the freeway to God knew where, and her palms were sweating, her pulse fluttering.

"Because you, my dear, are going to bring me my heart's desire." With his bright smile firmly in place, he smoothed his hand over her knee and partway up her thigh.

A fresh bolt of fear froze her in place.

Oh, God. This was a nightmare, and it had all happened so fast, was so unbelievable. Why in the world would someone kidnap her?

The question no sooner formed than she knew the answer. These were the men from last night, from Panama, and unbelievably, they had tracked her to Denver.

"You are much prettier than your photograph," Conseco continued, pulling a piece of paper out his breast pocket and unfolding it for her to see.

Or not so unbelievably, she thought with a sick sense of realization and heightened fear. She'd left one of her flyers for the showing on Kid's kitchen table.

"Peter Chronopolous?" Conseco said. "You know him, no?"

Oh, God, Kid. She'd brought this horror down on his head.

"He will come for you, yes?"

"Yes," she managed, knowing it was true, knowing Conseco knew it was true.

The bright smile faded. "He is a killer, this man, *el asesino fantasma*. He has killed many men. He killed this man's son." Conseco gestured at the man on the other side of her.

Without thinking, Nikki looked, and immediately wished she hadn't. The man on the other side of her was grim-faced, his gaze full of burning hate. Like Conseco, he was expensively dressed in a black suit and tie.

"How many, Uncle, has *el asesino* killed? Besides your own dear Ruperto?"

"Between our men and the NRF freedom fighters, we have counted thirty-four dead since you ordered the other gringo crucified."

Nikki felt the blood drain from her face, the full, shocking realization of her predicament suddenly becoming horrifyingly clear. Kid's brother, J.T., had been crucified—and these were the men who had done it. The barbaric act had set a whole series of events in motion, including Kid's mission, and if what these men were telling her was true, the deaths of thirty-four men.

Thirty-four. It was nearly inconceivable, but in her heart she knew.

She knew what Kid had done.

"And how many ghost killers, Uncle?"

"Two, maybe three." The uncle's expression did not change, and he did not take his eyes off Nikki, not for one second.

She didn't take her eyes off him, either. She was mesmerized, like prey held in a snake's hypnotic gaze. His eyes were dark, and cold, and empty of everything except the fire of his hatred for her. He wanted her dead, and he wanted her to suffer. The message was clear and almost beyond her comprehension. They were strangers.

Thirty-four men in seven months. Oh, God, Kid. Hawkins had been with him, and Creed, but my god, what they'd done.

No wonder no one told her anything.

No wonder he hadn't come home.

No wonder, when she'd asked how everything had gone for him in Colombia, Creed had smiled that strangely dangerous smile he had and said only one word: "Successfully."

"Plus our two men from last night, Tío Drago," Conseco prompted.

"Thirty-six," Drago corrected himself.

Conseco grasped her chin in his hand and pulled her head around, making her give him her undivided attention. "This man will die, Nicole Alana. He is a plague on my family, my business, and my friends. And for you, his *novia*, his sweetheart, he will come to me."

"Yes," Nikki said, believing it with all her heart, counting on it, hating it, and helpless to stop it.

Kid would come for her—if he could find her. She hadn't recognized a landmark since they'd left LoDo, didn't know where they were except in a part of Denver where she'd never been, probably a part where she shouldn't be, given the sudden old and run-down look of the buildings.

Drago, the man was called who hated her, *Tío* Drago, and he was going to do something horrible to her. She knew it as sure as she was sitting there feeling her skin crawl and her heart pound. When the Cadillac turned into a dark alley and pulled to a stop behind an old brick building, a sob escaped her. Wherever they were, this was the place. She had an imagination. She read the newspapers, and terrifying things happened to women. It would be what she did to Travis, only worse, with real pain, and real horror, and real blood—hers.

When the door was opened and they pulled her out of the car, she made a desperate attempt to free herself, twisting and kicking and screaming, but even to her own ears, her screams were little more than gasps for breath, and her kicking and twisting got her nothing. She jerked backward, trying to pull her arm out of Conseco's grip. For her troubles, he cuffed her up the side of her head, the flat of his hand coming up hard against her cheek and ear and almost knocking her senseless. She slumped toward the ground, held up only by the arm he still hadn't released. Then Drago took her other arm, and the two of them dragged her toward a large opening that led into the basement of the building.

"Get the ropes out of the trunk," Drago said, and Nikki felt her stomach churn. Oh, God, how many times had she tied Travis up, subduing him with her make-believe bondage, and then "torturing" him with her lights and music and the strange journey of her artistic compulsions?

Too many, she thought. Too many times not to know what was going to happen in the basement. She wanted to throw up, something, anything, to make them let her go.

Behind her, even with her ears ringing, she heard a commotion taking place at the car when the trunk was opened—and then there was another hostage being dragged onto the platform that had lifted to fill the opening into the basement. It was a service elevator, and in the next second, it ground into action, heading back down into darkness.

KID stood absolutely still in the shadows of the Aztec's basement, his breath soft, even, soundless, every muscle coiled with barely repressed energy, his brain screaming.

Nikki.

They'd tied her wrists together and hung her from a ceiling rafter by a length of rope. She was only about a foot off the floor, but it might as well have been twenty. All her weight was hanging from her arms, and it had to hurt like hell. Her dress had ridden up, exposing her from the hips down.

She still had her underwear on, and her stiletto heels, and he was grateful for both those things—but not enough to spare anybody's life. They'd doused her in water from her head to her toes from a pump that drained into the floor, and she was shivering all over, her teeth chattering.

Savage, she'd called him this morning and again tonight.

She'd been right.

The boy who had phoned the gallery from the trunk of Conseco's Cadillac was next to her, hanging by another length of rope. A Rat, Travis had called him, Fast Jack Spencer, but obviously not fast enough to escape Conseco. A soaking wet Rat; he'd been doused, too.

Kid looked around the rest of the room. There were two guys watching the hostages, both Colombian, neither of them Juan Conseco or his right-hand man, his uncle Drago Conseco. A third man was standing by the stairs, a local guy. The clothes the men were wearing and their demeanors gave their different nationalities away in an instant. All three were armed.

He checked the far corners of the basement. If there was a loose narco-terrorist in the dark somewhere, and Kid started this rumble without knowing where, the guy might get off a shot before Kid could take him out. So he waited, and he watched, and he tried to hear over the loud music and the bar crowd packing the club upstairs. Nikki was the bait, and they weren't likely to kill the bait before they got what they wanted: him. But there was no reason for the boy to die by a stray bullet tonight, and Kid was going to do his damnedest to make sure Fast Jack didn't.

The boy's phone call had been the advantage Kid had needed.

A force of local DEA and FBI agents was forming somewhere in Denver, and Lieutenant Bradley had gotten authorization to use the SWAT team, but they hadn't arrived yet, and Kid wasn't waiting. The authorities wanted Conseco. He wanted Nikki, and the setup sucked for a hostage rescue.

There were three ways into the basement, and three ways out: the stairs, the service lift, and the elevator. Groceries, supplies, and booze were delivered to the Aztec's basement storeroom from the alley, via the service lift. He'd come down the stairs from inside the club. A small elevator on the west wall had to be how the supplies were hauled upstairs to the bar.

The service lift wasn't the best setup for a SWAT team takedown. Narrow, and surrounded by a virtual landscape of crates and boxes, it would be damn difficult to breach with the lightning-fast speed necessary for a successful rescue. The elevator was an absolute no-go, and the stairs weren't much better. He'd made it with a beer in his hand, a shit-eating grin on his face, and a line of bullshit ready to go.

He needed to get Nikki out, before things got complicated.

The sound of feet clattering on the rickety stairs had him shifting slightly to see who was coming down from the club on the main floor.

"Baby Duce headed your way," Skeeter said in his ear, her voice coming through the earpiece of his radio. "Shot-caller for the Locos. Guaranteed badass. He looks nervous as hell, like he could crap a kilo any second."

Crap a kilo?

Somebody needed to wash Skeeter's mouth out with soap.

But she was right. When the Latino came into view, he was pale, twitchy, looking like somebody who was trying way too hard to keep his cool, and he, too, was packing a piece.

Skeeter was upstairs in the Aztec bar with Travis, blending in with the crowd and watching the stairway door. Kid didn't know where Conseco was, but the Cadillac was parked at the front entrance to the club, so he was guessing the crime lord was upstairs somewhere. Not on the main floor with the band, and the booze, and the crowds of people, but probably higher up in the building. Skeeter said at one time there had been apartments for rent at the Aztec.

Juan Conseco in Denver. Smith was going to crap a dozen kilos when he heard. The feds were in a frenzy over the news. Kid could hardly believe it himself. The guy must really hate him to have followed him all the way to Denver.

Drago Conseco, if he was with Juan—and Kid's money said he was—had plenty of motive for leaving the safe confines of the Conseco compound in Medellín. Revenge.

Relatively safe compound, Kid amended. He hadn't had any trouble breaching the walls of Conseco's fortress to kill Diego Conseco, and he hadn't had any trouble tapping Drago's son, Ruperto, at his breakfast table.

"This is going from bad to worse," Skeeter said in his ear. "Here comes another Loco heading your way."

Five to one. The odds were piling up against him, but with the thirty-shot magazine on his .45, Kid knew he could take them all out and still have twenty-five shots left.

One of Conseco's guys was talking to Baby Duce. Kid couldn't hear what was being said, but neither of them looked happy. Conseco's guy was grim-faced and angry, and Duce looked scared and angry, like he'd screwed up. Baby Duce kept pointing at Fast Jack Spencer, which made Kid wonder just how much trouble the Rats had gotten themselves into. The girl at the gallery, Jane, had said the Parkside Bloods were looking to take the Rats down tonight, but that wasn't Kid's problem.

Nikki looked terrified, and almost blue from the cold. That was Kid's problem, and he was damn close to letting it make him do something stupid. Fast Jack was shaking with the cold, too, and he looked plenty scared, but he wasn't terrified, far from it. He'd been watching everybody and everything, his gaze narrow and calculating, and Kid knew if he gave the boy half a chance, Fast Jack would take it and run.

He scanned the room one more time. There weren't any other narco-terrorists in the basement. They would have come out into the light at the start of the argument, especially when the odds had started shifting in the Locos' favor.

With an abrupt gesture, Baby Duce backed off, and he kept backing off, all the way to the stairs, taking his homies with him.

In less than a minute, Kid was left with just the two Colombians. It took him far less than that to lean out from behind the tower of boxes and squeeze off four silenced shots, less than two seconds, two body shots apiece. The Colombians dropped to the floor.

And *kee-rist*, there he was, killing people in front of Nikki again.

In five steps he had her in his arms and was reaching up to cut her free.

"K-kid." She was shivering uncontrollably, her voice raw with fear.

"Shhh, baby. I'm getting you out of here." His knife went through the rope, and she collapsed into his arms.

Without letting go of her, or taking time to cut the bindings on her wrists, he stepped over to the boy and cut him free. Fast Jack dropped like a cat to the floor and, just as Kid had predicted, took off for the service lift to the alley, working the knots on the rope around his wrists with his teeth. With Nikki in his arms, Kid was right behind him.

The boy scrambled onto the lift and hit the UP button, but the doors no sooner opened above him, out into the alley, than somebody yelled, "It's Fast

Jack!" and all hell broke loose with a burst of automatic fire careening into the basement.

Geezus. Kid dove with Nikki behind a tower of crates and hoped to hell they were full of something that would stop an automatic round. Almost immediately, Jack landed on top of them, a pile of fast-moving arms and legs.

Kee-rist. What kind of trouble was the kid in that everybody wanted to grease his ass?

The service lift was grinding its way up, but he could hear the guys in the alley already jumping down onto it, not waiting for it to come to a stop. With one swift cut, he freed Nikki's hands, held on to one of them, and took off running for the stairs.

"Five Locos coming down the stairs, heading your way," Skeeter's voice echoed through his earpiece.

Fuck. He made a fast right at the next tower of boxes and sprinted with her to the elevator. Fast Jack, the little bugger, was already inside and reaching for a floor button. Kid slammed into the door before it could close, then shoved Nikki inside, behind him.

"Main floor, Jack," he said to the kid, now praying for the damn doors to shut. It sounded like the guys from the alley were invading. "And if you ever try to cut me out again, *I'll* be the one who takes you down."

Jack at least had the decency to look remorseful. "You were headed for the stairs, not the elevator."

"The stairs got busy." He shrugged out of his jacket and put it on Nikki, making sure she got her arms inside the sleeves. The boy was shivering, too, but he was a guy, and he was on his own. Besides, he looked tougher than snot—wiry, fierce, even a little wild-eyed, but still not terrified.

"So's the damn main floor gonna be busy in about thirty seconds," Jack said.

"So where are you going?"

"To the roof," Jack said.

Well, they sure as hell weren't going to get there very damn fast. The elevator was moving at a crawl.

Kid pulled Nikki under his arm and squeezed her, trying to impart some warmth, while still keeping his gun hand free.

"What's on the roof?"

"A fire escape that runs all the way down the north side of the building," the boy said.

Sounded good to Kid.

"Talk to me, Nikki," he said, shifting his attention to the woman shivering in his arms. "Are you okay?"

"Y-yes." She nodded, her teeth chattering.

He'd have to take her at her word for now. They were far from out of this mess.

"You need to get her out of here, man," the boy said. "Before the Bloods and Locos and the rest of those badass uptown barrio boys chew up the Aztec Club. They ain't gonna like that you capped two of their guys."

"Who was shooting at you from the alley?" Kid asked. The gunmen had yelled the boy's name.

"Parkside Bloods."

Of course. The Parkside Bloods had Fast Jack at the top of their menu tonight. "What about the Locos?"

"All upstairs."

"Badass uptown barrio boys?"

The boy shrugged. "You left two dead ones in the basement, man. I don't know where the rest of them are."

"Do you know how many there were?"

"Five got out of the Cadillac with the woman."

That left three from the kidnapping crew, and depending on where Conseco was in the building, the cocaine king might or might not know that his whole night had just gone straight to hell.

"Skeeter," he said into his mike. "Two Colombians down. At least three more still alive. I've got Nikki and the boy. We're in a service elevator that runs up the west wall. Can you see the elevator door?"

The sound of a woman screaming delayed her response. He knew it wasn't Skeeter. Skeeter did not scream.

Then shots sounded.

"*Holy shit*, Kid. I've got Bloods coming in the back, and Locos pouring in the front, and a whole bunch of people trying to get out of the middle."

"Where are you?"

"Behind the bar with my head down, cowboy. Do not get off on this floor. I repeat, do not get off on this floor."

"Where's Travis?"

"AWOL. On his own. I lost him."

"Looks like your plan wins," he said to the boy. To Skeeter he said, "Any sign of the feds or Lieutenant Loretta?"

"Not down here in the slopped beer and old cigarette butts, and that's about as far as I can see, until the shooting stops. This is bad, Kid. Turf war galore."

"We're headed toward the top floor and will come down the fire escape on the north side of the building."

"Roger."

He had Nikki, and he was taking her out of there. The feds could have Conseco.

CHAPTER

23

THE HIGHER THEY ROSE in the building, the quieter it became, eerily so. Then the indicator lights on the control board flickered and died, and the elevator shuddered to a stop.

"Wh-what happened, Kid?" Nikki's hand tightened in his. The boy swore under his breath.

"I don't know." *Dammit.* "Skeeter," he said into his mike, but got no response. "Skeeter."

Her radio was either dead or turned off, and he couldn't imagine that she'd turned it off. He wasn't going to freak, though. Skeeter knew how to take care of herself. He hoped to hell Travis did.

He reached inside his jacket pocket for his cell phone, but couldn't get any reception—nothing. No one could hear him now.

"Are we trapped?" Nikki asked, huddling closer to him. She was shaking like a leaf.

"No, honey. I can get us out of here." Guaran-fucking-teed. There wasn't a goddamn elevator in the world he couldn't take apart. He had Nikki, and she was alive, and that was all that mattered. Everything else was merely incidental—but he still needed a plan.

A tiny red dot of light appeared inside the elevator and started moving over the walls. He followed it to its source—the boy.

"Night vision flashlight?" he asked.

"Yeah. I always keep one with me. I work in the dark a lot. It's handy for seeing what the hell you're doing."

No shit.

"Give me a hand," he said, digging the tips of his fingers into the break between the doors. Between him and Fast Jack, they pried the doors open, but there was nothing but wall on the other side.

"Show me the ceiling." That was their next best bet for making their escape.

The ceiling panels were screwed in, the screws exposed through age, not design, with the inside of the elevator stripped down to basics.

The boy proved invaluable again, when he produced a knife. Not a street fighter's knife, but a handy-dandy, twenty-function Swiss Army knife.

"You keep this with you all the time, too?"

"Just in case," the boy said.

Yeah, Kid usually had a whole lot of "just in case" stuff, too, but tonight he mostly had guns, and they sure as hell couldn't shoot their way out of an elevator.

Once they got one of the ceiling panels off, Kid boosted himself on top of the elevator; finally, a bit of luck. With Fast Jack's flashlight, the beam of which was hardly bigger than a quarter, he could see they weren't very far from a floor.

"Jack, get your butt up here," he said, reaching his hand down.

Jack took hold, and Kid swung him up. *Geez*, he doubted if the boy weighed a hundred and twenty pounds, but he was strong. When Kid put him on his shoulders, Jack didn't have any trouble prying the doors to the floor open all by himself. Light flooded into the elevator shaft, and like the Rat he was, Jack scrambled off Kid's shoulders into the hall, and disappeared from sight—instantly, without a backward glance.

Hell. Kid wasn't going to worry about him. The boy obviously knew how to take care of himself in a bad situation. He just hoped Jack didn't blow everything and get them all in more trouble than they were already in.

"Come on, babe." He reached down for Nikki and pulled her onto the top of the elevator, and then, for a couple of seconds, no more, he just quit—quit worrying, quit fighting, quit thinking. All he did was hold her, and bury his face in her hair, and breathe her in, and thank God that she wasn't hurt.

"Oh, Kid," she sighed, melting against him. "I knew you'd find me. I-I just didn't know if it would be in time. They were going to . . . going to . . ."

"Shhh, Nikki." He tightened his arms around her. He knew even better than she did what Conseco would have done to her, and he didn't want to hear the words spoken out loud. He didn't have the strength for that. He'd been in Colombia for too long. He'd seen too much.

"How did you get to the club so fast?" she asked. "How did you know?"

"The boy," he said. "Fast Jack. He called from the trunk of the Cadillac and told us exactly where you were being taken."

"He called you from the trunk?"

"Yeah. Crazy, huh?" It *was* crazy. "He was hiding in there and ended up in the middle of your kidnapping."

She let out another heavy sigh. "God, Kid. It's been crazy since you showed up at Sandovals' last night."

He knew that, too, and he wasn't too proud of it.

"Don't worry, Nikki. This is the last of it. I swear. I'll get you out of here, and you'll be out of trouble, forever." Because he was going to hunt Conseco down and kill him—no matter how far he had to go, no matter what he had to do. Conseco had made one big-ass mistake leaving Colombia, and if Kid didn't get him tonight, someday, the bastard would make another. When he did, Kid would be there.

"Come on. Let's keep moving." Revenge would have to wait. Right now, he had to think about Nikki.

Standing up, he boosted himself up into the hall, and then reached down for her. The sign next to the elevator showed a number three. They were on the third floor. The Aztec was five stories high.

Once she was up, he had them on the move. She started to speak, but he put his finger to his lips. He didn't know who was on the floor with them.

The elevator was on the west wall, and the fire escape was on the north, so he checked all the rooms on the left side of the hall, dragging her with him, moving fast, but none of them had the fire escape. It had to be all the way to the east, near the northeast corner, but when they got back out into the hall, there was nothing but a blank wall to the east. He had to find another way.

Shit. He was starting to feel like a rat in a maze.

At the first intersecting hallway, he saw a red exit light at the far end. Holding her hand, he took off, heading that way. They could get to the second floor from the stairwell, avoiding the firefight on the first, and still get out of the building. Climbing down from the third floor was too risky with Nikki on his back, not when she was shivering and might be too cold to hold on.

Jack, the little Rat, really had disappeared, and Kid wished he knew how and where. Disappearing was exactly what he wanted to do with Nikki. Dead Colombians in the basement, gang war in the bar, and Juan Conseco somewhere up here on the upper floors—Kid wanted the fuck out of the Aztec Club.

The instant they entered the stairwell, he heard gunfire, and it sounded a lot closer than three floors down. *Shit*. The gang war had made it to the second floor. He wasn't going to run a gauntlet of bullets with Nikki in tow, so he took them up, but didn't get more than a couple of steps before a door banged open below them, and all hell broke loose. It sounded like dozens of people were fighting their way up the stairs. It only took him a second to figure out why.

"Kid," Nikki said, turning and looking behind them. "I think the building is on fire. I smell smoke."

The unmistakable smell of it came to him on the air, and just as quickly, a blast of searing heat rolled up the stairwell.

Geezus. "Come on, babe. Let's *go*." Holding her hand, he took off up the stairs.

If things had been great before, they were perfect now. The friggin' gangsters had set the club on fire.

Another door banged open—the second-floor door, he guessed—and the noise level tripled, girls screaming and squealing, guys shouting, feet pounding, lots of shoving, pushing, and swearing.

Kid could run, but a frozen, shivering Nikki trying to do stairs in a pair of stiletto heels practically put them in reverse. He swung her up on his shoulders in a fireman's carry, the banana-clipped pistol still in his hand, and he took off.

He was fast, a verifiable track star, but within seconds, two Locos in do-rags passed him like he was standing still, and the horde kept coming, panic turning them into world-class Olympians. It was going to be a freaking circus on the roof, especially since from what he could see, the guns-to-dudes ratio was running at about fifty percent.

Worse than all of it was the smoke. It was quickly getting thicker, becoming a pall. The people below him were struggling to breathe. Drug lords and gang-bangers were one thing. Fire was another. It struck solid, cold dread in his heart. He couldn't outshoot it or outwit it, and he wasn't at all sure he was going to be able to outmaneuver it. Going up in a burning building was a bad idea, and he knew it, but there sure as hell was no way to go down, not in the stairwell, which was beginning to feel like *it* was on fire.

He hoped to hell Skeeter had gotten out of the bar.

At the fourth-floor exit, he fought his way to the door, but it didn't open. Doing his best to hold back the tide of people threatening to sweep him and Nikki away, he put her down next to him, in the small eddy of space he made with his body.

"Hold on to me!" he yelled above all the noise, and felt her hands tighten into fists on his shirt. Then he put his shoulder to the door. It gave a little, which encouraged him, so he hit it again, harder. Something was blocking the door from the other side. If he could move it just a few inches, he and Nikki could slip through. Their chances of getting out of the building from the fourth floor were better than from the fifth, and the roof was going to be a disaster.

Then the worst happened. One second Nikki was behind him, holding on to him, and the next she was gone, swept up in the tide of panic and people rolling like a juggernaut toward the top of the building.

"Kid!" she screamed, then disappeared from sight.

Shit. Kid threw himself into the crowd, using every physical advantage he had to fight his way up the stairs. In glimpses and pieces, he saw her up ahead of him, barely keeping to her feet, and his first fear became that she would get trampled. Then someone knocked her down, and the next time he saw her, she'd lost his coat and her dress was torn.

Goddammit. He had to get to her—but he couldn't, and the smoke and the heat were getting worse.

When he burst out onto the roof, it wasn't much better, but he didn't think Nikki was behind him. Everything in the stairwell had been sweeping up, carried by the force of all the people trying to escape.

There were dozens of them, maybe a hundred, coughing, wiping tears from their eyes, running this way and that, trying to figure out which way to go. But he didn't see Nikki anywhere.

Then he felt a stray breeze cut through the smoke billowing up all around. So did everyone else, and still caught in the crowd, they all stumbled toward it. In just a few feet, he realized that despite all the smoke, only the front half of the building was on fire. The flames were bound to spread and turn the whole building into a chimney, but they hadn't yet, and help had to be on the way. Loretta's SWAT team and the DEA, the FBI, all those guys must be getting close.

"There's a fire escape," someone yelled, and everybody swarmed in the guy's direction.

Kid held himself against the crowd, searching faces. Then he saw her, and his blood ran cold. Two men had hold of her arms, dragging her along. The third had a gun to her head. They were all moving with the crowd, heading for the fire escape, and in the next instant they disappeared into the smoke and all the people.

"*Conseco!*" he shouted, his feet moving him forward, slowly at first, then faster. "*Juan Conseco!*"

It was hard to make himself heard over the sounds of the fire and all the crying and shouting and running. It was even harder to keep Nikki and the Colombians in sight. Smoke was drifting everywhere. People were in the way. His gun was drawn, ready, but there wasn't a clear shot, not in the smoke and confusion.

"*Conseco!*" He had to get them to stop. "*Soy el asesino fantasma! ¡Estoy aquí!*" *I am the ghost killer. I am here.*

Here for you, you sonuvabitch.

He called out again, working his way through the

crowd, and when the smoke cleared again, he saw them.

They'd stopped and closed ranks, and they were waiting, looking for the man they'd come to kill.

Nikki had gone limp and was being held up only by the large man who had his arm around her waist. Juan Conseco was on the man's left.

The third man was nowhere in sight.

A dozen people were between him and the Colombians, and Kid waited for the space to clear.

Over by the fire escape, it was pandemonium. But Kid didn't give the chaos a thought. His mission, the focus of every ounce of energy he had and every breath he took, was staring at him from behind the two semiautomatic pistols pointed through the crowd, straight at his head.

That was their first mistake.

"*El asesino fantasma*," Conseco called out over the distance separating them. A smile crossed his face. "So, my ghost killer, in the end it comes to this? That *el asesino* is outgunned?"

Kid didn't think so, not with only two guns to his one, and Nikki useless as cover.

A fresh surge of panicked club-goers stumbled between him and Conseco before the first group finished passing through, all of them doubled over, coughing from the smoke, and oblivious to the danger they were in.

Kid bided his time, counting the split seconds before he'd have a clear shot.

Then he felt the muzzle of a gun come to rest on the back of his neck.

The third man.

"Drop your weapon."

"Tío Drago." Conseco's smile broadened. "*Un momento, por favor.*" A moment, please.

One moment, please, before Conseco let Uncle Drago blow his head off, Kid figured.

Fuck. He wasn't worried about himself. Having your head blown off was a pretty fucking painless way to go, especially with the muzzle pressed against a guy's brain stem. Hell, no. He wasn't going to feel a goddamn thing. But that wasn't what was going to happen to Nikki.

Kid let the .45 drop to the ground, then took a breath, staying calm.

Conseco wanted a moment for a reason, and every single moment he took worked in Kid's favor.

"Thirty-six men, *el asesino*," the cocaine king called out, "and still you have failed. Your brother's true killer is alive and well, my friend."

Fuck you, Kid thought.

Conseco's smile faded, and Kid saw all the hatred he felt for the man being returned in full measure.

"For the true believer," the man said, his voice low and deadly, "the sign of the cross is the sign of salvation."

With a slow, deliberate motion, Conseco drew a line down the middle of his chest, then another from side to side.

Kid got the message, loud and clear, and he took another breath, waiting.

"It will be a bloody salvation for the woman, too, you fucking ghost killer."

Double fuck you.

"Drago—" Conseco began, but Kid had already moved, twisting and striking out at Drago even as the man fired. The shot went wild, but somebody sure as shit hit Drago. Kid felt the slug impact the man at his back, felt him slump over.

Another shot came out of somewhere, then another. Kid saw the man holding Nikki stagger back, his hand coming up to his chest. He saw Nikki fall to the ground.

And he saw Conseco's eyes grow wide in shock as he looked down at himself. Then another shot hit him, and another smacked into the man who had dropped Nikki.

A fucking 9mm, Kid thought, diving for the .45 caliber he'd dropped. In the split second it took him to fire off two shots of his own, the party was over.

Nikki was pushing herself up, coughing. Kid raced over and knelt by her side, drawing her to him, while he scanned the crowd, trying to figure out who had fired.

From out of the smoke and darkness came just about the last person he would have ever expected: Nikki's angel, Travis James, holding Kid's 9mm like he knew what he was doing.

And he obviously did.

"Are we clear?" Travis asked.

"Clear," Kid said, still not quite believing what had happened. "Skeeter?"

"We got separated in the bar, but the last time I saw her, she was kicking down a door."

"Good girl," Kid said.

"The best," Travis agreed, kneeling next to Nikki and shrugging out of his coat. "Hey, babe."

"Hey," she said weakly.

Travis put his coat around her, and Kid pulled her closer. Her arms went around him.

"We've got to get off this roof," he said. There were still people running around all over, jostling for the fire escape.

"Yeah," Travis agreed, looking around. He started to rise, when they both heard it, the sound of sirens.

The cavalry, the fire department, and Lieutenant Loretta had arrived.

CHAPTER
24

***

SKEETER HAD KICKED a door down, but not without getting a little sooty and scorched first.

"*Geezus*, Kid. When you bring a party to town, you really bring a party to town."

They were all sitting in Kid's 1967 Pontiac GTO, a beautiful beast named Corinna, watching the Aztec burn down, the gangsters get busted, and Fast Jack trying to talk Lieutenant Loretta out of taking him downtown.

The heater was going full blast, and Nikki was cuddled up next to him in the front seat, her wrists bandaged by one of the ambulance crews.

Loretta wanted to talk to him, to talk to all of them. It had been a helluva night, again, and it was far from over. He was going two for two, and still racking up kills, but his weren't the ones he was thinking about.

"God, I couldn't believe it when that Blood set his Zippo to those damn curtains. Everybody knows the Aztec is a dump just waiting to burn." For a change, it was Skeeter in motormouth mode, sitting in the backseat with Travis, almost single-handedly carrying the conversation.

"*Was* a dump," Kid said, watching another whoosh of flame shoot up from the roof.

Gang wars and cocaine kings had been a lethal mix.

He lifted his gaze to the rearview mirror and looked at Travis. *What in the hell*, he wanted to ask, *has Skeeter been teaching you down on the firing range?*

Plenty, was the obvious answer, but Kid would bet anything that Superman's hand had been in a lot of what he'd seen tonight. Shooting well was one thing. Shooting to kill was an entirely different animal, and nobody taught the importance of winning the fight better than Christian Hawkins. Every day, in every way, no matter the odds, no matter what you had to do—win first.

Travis had won the fight for all of them.

From the backseat, the guy shifted his attention from Skeeter and met Kid's gaze in the mirror.

Kid gave him a short nod, and after a long, thoughtful look, Travis nodded back. Then he returned his attention to Skeeter.

"Once I got the door open, it was an *ex-o-dus*, I tell you. I almost got run over, getting out of there."

Skeeter continued her ramble, with no end looking to be in sight, until Lieutenant Loretta's knock on the driver's side window.

"You know the drill, Peter," she said, bending down to look in the window after he rolled it open. "Downtown. My office. Let's go. And Mr. James, if your life is going to get any more exciting, you're going to need a concealed carry permit."

Yes, sir, it was going to be one helluva long night.

NIKKI was safe, Travis told himself for the hundredth time.

Kid was safe. Skeeter was safe. The party was over. The gallery was a mess.

And he'd killed three men, unless those last two went on Kid's tally. Travis knew for sure Kid's rounds had put them down, where they'd still been standing after his.

Everyone had left Toussi's, even Suzi. There was no one left except Jane—and him, because he'd come here instead of going home after the endless debriefing at the police station.

He brought his hand up and dragged it back through his hair, looking around. All these paintings of him, he thought, and none of them quite right anymore.

His life had taken a turn.

"Travis?" Jane said, crossing the gallery.

In answer, he held his hand out to her, and to his

amazement, she walked over to him and took it in her own.

"Do you want to sit together?" she asked.

"Sure." Sitting was probably a good thing for him to do for a while. He needed to think.

Together, they walked over to one of the gallery's large upholstered couches, and again, she surprised him by sitting close and letting him have his arm around her.

She was warm and solid, and after a moment, he pulled her deeper into his arms, holding her close.

"That was scary tonight," she said. "What happened to Nikki."

"Yeah." And she didn't know the half of it.

"I don't want to be alone tonight," she said. "Not in here. Not after what happened."

"I thought you might like some company." It's why he'd come back, to check on her, make sure she was okay, knowing she might not want to be alone.

"That's not an invitation or anything."

He grinned. He'd known that, too. "Yeah, I pretty much figured out you didn't want to sleep with me, when you told me I scared you and ran off."

"I never said I didn't want to sleep with you."

He slanted her a look. "Do you?"

Sex would be so wonderful right now. To just get lost in her body. To be warm and naked and let the whole thing get completely hot and out of control.

He'd love to do that.

Really love it.

"No. Not tonight. I still haven't figured some things out."

Well, he couldn't blame her there. He, too, had a few things he hadn't figured out.

"About me?" he asked, just in case he could explain something, anything, and have a chance to sleep with her. It would be so perfect. He'd take such good care of her.

"No, about me."

Yeah, well, she was pretty much a mystery. That was for damn sure, he thought, letting out a sigh.

"Sometimes talking to someone else can help you figure stuff out about yourself," he said. It was true. He got paid seventy-five dollars an hour to listen to people talk about themselves. Once he had his doctorate, that price was going through the roof. He wasn't greedy. He just had plans that he wasn't sure the traditional medical community would be interested in financing. Or rather, he'd had plans. He wasn't sure now, what he needed to do.

Nikki had been kidnapped, right out from under his nose. What kind of a dream world had he been living in?

He needed to find out.

Slacking off in Boulder, safely ensconced in academia, he'd thought his EMT work was about as gritty as it could get. It was important; he knew that. But it was also always after the fact. People got hurt. People died. And after whatever awful thing that was going to happen happened, he went in and picked up the pieces.

So who tried to keep the pieces from breaking in the first place? What kind of man did that take?

"And sometimes it's nice to just be quiet with someone," she said.

"Sometimes."

"It's almost morning. Can you stay until then?"

She was so beautiful, so different, and he had a feeling her pieces had been broken lots of times and nobody had come to help her pick them up.

He needed to think about that, and about what had happened tonight, about what he'd done, and how easily he had done it. He hadn't questioned his actions for a second. There hadn't been time. Skeeter had spent months working with him, Skeeter and Hawkins, and tonight, when he'd finally made it to the roof, when he'd seen Nikki hanging from that bastard's arm, limp, and when he'd seen Kid with a gun being held to his head, there had been no hesitation, no decision to be made, and no regrets. He'd done as he'd been trained.

"Yes," he said. "I can stay until morning."

"NIKKI?" Kid asked, coming back across his loft to where he'd left her in a pile of blankets and pillows in front of the fireplace. He had a mug of cocoa for her, and another shot of tequila and a beer for himself.

It was way past wind-down time.

"Hmmmm?"

"Are you still awake?" He'd bundled her up pretty heavily after her bath, and after setting their drinks on the table, he got under the blankets with her.

"Hmmmm," she sighed, wrapping her arms around him.

He'd brought her to Steele Street after they'd finished at the police station, wanting the rock-solid security of the place. Conseco was dead, and Drago, and Kid hoped to hell the bounty had died with them, but only time would tell.

Travis had gone back to Toussi's to be with the dark-haired girl; at least, Kid figured the girl had been the reason he'd gone there. Skeeter had been too wired to come home, and she'd hit the streets, taking Corinna and heading toward the Midnight Doubles, the illegal car races that took place east of the city, but Kid had learned a long time ago not to worry about her.

Besides, he had another concern right now, more pressing than whether or not Skeeter was going to smoke the competition at the Doubles.

Kid had rings.

Two of them. Gold.

Reaching up, he slipped the chain holding the rings off over his head.

"Nikki, do you remember the night we met?"

She lifted her head from where she was resting against his chest and looked up at him.

"Yes."

"And the story you told me, about the pony and your parents?" Her parents had died in an earthquake while excavating Inca ruins in Peru, and as a young child, Nikki had thought she could save them, if only she'd had a pony to take her to South America.

"Yes." She tilted her head to one side, her expression growing more curious.

"I never forgot that story."

"The pony story." She let out a small laugh. "Kids think the craziest things, don't they."

"Not so crazy, Nikki," he said. "Having a pony really helped."

She grew very still in his arms, then her gaze fell on the rings in his hand.

A tremor went through her, and she brought her hand up to her mouth.

"They're yours now, Nikki, yours, and Regan's, and your grandfather's."

"Oh, Kid."

"They're pretty scratched, and I didn't disturb them any more than necessary, your parents, I mean," he said, feeling her tremble, watching disbelief turn to understanding and then sadness in her eyes. "I only lifted their fingers, just a little, just enough to get the rings off." A lot more than that had happened, and he'd tell her grandfather everything, about how unstable the dig had been, about how the whole thing had damn near slid down the mountain while he'd been in the grave site where Rob and Lisa McKinney had died. Wilson would want to know, but not Nikki.

She didn't like bones, and she wouldn't want to hear about the ones that had been broken, or about how her mother's hand had been crushed. He would protect her from that much—because he loved her.

She reached for the rings and took them into her hand, letting the chain slide through her fingers.

"You did it, Kid." Awe turned her voice soft, tremulous.

"Yeah." He had. Against the odds, when it seemed that he wouldn't be able to do anything else for her ever again, he'd found her parents and salvaged their wedding rings. It had been harder than he would ever tell her, but looking at her face, it was all so simply perfect.

"Oh, Kid," she said, closing her hand around the gold bands and holding them close to her heart. "How can I ever thank you?"

And the answer to that was also so simply perfect.

"Marry me, Nikki. Be mine." He cupped her cheek in his palm and smoothed his thumb across her soft skin. "Be mine forever."

CHAPTER

25

❖

"Isn't this great, honey?"

Nikki peeked out from under a pile of blankets and quilts and felt the cold, frigid air settle over the top half of her face, the only part of her she'd dared to reveal. Even her hair hurt, it was so damn cold.

"We're in a yurt, Kid." A yurt, in the middle of nowhere, miles from the nearest road, even more miles from anything that remotely resembled civilization, and her husband was standing in the open doorway, in what she had to admit was some very fine-fitting black long underwear, grinning like a fool.

God, he looked like a piece of sculpture, a long back, buns-o'-steel, thighs that made her melt, the whole six feet of him encased in some special, high-tech, warmth-retaining spandex stuff.

Well, it worked. She was starting to retain a little warmth just by looking at him.

"Yeah, a yurt. Isn't it cool?" He turned back to look out the door, at snow-covered mountains, and snow-covered trees, at the snow piled up outside the door and their snow-covered skis, and at more snow falling from the sky, big, fat flakes. "I always wanted to do this, like since I was ten years old. I couldn't believe it when you said you wanted to go camping in a yurt. I mean, it freaking amazed me."

She'd freaking amazed herself, too. She'd never considered herself a very good liar, but she'd sure pulled this one off. He'd obviously forgotten the night he'd let his heart's desire for this particular adventure slip.

She would never forget it. Not the whole wild twenty-four hours. He'd saved her life, hers and Fast Jack Spencer's, who was incredibly darn lucky to have ended up in juvie instead of the state penitentiary. Skeeter had worked some magic there, along with Christian Hawkins, to keep Jack out of the slammer. But his debt to society was a long way from being paid. He was going to be stuck in the ragged wasteland of western Colorado for the summer, digging dinosaur bones for her grandfather in his jobs-training program for criminally convicted juveniles. The rest of the Rats had been picked up and were in the social services system. It was going to be a long process getting them all sorted out, or in many cases, getting their family situations sorted out. A few of the older ones had simply disappeared, slipped free, unwilling to be wards of the state, even more unwilling to go back to the bad family situations that had put them on the street in the first place.

Secretly, Nikki thought Jane Linden and Fast Jack deserved some kind of medal for feeding and housing all those kids with little more than their wits and sticky fingers to get them by.

Jane, of course, had not been charged. All she'd tried to do was help a bad situation that had long since been out of her control. Nikki didn't know what was going to happen between the girl and Travis, but she was hoping they could work through the gulf seeming to separate them. At least that had been her hope before she'd gone to Panama. Since the night the Aztec had burned, and what had happened there, Travis had become more and more withdrawn, spending more time with Christian Hawkins than with anyone, even disappearing for days on end sometimes. For the first time since they'd become best friends, he was holding himself apart from her, keeping his own council, his own secrets. The last few times she'd tried to paint him, it had been hopeless.

She knew what had done it: the killings at the Aztec. He didn't seem to be suffering any ill effects from his actions, but he'd been changed. She didn't understand it, not really, even though Kid had explained it to her the best he could, before finally just giving her the quick, two-word bottom line—guy stuff—and his advice: Leave the guy alone; he'll figure it out.

She and Kid had figured out all kinds of stuff, fun stuff, serious stuff, how to fall even more in love stuff.

"What a cool honeymoon, huh?"

Oh, yeah, it was cool. Below zero last night. She didn't think a honeymoon could get much cooler than theirs, not and still have two live honeymooners in it.

Yurt camping.

Had she been insane?

"Are you ready for some coffee, babe?" He *finally* closed the door, for all the good it did.

"Yes, please." God, what an incredible liar she'd turned out to be all the way around. She'd said "yes, please" to Kid's coffee, as in "Please give me a cup of sludge, Kid," except Kid's camping coffee was even worse than his at-home coffee. It was instant, to match the milk.

Instant milk.

A small shudder went through her at the thought. What she wanted was a caramel macchiato with steamed whole milk and whipped cream on top.

He'd stoked the fire up and gotten it going before he'd decided to stand in the open door and freeze his whatevers off, and she could almost feel the tendrils of heat reaching the bed.

Almost, but not quite, not yet, but the bed, well, she had to admit there were some benefits to yurt camping, especially luxury yurt camping, like gazillion-thread-count sheets and silk-and-velvet duvets on down quilts. For a price, the yurt keepers would have snowmobiled in a caramel macchiato, but what she and Kid had wanted more than designer coffee and gourmet meals delivered was privacy—and her peek out the door had proved they definitely had privacy for as far as the eye could see.

There was nobody out there, not until the next yurt, or back at the lodge, which was a good three miles down the trail.

Three miles on cross-country skis, she'd discovered, wasn't as daunting as she'd expected, even in the snowstorm that had caught them halfway to the yurt yesterday. And "Luxury Rough," as their package was described, wasn't all that rough, not with Kid Chaos ramrodding the expedition.

For starters, he carried all the gear and didn't know the meaning of the word lost. Snowstorm or not, he'd guided them along a trail she couldn't even see until they'd made it safe and sound to the yurt. As a matter of fact, she hadn't even been able to see the yurt, until he'd opened the door. It had been such a whiteout, and she'd been so deeply huddled in her hat and coat, like a turtle, with barely her eyes peeking out, kind of like this morning. As far as getting lost, there was no such thing anymore, he'd told her, not since the widespread availability of the Global Positioning System.

Could have fooled her. She was lost, lying right

there in bed with a GPS on the table next to her. She didn't have a clue where they were, other than the San Juan range of the Rocky Mountains, somewhere outside of Telluride, Colorado.

Of course, she didn't have his somewhat obsessive need for bearings, and positions, and lat-longs. She was with him, and that was as "unlost" as she'd ever been. She'd thought he was the storm in her life, but she'd discovered he was really the rock, the one steady thing she could hold on to when all else failed. He would go through hell itself to find her and keep her safe. She'd watched him do it, and watching Kid Chaos fight his way through hell was a profoundly amazing sight.

"You know what we could do today?" Kid asked.

Stay in bed?

"We could build a snow cave." He was grinning like that long-ago ten-year-old.

Snow cave. Hmmm. She ran that around in her brain for a couple of seconds, but couldn't get any further than "Why?"

There was snow everywhere, all of it beautifully arranged by Mother Nature. She didn't really see the need to shove it around and get her mittens wet. Actually, it was too cold for her mittens to get wet, and she had special mittens now, with liners and over-mittens, and doodads for hooking them to her coat. She had a lot of things she'd never had before, like gaiters and skins and Gore-Tex. The only thing silky in her honeymoon wardrobe was her own set of long underwear, which he'd shimmied her out of early last night.

"Because the snow is perfect for packing. We could build a really nice one this morning, and then have lunch in there, or spend the night."

Her eyes widened in alarm. He had to be kidding. They were already in a *yurt*, for crying out loud. They were already camping in the wilderness, and he wanted to take the whole honeymoon expedition down a notch to a . . . a *snow cave*?

God, even the words "honeymoon expedition" were an oxymoron, or should have been. The situation was outlandish, but oh, it had made him so happy to plan and organize and pack and repack the supplies for their wilderness ordeal.

Still, there were limits.

She pulled the covers back up over her head and uttered one word into the blankets: "No."

"I bet you'd be good at it," he said, his tone cajoling, as if he actually thought he could talk her out of bed and away from the fire. She could tell from his voice that he was walking back toward the bed. "You could sculpt angels at the entrance."

That might be fun, but the rest of it didn't sound like any fun at all.

"And we could decorate it with the cranberry juice and make a big sno-cone out of it."

Okay. Maybe it could be fun to freeze her butt off outside packing snow into into a big hollow ball, then staining it with fruit juice and sitting inside.

She thought about it for a second, then changed her mind.

"No." He was nuts.

"Ah, geez, Nikki. What are we going to do all day, if we don't go out and play in the snow?"

Try to stay warm. The answer was so obvious, it wasn't even a question in her mind.

"Come on, Nik. Be a sport."

She felt part of his weight come down on the bed.

"I am *not* a sport," she said inside her silk-and-velvet cocoon.

"Not a sport?" he asked, settling more of his weight on the bed. "Then what are you, baby?"

The covers lifted for him to slide inside, and she started scooting to the other side as fast as she could. Darn it. He was going to be six feet of frozen Popsicle.

But he wasn't. He was warm, and naked, and he had her in his arms before she got even two inches from her spot.

"Umm." He nuzzled her neck, pulling her in close to his body. "You're soft."

And he was hard, everywhere, even after practically standing outside in the snow.

He took her breast in his mouth and teased her with his tongue, which she absolutely loved. "You're sweet."

Moving up to her mouth, he sucked on her lips, then slid his tongue inside and ravished her, all the while pressing her back into the bed. She had a feeling the old snow cave was sliding down to the bottom of his "To Do" list pretty damn fast. If he was going to do anything this morning, it looked like it was going to be her, which she absolutely loved.

"Hmmm. Soft and sweet." He kissed her lips again. "You must be a doughnut."

She giggled. A doughnut. "You're a doughnut."

"Me? Soft?" He laughed. "I don't think so, honey. I'm hard and—"

"Yummy."

"Yummy sounds soft." He smoothed his hand up over her knee, then higher, and she opened for him, anticipating his touch. "How about—"

"Delicious, *mmmmm.*" Kid Chaos had magic hands. He moved his thigh over hers, and she felt him, hot and heavy between her legs.

"No, babe. Delicious *mmmmm* is you. I'm..." He pushed up inside her, and she all but melted beneath him. It was always so glorious, the way he made love to her. She ran her fingers up into his hair and brought his head back down to hers for another kiss, moving with him, breathing him in, letting him take her higher and higher.

She was so in love.

"Taking me to Paris," she murmured a long while later, finishing his sentence after it had trailed off.

He let out a short laugh. "Yes," he said, slowly easing himself out of her. "Paris."

A year in Paris for a week in a yurt, and she still wasn't sure she'd made a good deal, except in the marrying of him. Of that, she had no doubts. She'd take Kid Chaos any way she could get him, anywhere, any time—every time.

ABOUT THE AUTHOR

Tara Janzen lives in Colorado with her husband, children, and two dogs, and is now at work on her next novel. Of the mind that love truly is what makes the world go 'round, she can be contacted at *www.tarajanzen.com*. Happy reading!

Don't miss
Tara Janzen's next novel
of heart-stopping action,
nail-biting suspense,
and breathless passion.

Read on for a sneak peek of

CRAZY LOVE

ON SALE SUMMER 2006

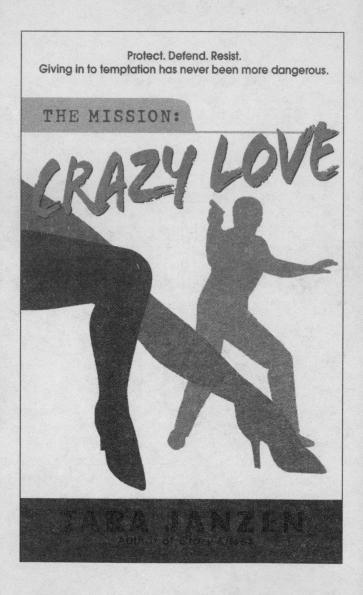

Protect. Defend. Resist.
Giving in to temptation has never been more dangerous.

THE MISSION:

CRAZY LOVE

TARA JANZEN

Author of *Crazy Kisses*

CRAZY LOVE

ON SALE SUMMER 2006

PINK.
Sweater.
Short.
Skirt.
Long.
Legs.

Dylan Hart flipped his cell phone shut and rubbed his hand over his forehead, trying not to stare at the girl on the other side of the office. She was out to slay him, his nemesis, the bane of his existence—Skeeter Bang, five feet eight inches of blond bombshell leaning over a computer.

Jail.

Bait.

She knocked a cigarette out of the pack of Mexican Faros on the desk and struck a match off her belt.

"Put that out," he ordered. She knew there was no smoking in the office.

"Make me," she said, then stuck the Faro between her lips and inhaled, holding the match to the end of the cigarette. A billow of smoke came out of her mouth when she exhaled.

Make me?

Dylan was the boss of 738 Steele Street in Denver, Colorado, second in command of Special Defense Force, SDF, a group of tough-as-nails black-ops shadow warriors who specialized in doing the Department of Defense's dirty work.

Make me?

"Put out the damn cigarette, Skeeter," the man working at the last computer said. "And if you bend over that desk one more time, I'm going to paddle you."

Thank you, Superman, Dylan thought.

The girl was out of control, but Superman, a.k.a. Christian Hawkins, had kicked more ass and taken more names than most men alive. He could handle Skeeter Bang, and honest to God, they had bigger problems, much bigger, like the phone call he'd just gotten from General Grant—and of course, there was still that little problem of the death sentence he'd picked up on his last mission. Wouldn't want to forget about that now, would he?

Yes. Actually, he would, but forgetting about it wasn't very goddamn likely.

"Skeeter," Hawkins warned her again.

And the chit put it out, just like that, without batting an eyelash or missing a beat. Though who the hell would know if Skeeter batted her eyelashes? The girl *always* wore sunglasses, and a damn ball cap Dylan was about ready to burn, literally, put it in a trash can and blast it with a flamethrower.

He was hardly ever at Steele Street to see her, and then even when he was there, he couldn't actually see her—which was all for the best. Just the way he liked it.

Except now he had this walking time bomb thing going, and if it turned out that things weren't going to go his way and the whole damn shooting match was going to be over, well, if that's the way things were going to be, maybe he should tell her how he felt.

Or maybe not.

Shit. He was such an idiot. He shouldn't have come home. He should have just toughed it out in Indonesia.

"So what did General Grant want?" Hawkins asked, gesturing at the cell phone Dylan still held in his hand. General Richard "Buck" Grant was SDF's commanding officer at the Pentagon. He deployed them, paid them, and made sure damn few people beyond the secretary of defense had a clue what they did for a living. They trained at Quantico and Fort Bragg, lived in Denver, flew out of Peterson AFB or Buckley, and were the only group of special-forces operators in the world with a twenty-year-old girl on their team, even if she was just the office manager and their computer tech.

She also just happened to be one of the best auto mechanics they'd ever had at Steele Street—which was saying a lot, considering that most of SDF was made up of a bunch of former juvenile-delinquent car thieves who'd stolen, chopped, and rebuilt more cars than anyone else in the history of Denver. To the cops and the gangs, the short alley called Steele Street in lower downtown was still synonymous with grand theft auto, no matter that none of the guys had stolen a car in years.

Guys—that was his point. Every teenaged thief at Steele Street had been a guy. General Grant had started SDF with those same guys, all guys, until three years ago, when Hawkins had dragged home a spooky, baby-faced street rat with long blond hair and twenty stitches holding her face together.

Geezus. They all needed their heads examined.

"Dylan?"

He jerked his attention back to Hawkins. The expression on his friend's face told him he'd been caught red-handed, staring at her ass again. *Dammit.* He hadn't even noticed her the first two years she'd been at Steele Street—and then one day, he had noticed her, noticed that suddenly she had more curves than a Camaro, that her stringy blond hair had turned into a platinum waterfall, and that though she was still spooky as hell, she wasn't spooked anymore. She'd been standing on her own two feet, in combat boots no less, with confidence radiating off her like a supernova.

He'd been noticing her ever since. He couldn't seem to help himself, which pissed him off to no end.

Ignoring Hawkins's knowing grin, he cleared his throat.

"Grant's concerned about some documents he saw at Senator Whitfield's mansion tonight, about an hour ago," he said. "He thinks they might be part of something called the Godwin File." Concerned was putting it mildly. Apoplectic was more like it—which meant maybe Dylan ought to stop getting distracted by Skeeter's butt and start focusing on the job he got paid to do.

"An hour?" Hawkins said. "He didn't waste any time getting ahold of us."

"No," Dylan agreed. The general knew better than

to drag his feet on something as volatile as the Godwin File, if what he'd seen really was the Godwin File. Most people doubted that the documents actually existed.

"And what does Grant want us to do with this file?"

"Steal it." That was the mission. Steal the damn thing and bury it, before it blew up the careers of half a dozen congressmen and another half dozen major players at the Pentagon.

"From Senator Whitfield?" Hawkins's gaze sharpened with interest.

Dylan knew it sounded nuts. Stealing from a United States senator was the kind of mission guaranteed to get somebody's ass thrown in Leavenworth, even if the thieves worked for the Department of Defense—*especially* if they worked for the DOD. On top of all the regular "thou shalt not steal" laws, federal law explicitly forbade the use of military personnel for operations within the United States. More than once, though, when a situation had gotten sticky enough, Grant had shuffled him and a couple of the guys through the FBI's payroll so they could follow through on a mission without having their backsides completely exposed.

Grant hadn't mentioned any shuffling tonight, but Dylan knew their commanding officer always did his best to cover their asses and their tracks. Of course, under normal circumstances, Buck Grant and Arthur Whitfield were on the same side, America's side, and under normal circumstances, U.S. Army generals did not go around authorizing the theft of top secret documents from senators—but nothing about the Godwin File was normal.

It was a legend, a myth, a time bomb that had been

lurking in the murky waters of the Defense Department's rumor mill for over a decade. It was the bogeyman sitting at the intersection of U.S. foreign policy and clandestine operations, and if the rumors were true, it had been a death warrant for a CIA agent stationed in the Middle East, two Israeli Mossad officers, and a foreign ambassador under their collective protection, just the sort of dirty laundry nobody wanted aired, especially the people whose names were on the orders.

"Whitfield has an appointment to see the Chairman of the Joint Chiefs of Staff Monday morning at nine a.m. Grant wants the file to disappear before the meeting."

"So we're heading to Washington, D.C."

"I am." It was a one-man job, and given his current condition, he wanted to keep it that way. The last thing he needed right now was a partner breathing down his neck. Fortunately, it was a non-issue. All the other SDF operators were assigned elsewhere, except Hawkins, and he wasn't going anywhere, not this week, and probably not next.

"You're going to need somebody to watch your back," Hawkins said.

"And that would be?" Dylan asked, giving the other man's leg a pointed look. A cast went from just below Hawkins's knee to down around his foot. The broken ankle was compliments of a successful mission six weeks ago in Afghanistan that had netted the United States armed forces a long-sought-after terrorist leader. No one was naming names at this point. Hawkins, with two other SDF operators, Creed Rivera and Kid Chaos, had done their jobs so well, word had yet to leak out that the terrorist leader was even missing, let alone that he was sitting in a cell in

Guantanamo Bay. Besides, Superman had other things to take care of this week.

In answer, Hawkins flicked his gaze toward Skeeter.

A shiver of alarm skittered down Dylan's spine. He couldn't be serious. Skeeter? On a mission?

No way in hell.

Especially one of his missions, which all required deception, deceit, discretion, and stealth of the highest order, not to mention plenty of sheer, unadulterated nerve. He was a thief, the best. Big things, little things, cars, computer chips, ideas and identities, fingerprints, information, jewels, gems, high-tech junk, a nuclear war head out of Tajikistan, or seventeen million dollars out of an Indonesian warlord's black-money slush fund: whatever General Grant wanted, Dylan delivered. Those were the terms of his freedom, and they hadn't changed in the nine years since the general had first proposed SDF to the U.S. Secretary of Defense. An elite force of highly expendable men had appealed to the man who had been the secretary then, and to the two who had followed. SDF had a commendable reputation, but dozens of successful missions hadn't changed Dylan's situation. The other members of SDF, most of whom had been in the military, could come and go as they pleased, but he was always on borrowed time. The CIA still wanted his ass in a federal prison for his involvement in a dicey operation in Moscow back when he'd been a green kid smart enough to get what he wanted, but not smart enough to stay out of trouble while doing it. To date the agency had consistently been outgunned by General Grant and Dylan's benefactor in the State Department, a man code named White Rook. It was a situation Dylan wasn't going to allow to change. He'd be damned if he went to prison, which meant he couldn't afford failure, ever.

So he didn't fail, ever.

He shot Hawkins a cold look and silently shook his head. He wasn't taking Skeeter to Washington with him. He wasn't that insane, or that selfish. Not yet.

"Don't talk about me behind my back like I'm not in the room," she said, continuing to tap on the computer's keyboard without so much as glancing over her shoulder.

Dylan swore under his breath. The girl *was* spooky. Neither he nor Hawkins had said a word, but she knew.

"You're not going," he said clearly, not wanting there to be any doubt in anybody's mind, most of all his own.

"She's good," Hawkins insisted. "Steady as a rock and practically invisible when she wants to be."

And when would that be? Dylan wondered, arching his eyebrow at his friend.

Hawkins didn't blink, and against his better judgment, Dylan let his gaze slide back to Skeeter.

Forget it. She was outrageous, the cosmic opposite of invisible. Her pink sweater was sleeveless, practically Day-Glo, and absolutely, positively laminated to her body. Her black leather miniskirt hugged her hips like a second skin. She had Chinese tattoos inked into the upper part of her right arm. Underneath her black tights, a lightning-bolt tattoo streaked up her leg from her ankle and shot over her hip, up under her arm, up around her back, and down over the top of her shoulder. He'd never seen the whole thing, couldn't see it now, but he knew it was there. She had that perfectly silky, perfectly straight, perfectly maddening platinum-blond ponytail that went all the way to her butt, and every day she managed to work a little chain mail into her outfit. Today it was her belt and a knife sheath. Add the mirrored sunglasses and the ball cap and she was nothing short of a piece of work.

A piece of work with a button nose and the softest, most perfect skin he'd ever seen on a woman. She was built like a centerfold, dressed like a goth princess, and had the face of a cherub. Every time he looked at her, he felt like the world's biggest fool.

So he tried not to look, tried not to come home very often. Hell, he hadn't been to Denver five times in the last seven months, but he'd already overstayed his welcome tonight. He could tell by the pain running down the middle of his chest. She gave him heartburn.

At least that's what he called it.

"No," he said. Hawkins was crazy if he thought she was invisible. Dylan saw her everywhere he went, from Bangkok to Paris, from L.A. to the Beltway. He saw her in his sleep. He'd spent one night in her company last January, chasing Creed Rivera across the city through the blizzard of the century, and he honest to God hadn't been the same since. Hour after hour of talking with her, being with her, and damn near dying of fear for her life had only exacerbated his incredibly inconvenient obsession. He was so out of line to want her the way he did.

"She can shoot and loot," Hawkins said.

The hell she could.

"Who has she ever shot?" he asked, then didn't wait for Hawkins to tell him, because he already knew. "No one, that's who."

It was impossible. Office managers and computer techs did not go out on missions, not even with an outlaw outfit like SDF. Sure, he'd taken her with him to find Creed that night, but only as a computer tech, not as an operator. And yes, things had gotten out of hand, and yes, she'd gotten into trouble up to her neck and gotten back out all on her own, but none of it had been planned.

Again, Hawkins didn't blink, just held his gaze, steady and sure, until Dylan finally got the message. Another shiver of alarm raced down his spine and damn near stopped his heart cold.

"What's been going on around here?" he asked, very quietly, very calmly, very certain he wasn't going to like the answer.

"It's a natural progression," Hawkins said, unperturbed. "She's been training for almost three years, and she's good, really good."

"Where was she good?" He couldn't believe this.

"Colombia. Kid and I took her with us as backup on the personal security detail we did for Occidental Petroleum in Bogotá."

"The one where two members of the National Revolutionary Forces were killed during a kidnap attempt?" He'd read the report, which hadn't had Skeeter's name on it anywhere. The FNG's, Fucking New Guy's, name had been on the report, Travis James, but not Skeeter.

Hawkins nodded, then hit a couple of keys on his computer when it beeped.

"She got the first kill," he said, looking back to Dylan.

Dylan, who couldn't breathe.

"They were waiting for us in the lobby of the hotel we were using as a safe house," Hawkins continued. "It was close quarters combat, textbook CQC. She beat Kid on the draw, which neither you nor I could do on our best day."

She'd beaten Kid Chaos on the draw—and Dylan still couldn't breathe. She'd been in battle, with people shooting at her, trying to kill her.

"Has she been anyplace else?" he asked, his voice still so very calm.

To his credit, Hawkins finally looked uncomfortable. "Kabul."

"Afghanistan?" he asked, just in case, unbeknownst to him, there was a Kabul, Kansas, or a Kabul, Kentucky, like there was a Paris in Texas.

"Mostly just in Kabul, but a little bit up the Gayan Valley toward the Pakistani border."

Dylan's gaze went back to Hawkins's cast. "Where you almost got blown to smithereens?"

Hawkins shook his head. "We'd sent her back to the capital before we went up into the mountains."

"But she saw action."

It wasn't a question. He could see the truth on Hawkins's face.

"An ambush. The Special Forces soldiers we were with weren't too happy to have her along, and the Afghan Militia guys were downright horrified, but when the Taliban hit, she didn't hesitate. The girl kicks ass, Dylan. She can hold her own, and she can certainly keep your back in Washington, where she's a damn sight more likely to get hit on than hit."

Unlike Skeeter, Dylan made no claims to clairvoyance, but he'd just gotten a very bad vibe.

"Hit?" he asked, working hard not to choke on the word.

"Skinned," she broke into the conversation, turning around and giving him the full benefit of her mirrored gaze.

Skinned. His heart lurched to a stop, then started back up on a ragged beat.

"It burned my pants, grazed my leg, and was gone. I didn't even feel it," she finished.

Bullshit.

He shifted his attention back to Hawkins. He'd trusted Christian Hawkins with his life more times than he could count, real "end of the line, so help me, God" times—but he no longer trusted the man with hers.

It was a wrenching realization.

For seventeen years, trusting Christian Hawkins had been the bedrock of his life. They'd been to hell and back, firefight hell where the odds had been against their chances of survival, the hell of losing two of their SDF brothers, and the black hell where a man was more dangerous to himself than anybody else on the planet. They'd pulled each other back from the razor's edge more than once, and once was all it took to cement a bond that went deeper than blood. If asked, Dylan would have said nothing would ever come between them, nothing could shake their friendship. They were solid.

But Skeeter had gotten "skinned" on a black-ops mission in Afghanistan, of all the goddamn places for her to be, and Dylan's trust in Hawkins's judgment was shaken to the core. He'd known Christian was training her, and he'd known that what had started as a course in self-defense had turned into something far more demanding, far more serious. The girl had proven adept, skilled, and too uniquely suited to the clandestine world in which they worked not to be brought deeper into the fold.

But not as an operator in the line of fire. Never as an operator. Hawkins should have known that.

Keeping himself carefully under control, Dylan slowly rose from his chair. He was going into his office, his private office, where he could close the door and drink himself under his desk.

He didn't have a choice.

He couldn't afford to say something he was bound to regret, not where Hawkins was concerned, and his nerves were just a bit on edge. He needed a break, a vacation, something, before he snapped, and if he was still alive after he took care of General Grant's Godwin File disaster, he was going to disappear for a while, go someplace and see if he could get this head back on straight. Skeeter Bang was not for him, and he needed to convince himself of the fact before he did something irredeemably stupid. He had enough sins on his head without adding her to the list.

At the door to his office, he stopped and turned, his gaze meeting her damned mirrored sunglasses. It was probably a bad idea, but he had to say something—just a little something straight from the heart.

"I think it might be best if . . ." He stopped, recognizing a weak start when he got off to one. What he needed was to be honest, forceful but kind. He needed to use the authority of his position, and yet be reasonable.

And so he began again, his voice carefully modulated with all the kind and reasonable honesty he could muster.

"If I ever . . . *ever* . . . hear of you going out on another mission, so help me God, Skeeter Jeanne Bang, I'll bust you back down to grease monkey so fast, it'll make your head spin, and then I'll ship you up to Commerce City to work in the garage, sweeping floors for Johnny Ramos."

His words fell into an abyss of silence.

Okay, so it had been a carefully modulated threat, but it felt good, and he would deliver on it in a heartbeat. Guaranteed. And if he did say so himself, he was pretty damned impressed with how calm and steady he'd kept his voice. Listening to him, no one would ever guess how badly his heartburn was suddenly acting up. The pain was like a knife in his chest, and the nausea was about ready to double him over.

He turned to go. She'd killed a man and been hit by a bullet, and he needed a drink.

"Screw you."

He froze where he stood, his hand on the doorknob.

Screw you?

He wanted to paddle her himself, then shake her, then sit her down in a chair and explain to her why she must never, ever get herself in a situation where she could be shot at again—and then throw himself at her feet. It was all so tragically stupid he couldn't bear it. He'd never been a sap over a woman, and she barely qualified for the designation. He knew exactly how much older than her he was, to the day, and he couldn't quite fathom his fascination. He'd never been attracted to younger women. So what was different about her . . . except everything.

Screw you?

He wasn't going to dignify the remark with a reply. He didn't dare, not when he'd fantasized about it more ways than she could possibly imagine. Scotch on the rocks was what he needed, something cold and serious. He did not need an argument with a tattooed, clairvoyant street rat who just happened to be the woman of his dreams.